UNSHAKABLE

UNSHAKABLE

**DOUGLAS
THOMPSON**

Copyright ©2023 by Douglas Thompson
ISBN 979-8-218-19040-8

TYPESET @ 2feetpro.com

I dedicate this book to my heavenly angel,
my father, Big Doug T.
You always told me I could do anything, pops.
I love you always.

Acknowledgements

All praise to Yahweh.
Thank you to my main man Mike,
who pushed me to complete this book.
My boy Elton, who kept me motivated
and out of trouble while I completed the book.
Thank you to my mother, Patrice and my sister Yashena
for always pushing and believing in me.
Thank you to my children,
for always being the drive that I need to get through life.
Thank you to my backbone, my better half, Cocoa
for always keeping me sharp and on my toes.
I greatly appreciate you Queen, for never taking no for an answer, yet keeping me balanced.

I love you all, and this is only the beginning.

INTRODUCTION

Ring…. Ring…. Ring

"You have a collect call from: 'Kedar'… an inmate at Autry State Facility. To accept this call press 1."

The receiver pressed 1 to accept the call and waited for the caller's greeting on the other end of the phone.

"Hello?" said Kedar.

"Hola my friend!" replied Escobar. "I've been waiting for your call."

Kedar took a long drag from his Bugler cigarette. He smiled to himself then replied, "I've been patiently waiting to make this call."

"What can I do for you today?" Escobar asked.

"Shiiiit, it's about that time, my friend!" replied Kedar.

"Do I need to make arrangements to come and pick you up?"

"Naw my friend. That won't be a problem."

Escobar chuckled. "Well okay then. Have it your way. Do you have a pen?"

Kedar sat his cigarette on top of the phone while he retrieved a pen and paper from his pocket. "I'm ready when you are," he said into the phone.

"You better be. 470-555-0766. Call when you're situated," Escobar replied.

"Will do, my friend." Kedar then put the receiver on the hook and took another pull from the cigarette as he thought to himself, "It's on now."

CHAPTER 1

Kedar had woken up this morning feeling rejuvenated. He rolled out of his bunk and opened his locker. He grabbed his toothbrush and toothpaste. He began his routine of brushing his signature Colgate smile. Kedar had been told all his life that he had a beautiful white smile to go with this dark-skinned complexion. He ran some warm water on his face cloth and then began to wash his face. Kedar could see the slight change within himself, but the last ten years behind these walls had kept him well-preserved. He finished cleaning the sleep from his eyes, then stood back and took a look at himself. His skin glowed like never before. The tattoos on his body stood out more, especially since he had been going in hard with his man Mike's weight training for the past nine months. Kedar was truly fit for a bitch and cut for a slut, but the hair on his face and head had him looking like Wolfman McClain.

He finished getting himself together as he put on his black socks, black Nike shorts, black 1's and finally pulled on his black wife beater. Some habits are just too hard to break, especially all-black everything. Kedar grabbed the remainder of his commissary, worth about $20, and placed it in a net bag, throwing it over his shoulder as he strolled out of his cell. He hadn't told anybody that today was his day to go home, not even his right-hand man Mike.

Kedar had already dropped $500 on his books, but Mike wouldn't see it until the following week's store call. It would come as a surprise to him. As Kedar walked across the top range, he saw Divine just finishing up on Schoolboy's haircut. So Kedar brought three razors off the brick so that he could get himself a haircut.

"What's the science, God?" greeted Divine.

"True wisdom and understanding comes from having knowledge of one's self," replied Kedar.

"Well put," said Divine as he shook the sheet and prepped Kedar for a cut.

"What's the bag for? Can I get in?"

Kedar smiled, "Naw, you can't get in because it belongs to you for this haircut. You 'bout to put me in the game wit' it."

"Say no more. How you want it?" Divine asked.

"I want a one all over to bring my dogs back out again," referring to his waves. "Even the beard out and round the back up."

"Aight, I got you."

"I need for you to do your thang and make me look 18 again," Kedar said. He was 35, but he truly looked as though he was still in his mid 20's.

Divine began to laugh, "Man, please! For that lil money, I can't perform no miracles." Both men burst into big laughter.

"Do the best you can then," Kedar said.

"I got you, God."

Divine began to put his craft to work on Kedar. As he chopped away at the top and then moving on to cutting off the facial hair, Kedar began to look younger. Divine was putting him in the game. Divine was doing Kedar's lineup as Ms. Jones came in with a cadet, for count.

"Count time! Count time! Let me get in and get out. I don't want no problems and you don't want no issues," she yelled out.

Ms. Jones was a little petite female, brown-skinned with a nice shape. Even though the prison was in a country ass area, she still looked good. The plus to it was that Ms. Jones was 25, no kids, and a career. To top it all off, she was a good ass mule. It was just that she was under the wrong guidance, this bum ass nigga Dre from Atlanta. This little chick was only trying to get some money but this tender dick ass nigga wanted a girlfriend. She wasn't feeling him like that though. He once stuck a nigga up for grilling and grinning all in her face. Ms. Jones was too scared to write him up and for that reason, and for that reason he just knew that he was in like Flynn. It also had been heard around the dorm that he might drop salt on the broad, damn near to the point of telling. So, to save her job plus to keep getting that chain-game money, she conversed with him periodically.

"Count time! Count time! Let me get in and out," she yelled again.

"Shiiiiiit, let me get in and out," one brother yelled out.

The men in the dorm began to laugh. Kedar and Divine both just shook their heads at the total disrespect that these cats show for the women that work there. It was beyond them how a man would call the C.O.'s all types of bitches, hoes, and broke muthafuckas, then turn around and ask her to bring the pack in to them. They just didn't understand them.

Ms. Jones walked over towards the table where Kedar was getting his hair cut. "K, is that you?" she asked as her brown eyes scanned Kedar up and down.

The cadet nudged her and whispered, "He's cute."

Ms. Jones' cheeks started to flush as she thought the same thing.

"My bad Ms. J. We 'bout to get up now," Kedar replied.

"Naw, naw, y'all good. 'Bout time you took that shit off your face. You were starting to look like a lil runaway," she said.

"Oh! Now you notice a nigga, when I get a haircut."

"Boy, please! The way you and Mike work out every day like y'all trying to participate in a triathlon doing your lil sit-ups and pushups then running up and down the stairs. How can I miss you?"

Kedar began to blush. "So you watching a nigga?" he replied, as he hit her with a signature smile.

"Oh. You got dimples?" said the cadet as she admired Kedar from head to toe. That made his smile stand out even more. The cadet blushed. "My mother always told me to never trust a black nigga with a smile."

"Well, your mama told you right because I'm a woman's drug and antidote," replied Kedar.

"Is that so?" smiled Ms. Jones.

"Pretty much. All you gotta do is tell me if you wanna get high or be revived and I'm there."

"Mmmhmm….. and what would your girl think, who we all know you getting fresh to see tomorrow at visitation, about being another woman's drug and antidote? As you call it," asked Ms. Jones.

"Well, let me see," Kedar said as he sarcastically gazed into space like he was thinking hard about what she had just said. "Since you asking, I truly don't know 'cause I have neither a girl or a visitation."

"That's what they all say."

"Seriously, I don't. As a matter of fact, I actually get out today," Kedar replied.

Ms. Jones sucked her teeth, "Boy, stop playing," as she put her hands on her hips.

"For real. Today is my day. That's why my man is putting me in the game," Kedar responded.

At this point, Divine stopped cutting and turned his face up towards him, "Kedar, you gone?"

"Yeah, my dude. Keep it down. Now make sure I'm ebony black ready because I'm going to go get me a modeling gig." They all burst out into loud laughter.

"Say no more," Divine said, as he continued to do his thing. Ms. Jones congratulated Kedar and said that hopefully he would stay out of trouble once he was out.

Dre came out of his room and screamed, "Come on with the count!"

The dorm got quiet. Dre sized up Kedar from the top range where he was standing. Ms. Jones told Divine that he had some nice work as she walked off. She walked around with the cadet and did a head count. As she was exiting the dorm, she cut her eyes back over at Kedar, giving her approval of his haircut. As the door closed behind the officers, Kedar could see Dre from his peripherals, congregating with his city niggas. Divine nudged him to let him know that they were on their way down the stairs. It was about five of them in total, including Dre.

Divine tilted Kedar's head to the side and began to line up his sideburns. He whispered to Kedar, "My tool under your stool if you need it." Then he tilted Kedar's head back up. Dre and his crew walked up while Divine was putting the finishing touches on Kedar.

"Which one of y'all next?" Divine asked no one in particular.

"Naw, we good," replied Dre as he looked Kedar over. In his mind, Kedar was just some blow up, which meant a front, working out with Mike every day. Dre couldn't even remember any altercation that Kedar had ever been in inside the dorm. Any time something popped, some kind of way Kedar's shit always got talked out. Dre, on the other hand, had always been 'hands on' and his quick temper always preceded his hands. Dre squinted his eyes as he looked over Kedar's haircut.

"Mannnn, the right side is just a tad bit off," said Dre as he touched the corner of Kedar's head.

Kedar quickly slapped his hand down. "Don't touch my fuckin' head!" Kedar knew that Dre was on some hating shit.

"You better watch yoself shawty," replied Dre as his partners began to clutch, positioning their hands at their weapons. "In fact," said Dre, "Why you all up in my bitch face keekee'n, laughing, giggling, and shit?"

Kedar grinned. "Well, you need to put yo' bitch on a leash," he replied as he began to finger fuck the tool that was under the seat.

"Is that right?" Dre smirked, as his crew began to close in. "You keep on with that slick ass mouth, and a nigga gon' see what that shit hit like," he growled.

Divine set the razors down and turned to tell Dre and his crew to back up, they were in too close.

"You better go find you something safe to do and get the fuck up out my personal space!" Kedar threatened.

Dre laughed out loud. "The nerve of this nigga to be popping shit while sitting down. You know, you a real disrespectful ass nigga, Kedar.

Kedar cut his eyes at Dre, "Why? Cause I try to stay sucka free?" No sooner than the words had left his mouth, Dre swung and hit Kedar in his jaw. The whole dorm grew quiet and all eyes were on them. All you heard was the echo of the "Ohhhhh" that had just sounded off. Kedar had taken that hit to the chin, as he rolled off the stool. He quickly caught himself with his left hand and pushed away from the floor. Just before Dre's crew was about to jump on him like a pack of hyenas, Kedar launched towards Dre. He came from under the sheet with an ice pick, sticking Dre in the neck and abdomen. Blood jumped from Dre's neck like a lawn sprinkler. Dre's crew quickly backed up. 'IT AIN'T ALL FUN AND GAMES ONCE THE RABBIT GOT THE GUN'

The Cert Team was walking by just before the fight broke out, which resulted in quick response time. They quickly ran inside the dorm screaming, "LOCK IT DOWN! LOCK IT DOWN!" Divine hurried and grabbed the pick from Kedar and said to him, "Go home!" Divine ran from the middle of the crowd and assumed the position before he slid the pick to the foot of the sergeant.

"Cuff him," the sergeant yelled.

BEEP. "10-10, Unit F1, need medical assistance..... LOCK IT DOWN NOW!!!"

CHAPTER 2

Inmates started to scramble everywhere. Some running to get to a room so they wouldn't be free picked (randomly called out). Majority of the men that were just sitting on the brick were covered in blood. Others running to put their phones away. From the look of the amount of blood that Dre was losing, it didn't look like he was going to make it. They knew that the Tact Squad would be there if Dre happened to die and NOBODY wanted to lose a phone that ranged anywhere from $1,500 to $2,500 a piece. Meanwhile, Kedar beelined to his cell and immediately began to take off his clothes. He had grabbed a razor on the way up and was now starting to shred his clothes and flush them down the toilet. One thing about a toilet in prison, the shit would flush a whole bed sheet without getting clogged up. Kedar quickly washed off and changed clothes.

The Cert Team went from room to room, asking questions and telling everyone to show their hands. If anything looked the least bit flakey, they tossed the cell. A couple of dudes took losses on phones and cigarettes, but they were only the ones that panicked and had locked themselves in their rooms. Kedar could only shake his head, as he thought, "How could these niggas be so damn careless, knowing full well that this shit in here is illegal?" ***Hell… if you stay ready, you ain't got to get ready.***

8

His heart pounded harder as the Cert Team made it to his room. He stood at the door in his t-shirt and boxers. He kicked himself in the ass realizing that he had not at least put his shoes underneath the bed. Kedar's shoes were covered in blood, and even though they were black, the crimson red glowed on them. As Kedar extended his hands out towards the Cert Team, another fight broke out in another dorm. "Whew," Kedar said to himself as he quickly grabbed the shoes and cleaned them. At this point, the only thing that Kedar could hope for is that Dre wouldn't tell, if he lived. Reason being was that Kedar was paroling out, not maxing out. D.O.C. would, for damn sure, hide his black ass if Dre or anyone else for that matter, told. Good thing he had a change of clothes, seeing that he really didn't even have a uniform because he had been slowly giving all of his stuff away. The bad thing is his other outfit was same black on black 'fit just like the one that he had just shredded. About two hours later, the Warden came strolling into the dorm with the Cert Team in tow. He stood in the middle of the floor with his arms crossed.

"Cert, I want you to tear this bitch up," the Warden screamed, as he began to pace the floor. "You muthafuckas stabbing, smoking, and kicking big shit on your phones, huh? So, it's muthafuck me, huh? For the record," he called out. "I can tolerate the smoking and can even tolerate the phone, to a certain extent but stabbing??!!! Hellllll NAWWW!" he yelled. Someone yelled from the back, "Man, why you fucking with us? You got the niggas that was involved, right?"

The Warden begins to laugh, "You know what? You're right. In part, I got a man in the hole, who claim that he did it. Only thing is, HE DON'T HAVE A LICK OF GOT DAMN BLOOD ON HIM!!!!" He screamed as he spread his arms out signaling to the pool of blood that was still on the floor and across half of the dorm. "Now, I want whoever DID the fuckin stabbing. Be a man and man up to your shit because if I have to dig and find you, you're not gonna like it. I have my staff looking into the video footage now, so come on out because the 'eye in the sky' don't lie," he said, referring to the cameras that were placed all around the compound. The Cert Team was now on the top tier. They picked up where they left off just minutes ago. They went into the door after Kedar's.

"Shiiiiit," Kedar thought. "I didn't tell on myself to get here. What makes him think I'm gonna start now?" At that moment Kedar heard his name crackle across the radio. "FUCK!!!" he thought. The Cert Team u-turned to his door. "Kedar Simpson? Cuff up."

Kedar was led down the tier by two members of the Cert Team. The Warden stared him down the entire way. "So, this is my culprit?" asked the Warden. "So, you like to stick people, huh?" he said to Kedar, menacingly. "You're fucking lucky that the trauma unit responded quick or else yo' ass would be getting booked for a body. Oh, but don't worry. Yo' ass is definitely on your way to a tier program for at least two years. Then, I'm going to send that ass to High Max afterwards. Look out that window because that's the last bit of sunlight you gonna see for about five years!"

"Uhh, excuse me sir," said Cert 1. "They just called for him to report to I.D. That's why we pulled him out."

"Oh. My bad. Where he going?" asked the Warden.

"He is being released, sir," responded Cert 2.

"Damn, you gonna miss all the fun that I got planned for the dorm," said the Warden. Kedar wanted to smile but he also wanted to punch the power-abusing Warden in his shit.

"I'm sorry. I'm gonna miss this one, sir," replied Kedar.

"Get him out of my face," said the Warden. It seemed like the Warden didn't want Divine, and that he was going to let him go. But boy, his temper was really going to boil once he realized that Kedar did indeed do the stabbing. Kedar just laughed to himself all the way out of the dorm. Once cleared, they gave him a $25 debit card and a bus ticket, then dropped him off. Kedar shook his head at how the law worked. They lock you up and you lose everything from clothes, cars, house, etc. Not to mention family. Some people even lose their kids. Then after you do all that fucking time, they give you a $25 debit card and a bus ticket. Pretty much saying, "Fuck you but that thank you for the time you did for us." Especially knowing they get paid anywhere from $500-$800 a day to house and feed an inmate. Prison is the biggest scam in America. They give you enough rations to make it to the next day, enough beams to build a trail to the moon and back. Then, they have you spend what little money you do have on some over-priced gas station food.

CHAPTER 3

    Kedar came to his senses, as he looked at the ticket. It was 2:30 in the afternoon, and his bus wasn't due until 7:30. Another damn five hours from now. Kedar decided to come up out of the khaki pants and button-down shirt that they had given him to put on upon leaving. He, for damn sure, wasn't about to wait and see if the prison would come back and get him. Hell, they would probably try to free world his ass now, he thought. So, he started walking, and thumbing for a ride, wearing all black. As he walked, he looked around at all the land. He was truly in the middle of nowhere. He passed by nothing but trailer parks.

    Kedar could see a shopping plaza in the distance and figured that it was about time now to call someone to come pick him up. Kedar was lost in his thoughts, thinking about his next move. He thought about how he was about to touchdown and cause hell. He hadn't notified anyone of his return, not even his twin daughters whom were his heart and joy. Back when Kedar caught his time, everyone had turned their backs on him. Everyone except his mother and his daughters. His baby mother moved on after about five years, claiming that the loneliness had gotten the best of her. He could only shake his head and give her his blessing to move on, and do what she had to do. The only thing that she had done positively and stuck to was making sure that the twins remained with his mother, who made sure they wrote him, and sent holiday cards. He was lost during his bid but humility had found him. Kedar was pulled from his thoughts when a car slid up next to him, kicking up a dirt cloud around him.

"Freeze, inmate!" A deep voice called out. Kedar stopped dead in his tracks. He took a look around and realized that he was around nothing but open fields to the left and right. He knew that if he broke out, and the muthafuckas caught him, he was as good as dead out there. So, he made a decision right then, running would only take energy from him, so he might as well give them all of the smoke that they were asking for. "Fuck it," he said. Kedar interlocked his fingers behind his head and slowly turned around. Kedar could see the prison uniform through the cloud of dust. During his whole bid, he hadn't seen too many C.O.'s that could hold their own, and being that he was fit and South Beach ready, this muthafucka was gonna have some big problems. As the dust settled, Kedar could see the officer standing on the ledge of the door.

"Kedar," the voice called out.

Kedar squinted his eyes, trying to see the face because the voice sounded too familiar.

"Why is your face balled up like that, K?"

Kedar's frown turned into a smile as his eyes settled on Ms. Jones standing before him. "Girl, you play too fuckin much!" He smiled. "What up, Ms. J?"

"That's Ms. Jones to you, inmate," she replied.

"Oh. We got jokes now? Well, I'm sorry to disappoint you but I'm a free man now."

"I see," Ms. J replied, as she slowly approached him. She stopped directly in front of him, sizing him up and down. Ms. J could feel his aura of defiance. She inhaled deeply, taking in his intoxicating masculine scent. Kedar stared deep into her eyes, attempting to see what was on her mind. He then broke the silence, "You gonna look at a nigga all day or you gonna give me a ride?"

"I'm sorry sir, I don't pick up hitch hikers," Ms. Jones replied.

"Lady J, you better stop playing. It's hotter than the devil's dick out here," Kedar said as he walked around to the passenger side of her car, opened the door, and got in.

"K! If you don't get your ass out of my car...," she yelled, still standing in front with her hands on her hips.

Kedar opened the door and placed one of his feet on the ground. "As cute as you are to look at, especially with your serious look and those cute lips poked out like some soup coolers, it's hot as hell. Just drop me off somewhere in town so I can wait 'til my bus comes. Please."

Ms. J burst out into laughter. "I know damn well you ain't talking 'bout my lips, with them big ass umbrellas you got."

"Girl, GET YO ASS IN THE CAR!!" Kedar said with authority. A shiver went down J's spine as she walked back to the car.

"I don't know who you think you talking to but put your fuckin' seatbelt on. I'm not trying to get pulled over with you in my car," she said, as she sat down and pulled her seatbelt on. They rode for the next five minutes in silence.

"Why yo' ass ain't at work?"

J cut her eyes over at him, like 'yeah right.' "Well, someone got stabbed on my watch."

"So, they fired you for that?" he asked.

"Naw, but I told the Warden that I couldn't cope with all that blood I saw. So, he gave me a week off, after I wrote the incident report up."

Kedar shifted in his seat, then turned towards her, "So what you wrote?" he asked.

"I told him that I was next door counting when it happened. Divine Taylor was cutting hair so I doubt that he did it. And that I heard Dremond Smith exchange words with one of the fellas in his crew during count but that Cert took each one of them out of the dorm after the altercation," J said.

"And he bought that?" asked Kedar.

"Hell, seeing that the cameras don't work, what was he gonna say? Then to top it all off, once Taylor knew that you was gone, he told the Warden that he was only trying to give the Cert the weapon because it was close to him and didn't want to be the one to blame for the situation."

"Huh?" Kedar lifted an eyebrow.

"He only got Taylor locked in the shower, so he gon' be back out probably later on today," J assured Kedar.

"That's what's up. I appreciate the look out."

"No. Thank YOU! Dre was such an asshole. He barely made it. They did find a knife on him though, so his ass is going to the tier after recovery. To add insult to injury, his homie Mitch gon' pull up on me, talking about a proposition," J explained to Kedar.

"Yo, you might need to cool it for a while," Kedar whispered.

J looked over at him. "What you mean?" she asked.

"Chill, Lady J. You ain't out there like that, but that bitch ass nigga was slick showing his hand. So, word of advice, be mindful of who you fuck with."

J began to bang on her steering wheel as tears fell from her eyes.

"Chill, Lady J. You aight?" Kedar reached over and wiped away a tear that fell down the side of her right cheek. His hands were so strong, yet they felt so soft and warm to the touch. "Chill now," Kedar continued, as he caressed her cheek. "A nigga just got out. I've been through all types of fist fights and knife fights and I came out without a scratch. So, I'll be damned if you kill me in a car on my first day out," he laughed. J joined in and laughed with him. It was interrupted by J's ringing phone.

"Hello," she answered, still sniffling. "Yes, Mrs. Jenkins. Understood. I'm on my way now."

"Is everything okay?" Kedar asked. "You probably got a lil shih tzu or something," he joked.

"For your information, I got a yellow jacket pit," J said sarcastically.

"Damn. Do you know the ticket on one of them? They some expensive ass dogs. How the hell can you afford one of them, if you don't mind me asking," Kedar inquired.

Well, to be honest with you, my ex left the dog when he left me. She was just a puppy at the time. I couldn't see giving her away to the shelter so I just kept her. I took her to the vet and later on I registered her. I was given all the paperwork and documents needed. Hell, her vet bills 'bout as high as my medical bills. But nevertheless, that's my baby and I can't see parting ways from her for nothing in the world," J explained.

"So, you don't have kids?" Kedar asked.

"She IS my baby. But I would like to have kids one day. But it gotta be with the right man. One who is gonna be a father NOT just a baby daddy. Do you have kids?" J asked Kedar.

"Actually, I do. I have a beautiful set of twin girls. Asia and Anastasia. And yes, I'm a father not a baby daddy. It's just that their mother wanted to move on, once they gave me my time. So, I said to hell with it. But I'm always there for my girls. My mother always made sure that she brought them to see me twice a month. Trust, I did the best that I could, given the situation that I was in. Furthermore, with a supportive mother like mine, they never went without," Kedar explained.

"That's good to know," J said, as she turned into her apartment complex.

"You live here?"

"Yeah. Just be quiet." J got out of the car and hit the alarm. As she entered the apartment building, one of the doors swung open.

"You hear that?" Arf. Arf. Arf. You could hear Ginger in the distance, going bananas. "That's been going on for the past hour or so," said Mrs. Jenkins. "The maintenance man came by to fix that leak but he was scared to go in. He said that it sounded like she was out of her cage. Oh my!" Mrs. Jenkins stopped in mid-sentence. "Who is this nice-looking fella?" she asked J.

"He's just a friend, Mrs. Jenkins," replied J.

"Well, I'm glad you got a friend. I was starting to worry about you. I thought you had joined the rest of the world and turned gay or something," Mrs. Jenkins stated.

"Mrs. Jenkins!" J exclaimed.

"What, child? Did I say something wrong? Hello young man. I'm Mrs. Jenkins."

"Hello, Madame," Kedar greeted Mrs. Jenkins.

"Oh! He got that French shit in him. Madame. I like that!"

"Mrs. Jenkins!" J said again, as she shook her head in embarrassment. "K, come on," she said to Kedar as she pulled him by the arm, marching up the stairs.

"Nice to meet you, Madame Jenkins," Kedar called out to Mrs. Jenkins, as he stepped up on the stairs.

"I thought I told you not to say shit," Lady J finally said. She put the key into the lock and opened the door. Her voice was caught in her throat, when Ginger came out running past her. Ginger headed straight towards Kedar. "Ginger, NOOOOO!" she yelled out.

Kedar stood still, then he slowly placed his hands to his side with his palms facing the ground.

"Ginger, no!" J said again. But Ginger was locked in, growling, snarling, showing her teeth. Ginger was waiting for Kedar to attempt to make a break or any type of move, for that matter.

"Shhhh," Kedar said to Lady J. Kedar clicked his tongue against his teeth twice, then he whistled twice. Ginger took another step towards him. He clicked his tongue again and whistled twice. "Easy girl," he said in a low whisper. Kedar never broke eye contact with Ginger. "Easy girl," he said as he repeated the click, whisper method. The hair on Ginger's back began to lay down. "Sit!" Kedar said with authority. Ginger's ass hit the floor while still looking at K. Kedar slowly spread his arms, as if asking for a hug as he eased down onto one knee. Eye contact still unbroken with the animal. Ginger began to growl. "Easy girl," Kedar repeated the whisper. Ginger then licked her tongue across her nose. Kedar was now eye level with the dog. He reached around with his right hand and began to stroke Ginger's head. As Kedar caressed the dog, he spoke to her in a calm manner, "What's the problem, girl?" Ginger licked her tongue across her nose again. "Shhhh," Kedar said as he stroked her head then down her back. He could see that her nose was a little dry. "The girl need some water," he said to Lady J.

"I see," she replied. Lady J swung around and scanned her apartment. She noticed that Ginger's cage was turned over, and her water bowl that was in the kitchen was also turned over.

Kedar stroked Ginger's head again, then patted her side. "Come on, girl. Let's get you some water." He walked past Lady J, heading to the kitchen with Ginger in tow. Kedar grabbed the bowl and filled it with water. "Here, girl. That's all you wanted," he said as he rubbed her head. Kedar turned from the kitchen and set the cage back upright.

"Wowwwww," said Lady J.

"What?" he asked.

"She don't like nobody. Not even my roommate."

"Really?" Kedar replied. "Well, they say dogs know best."

"Mmm. They also know their own kind too," Lady J responded.

"You got a lil slick ass mouth for someone that almost got me killed three times in one day. First, your boyfriend tried to stab me. Then, you try to kill me in a car accident, and now your dog just tried to eat my ass alive. I got to have a death wish fuckin' with you," Kedar stated.

Lady J roller her eyes. "But yet you still alive. Imagine that."

"Well there are other things I could be imagining," Kedar said as he stood up face to face with her. He was all in her personal space, but she didn't resist him nor did she push him back. He was so close that they were sharing the same oxygen. Kedar then grabbed J by the waist and pulled her closer to him.

"Don't do this, K," J whispered. Their noses were now touching.

"Do what? Lady J?"

"You know what I'm talking about," J said with her words coming out as gasps. She bit down on her bottom lip. Kedar gazed down at her, as the saliva now had her lips glowing. Kedar was getting an erection. Lady J felt his manhood growing, as it began to press against her navel.

I won't do nothing that you don't allow me to do," he whispered, as he leaned in for a kiss. Never letting his gaze move from her brown eyes, Kedar kissed J. Her lips felt so soft. He kissed her passionately. They struggled to keep their breath as they stood there exploring the insides of each other's mouths. Kedar then lifted J off the ground, as she wrapped her legs around his waist. J began to breathe heavily.

"Please. It has been a while."

Kedar kissed her lips. "What's a while?" he asked as he planted kisses on her neck.

"About two years," she moaned.

Kedar looked at J. "That's it? Try ten," he said as he lay her down on the couch.

J dropped her hands above her head. Kedar stood and eyed her all over in her uniform. The beast in him had just awakened. He snatched the shirt open, popping all of the buttons and exposing the black lingerie she wore underneath her uniform. Lady J had a nice lean body. Kedar had noticed the Universal Machine in the corner of the living room when he had first walked into the apartment. K began to place kisses all over her chest, as he unbuckled her belt. The snatching of the shirt had caught J by surprise, but it was arousing how he had control. She kicked her boots off and Kedar slowly slid her pants off. She had on a pair of boy shorts that matched her bra. Kedar noticed that her uniform did nothing but hid this nice physique that she had under it. J sat up and eased Kedar's tank top over his head. She inhaled deeply as she examined his muscles and ink work. She kissed his chest as she rubbed her hands across his perfectly formed six-pack.

"Damn," she thought to herself, "This is a perfectly formed black man."

J unsnapped her bra, showing off her 36C breasts with dime-sized nipples. Kedar dove into them head first, massaging one while sucking on the other. He alternated between the two, making sure to give them both the same amount of attention. He trailed kisses down her body, to her flat stomach. Kedar could see through her lace boy shorts, that she was perfectly shaved. He slid her legs out of the boy shorts one at a time, while he kissed her inner thighs. The moisture forming there told Kedar that J was indeed turned on. He slowly took her clit into his mouth while massaging her breasts. Kedar made sure that his hands never left her body. If he wasn't rubbing her, he was squeezing her or tasting her. Lady J arched her back, while Kedar's tongue danced around on her clitoris in a figure-8 motion.

Next, Kedar slid one finger into her. It felt as though he had just snapped on a rubber glove, the way her insides wrapped around his finger. He slowly slid his finger in and out of her, massaging her inside as he began to ease the second finger in. As Kedar guided his fingers in and out of J, he sucked even harder on her swollen clit. Her juices were flowing down his wrist and arm. Kedar took his free hand and guided J's hand to the back of his head, repeating the same motion with her other hand. Lady J now had Kedar's head palmed like a basketball.

"Put me where you want me," Kedar said between licks.

J arched her back even more, as she guided his tongue into her open, wet tunnel. She began to grind on his tongue that was dipping in and out of her. They locked eyes. The sexual chemistry was heated. Kedar gripped her thighs and started roughly pulling her down onto his tongue. J swayed her hips back and forth then around until she felt a shock wave coming in from her feet and traveling through her entire body. She tried to push away but Kedar had her locked in. He felt her body begin to tremble, so he pulled his tongue out of her and started to suck on her clit passionately. J could no longer contain the cries that had been trying to escape her mouth. "Please. Please. Please, K. Oh my God!" she cried out.

Kedar looked up at her and smiled. "Give it to me then," he commanded.

As if on cue, J came. "Ohhhh shit, ahh… ahhhhh…. Mmmm!"

Kedar licked up her juice, then went back to her clit again.

"Oh God. No! Please, K. Noooo. I'm begging you," she cried out.

"Yes," he replied. "Say yes."

"Yes. Yessss. Oh my. Fuck. Yesssss," J screamed.

"Now cum for me," K whispered.

Once again, as if on cue, J came again.

"What the fuck?!" she thought to herself. She felt as if her soul was depleted. J dropped her arms, not having the energy to hold them up any longer.

Kedar just sat and watched as her stomach rose up and down from her heavy breathing.

"Do you have a condom?" he asked her.

"I'm sorry. I don't," she replied. "I wasn't planning on having sex. Like I told you, it's been a while."

Kedar begins to pull off his basketball shorts. "Do I need one?" he asked.

J looked down at the 9½-inch dick that hung between his legs. "Oh my, God!" she thought to herself. "I have never seen anything so black and beautiful in my life." Not only did this man have length, but his manhood was at least two inches wide, with a curve. Not to mention, it was girthy.

Not waiting for an answer to his question, Kedar slowly spread her legs. He rubbed the head of his dick between her lips, then massaged her clit with it. He was lubing up his penis with her juices. As he slowly eased the head inside of her, she flinched then inhaled deeply.

"Oh, shit. He is spreading my insides," she thought to herself.

Truth be told though, Kedar was being ever so gentle and slow with her, slowly rocking his way in and out of her. Her body began to open up to him. As Kedar finally got halfway inside of her, J started to feel the curve of him. He went deeper and deeper, slowly grinding and digging in her.

"Oh my God," she cried out.

Kedar was now thrusting into her, their pelvic bones rocking back and forth. Kedar placed J's hands on his hips so she could let him know when he was too far in. She lifted her legs, allowing him to go deeper and deeper. Kedar grabbed her pedicured feet, and started to suck on one of her toes. As he stroked her insides and sucked her toes, J started to hyperventilate. She didn't know what to do with herself.

Kedar placed his free hand behind her neck so that she could see him at work. His penis now had a shine to it from her cum. Kedar looked down at her as she gazed down at his manhood pumping in and out of her. She was mesmerized by his work.

She started to talk to him, "That's it. Right there. Take this pussy. Deeper… deeper daddy. Mmmm. Don't stop. Yessss…. Harder…. Harder baby… ahhhhh… shit deeper, harder!" Her body begins to shake. Kedar moved his hands from the back of her neck to the front. "What the fuck?!" she thought. Then like a truck, it hit her. She was coming, but with K's hands wrapped around her neck. It was like euphoria. The orgasm was stuck in her head, wanting to be released. But this man, who was now fucking her harder and harder, was only allowing it to build up even more.

Finally, K looked down at her and asked, "Are you ready to cum?"

J could only nod her head. She felt like if she didn't, she would lose her fucking mind. Kedar didn't release her right then though. He fucked her harder and harder. Digging and stroking her like he had a point to prove. He leaned over and kissed her feverishly on the lips.

"What the fuck?!" she thought again.

"Are you ready to cum?" Kedar asked her again, this time with a slight growl to it.

"Yes…. Yessss," she thought, as tears of joy begin to fill her eyes. "Yes, please," she managed to say. "Ahhh… shiiiittttt!" She couldn't contain herself. The buildup was so strong that it pushed K's penis out of her. "Oh my God!" she yelled as she begins to squirt on his stomach. J didn't know whether to grab on to herself or Kedar. Her body wouldn't stop shaking and convulsing, as she cried and came at the same time. She couldn't do anything but collapse, as she slid off of the couch. Kedar picked her up, and looked into her eyes.

"Are you okay?" he asked.

"Hell no! What the fuck did you just do to me?" she yelled.

Kedar smiled and kissed her on her soft lips. J's body started to shake again.

"Hell no. Hell no. Hell no! Put me down," she cried out. Kedar did just that. J collapsed and rested, leaning over the arm of the couch. Kedar could see her juices sliding down the inside of her thighs. She had a perfect shaped ass, not too big but nice and round. He was getting aroused all over again. Kedar eased up behind J, and started kissing on the back of her neck. He slowly re-entered her from behind.

"Why are you doing this to me?" J asked.

"Can I at least get me one off, like you just did?" he asked, as he slowly slid in and out of her wetness. Kedar moved her hair from her face so that he could admire her beauty from that angle. J bit down on her bottom lip, and immediately felt his head throb inside of her. She arched up her ass and looked back at him, then bit down on her lip again. She felt Kedar throb inside of her again. J started feeling herself, she threw it back at Kedar while looking back into his eyes.

"Fuck me harder, K," she moaned through clinched teeth. His pulse now felt like a bass drum. Kedar stood her upright without breaking stride. J was now standing upright, with her face up against Kedar's face. His breathing was heavy and hot in her ear as he thrust himself in and out of her from the back. As Kedar reached around and began to massage her clit, she started to moan.

"Fuck me. FUCK ME!" All you could hear was her wetness, and the smacking of their skin. J lay her head back onto Kedar's shoulder as she bucked against him. "Now. You cum," she commanded.

"Ughhhhh," Kedar gripped her hips as he emptied his whole load inside of her. J continued to grind and buck back on his dick, refusing to let go of his now sensitive head that was stuck inside of her. Kedar's knees began to buckle.

J whispered, "Come for me, baby."

"Oh shit," Kedar moaned as he came again. Kedar fell over on J's back, knocking them both onto the couch.

CHAPTER 4

Kedar awoke a little while later. Lady J had powered him down. Well, it was safe to say that they had powered each other down. He looked over and saw her passed out, sleeping, like a newborn baby. Kedar picked her up and carried her to the master bedroom. On his way, he was able to get a good look at the mess they had made. They had knocked down, damn near, everything in their path.

"Damn, that shit was wild as fuck," he thought. Kedar made a mental note to straighten things up a bit for J. For right now though, the only thing on his mind was laying her down to bed and taking a hot shower. His stomach was sticky from when J had squirted all over him. Kedar looked around the apartment for an ashtray. When he didn't see one, he figured that J didn't smoke. Well, at least she didn't smoke inside of the house. Kedar didn't think anything of it though because, since when did he follow rules. He decided to smoke in the bathroom. Kedar headed to the bathroom. Ginger looked at him and went in the opposite direction, going to her cage. Kedar spun around remembering that everything in the cage had been knocked over. He headed back towards the kitchen.

He put some food in Ginger's bowl and placed it inside with her then locked the cage. Kedar looked into a closet in the hallway and grabbed a washcloth and towel. In the bathroom, Kedar started the shower and waited for the water to heat up. He allowed the hot water to beat down on his body as he lathered himself up.

Nesheya was in a state of awe as she entered the apartment. "What in the natural fuck happened in here," she said to herself. "Lady J," she called out as she walked to the kitchen to grab a bottle of water. Ginger began to growl. "Shut the fuck up, ol' stupid ass dog. I don't know why J won't get rid of yo' ass anyway." Nesheya called out J's name again but stopped short when she saw steam coming from the bathroom. Nesheya looked down and saw Kedar's shoes beside Ginger's cage. As Nesheya looked around the apartment some more, she noticed his shirt thrown over a chair and his boxers by her foot.

"What the fuck this bitch been doing?" Nesheya spotted an ID lying on the floor and picked it up. She examined the ID and saw a picture along with info belonging to one of the sexiest, chocolate niggas she had ever laid eyes on. "Damn! He fine as fuck! So, she got a nigga from the prison up in here fucking her lights out." She eyed K's bus ticket laying on the kitchen table. Nesheya shrugged it off and headed to her room. She was exhausted from her own festivities. She didn't feel like dealing with J and her prison love shit today. As she walked down the hallway though, she noticed Lady J's room door wide open. Nesheya peeked in to speak at least and noticed that J was in bed curled up like a newborn baby, sleeping. "Damn, that nigga worked my bitch out!" She slightly closed the door and continued to her room. She passed the bathroom door. Kedar had left the door wide open and furthermore, the shower curtain was cracked. Nesheya damn near dropped her purse and her water when she saw K's naked body covered in soap. "Damn, he fine as fuck. Good God! They sho' know how to make 'em in prison," she thought. Kedar turned to the side and Nesheya was able to see K's manhood. Nesheya's purse hit the floor.

"Lady J, is that you?" Kedar called out.

Nesheya didn't know what to say.

"Pass me some shampoo," he ordered.

Nesheya grabbed a bottle of Head & Shoulders and handed it to him. Kedar was still covered in soap. He even had his face covered in it.

"I just want you to know that I'm not tripping about you not giving me head, J. But just for the record, I'm a head fanatic," Kedar said, assuming that he was speaking to J.

Nesheya's mouth began to water, as she thought to herself, "How the fuck did J not suck on this big ass black dick?" She bit down on her bottom lip, and shook her head as she turned to walk out of the bathroom. It was like fate was taking place. The shampoo bottle slipped from Kedar's grip as he was taking it from Nesheya.

"Lady J," he said.

"Hmmm?" Nesheya replied.

"How in the hell you drop the shampoo when it ain't even in my hand yet? You clumsy as hell," K said.

"Umm hmm," Nesheya said as she hurried and picked the shampoo up from the floor and handed it back to Kedar. Kedar continued to wash his head with his face still covered in soap. Nesheya waved her hands in front of his face. "Damn, this is too tempting," she thought. "Fuck it," Nesheya kneeled down and slid the tip of Kedar's dick into her mouth.

"Ohhh shitttt… hold up. Let me get the soap outta my eyes baby," Kedar pleaded.

"Umm umm," Nesheya shook her head with his dick in her mouth.

Kedar was loving the game that J was playing, plus her moth was much warmer than the shower. Nesheya caressed his shaft as she sucked on his balls. She slid her tongue down the side of his manhood, then traced the vein underneath it coming back up to the tip. She slowly slipped the head back into her wet, fiery mouth. Nesheya began to lick and suck on the head of Kedar's dick, only allowing it to slip a little father into her mouth every so often. All at once, Nesheya attempted to deep throat Kedar and take his entire dick into her mouth. She only gagged herself.

"Fuck," she whispered. "This shit is too big for me to even be trying that shit," she thought. She started to jack it, she spit on the tip and massaged it while again caressing K's balls. Nesheya noticed the precum that had formed at the head. She flicked her tongue across it then sucked it up. Kedar's cum was so intoxicating to the taste. Nesheya wanted more of it, so she took his manhood into her mouth once again. She was determined to get what she wanted out of Kedar. Bobbing back and forth on his dick, Nesheya began to relax the muscles in her mouth so that Kedar's dick could easily hit the back of her throat. As Kedar started to thrust inside of her mouth and fuck her throat, Nesheya felt his dick get heavy. She could feel him throbbing in the back of her neck as he dug his dick in the back of her throat. Nesheya was waiting for the explosion. She wanted to taste him, devour him, consume every drop of his cum that he had to offer.

"Let me feel the inside of you again, J," Kedar asked. He was still under the impression that it was J that was having her way with him right now. "Then I'll let you finish," he added.

Nesheya slid out of her dress and panties, pussy soaking wet. She was extra ready. Kedar slid right in. He filled her up completely. Her pussy gripped his dick like a glove. Nesheya moaned as she threw it back on Kedar. Kedar's balls slapped her clit as he thrust in and out of her.

"Damn baby, you taking that dick," he said to her.

"Mmmhmm," she replied as she began to cream all over him.

Kedar slapped Nesheya on the ass hard, as he gripped her waist from behind.

"Fuck! Baby this ass feels fatter," Kedar moaned.

Nesheya came again, as if on cue, to K's sex talk. Kedar's dick began to throb. "Oh shit! I'm 'bout to cum baby," he moaned. The tingling sensation began to travel through his manhood.

Kedar let the water rinse the soap from his eyes. He didn't want to miss this view. Nesheya pulled off of Kedar's manhood and turned to drop to her knees. He opened his eyes.

"Oh shit!" Kedar moaned as he bussed into the redbone's mouth. Nesheya sucked even harder, as she squeezed and sucked every drop out of him. She looked up at Kedar with lustful eyes, as she licked her lips and smiled. She quickly jumped from the shower and grabbed her clothes off of the floor.

Nesheya looked back at Kedar then placed her finger over her lips. "Shhhhh. I wouldn't say nothing if I was you," she said as she smiled again and left the bathroom.

Kedar just stood there in shock of the turn of events that had just taken place. He shook his head. "I'm back in the world with snakes," he thought to himself. He stepped from the shower and proceeded to dry himself off.

CHAPTER 5

Once K was dressed he went out into the living room and began to clean up the mess that he and J had made earlier. By the time K was finished, he glanced at the clock. It was a quarter 'til 7.

"Oh shit," he thought. He quickly went in the room and woke up Lady J. She got up without hesitation and put on clothes. As she pulled on a pair of sweats and Kedar's tank top, he noticed her nipples were poking through his shirt. He instantly began to get an erection. She was fine as fuck.

"What?" J asked, when she noticed him staring at her. She was then pulling her hair into a ponytail.

"Nothing," he replied. Kedar simply smiled and continued to admire her.

"Come on boy, if you gonna make this bus." The words hit J as soon as they left her mouth.

Kedar could tell that the reality of the situation was sinking in on her. She looked saddened. He crossed the room and grabbed onto her. Kedar lifted her face to him with the palm of his hand and kissed her lips. "Come on Lady J. We got to go."

J shook off the emotions that she was feeling then grabbed her keys and purse.

"Why do you smell like my shampoo?" she asked.

"I took a shower while you were sleeping," K said.

"Oh, so you just made yourself at home, huh?"

Kedar laughed and popped her on the ass. "Let's go."

Kedar followed J, walking down the stairs. Just as they hit the bottom of the stairs, Mrs. Jenkins' door flew open. "I hope to see you again, young man," she spoke to K.

"You probably will, Madame," he replied.

"No, you won't, Mrs. Jenkins," J said and playfully pulled Kedar out of the door. J hit the unlock button on her keys, as they approached her Scion. She started up the car. Ella Mai's 'Boo'd Up,' came blasting through the speakers. J started to sing along to the song as she drove off. Ten minutes later, they pulled into the Greyhound Station. J turned the car off and sat back in her seat. K could clearly see the battle going on within her. He, himself was also battling emotions. He was wondering if he should tell her about how raw her roommate's snake ass was playing the game. Sensing that she was going through enough, he decided against it and waved it off. Kedar got out of the car and walked around to the driver's side. He opened the door to let J out. She didn't move. She just sat there with her arms crossed and a sad look on her face.

"Come here, Lady J," Kedar said as he pulled on her arm for her to get out. Once out of the car, he squeezed her tightly and kissed her on the neck. J's body began to tingle and melt into his. For some reason, she felt a security that she hadn't felt in a long time as Kedar held her. She leaned back and looked him in his eyes.

"Gone man," she said. "Cause shit starting to get real for me. I can't control my feelings, and plus you gotta go."

Kedar wrapped his hands around her small waist and planted another kiss on her lips. He was so passionate with it, he didn't want to stop. As he pulled away from her, he spoke, "I fucks with you, Lady J. Once I situate myself, I'ma call you. Then you can pull up to the city and I got you. Real nigga shit."

Those words put a smile on J's face because she knew he was sincere with his words. "Let me go and check and I'll be right back out," he said as he popped her on the ass again.

"Aight now K, you keep popping my ass like that, yo' black ass might don't leave," she said. What J didn't know was that, lowkey, it had crossed K's mind. But if he had learned anything from his bid, it was that if you start thinking with your dick, you'll have a lot more problems than fun. With that thought, he walked inside. When K entered the station, a white freckle-faced clerk by the name of Thomas greeted him. "How do you do, sir?"

K approached the counter in his normal swag and handed his ticket to Thomas. The clerk scanned the ticket. Thomas took a look over his shoulder at the clock on the wall. "I'm sorry sir, but Bus 19 to Atlanta, has already departed."

"What?!" K shouted.

"I apologize, sir, but we had an accident. Departure time was pushed up as a result. We had to send out a new bus to pick up passengers on the disabled bus. Were you not notified?"

He had to be bullshitting. "Was this a rhetorical question," K thought. Had he been notified, would he be standing here in front of him now? Kedar just shook his head. "No, I was not notified."

"I'm deeply sorry for the inconvenience, sir, but the next departure that we have is for 6 p.m. tomorrow," stated the clerk. "Or we can refund your money via check."

K clenched his fists. "Do it look like I want a check, bruh?"

The clerk looked at the ticket again, "Oh my."

"Oh my, what?" K asked.

"It seems that the state purchased this ticket. Are you getting out of prison or something? If so, then this ticket is non-refundable to you."

"Look, man. Just adjust the fucking ticket for tomorrow so I can get the fuck up outta this country ass town," K told the clerk.

Thomas sensed the tension in K's voice and began to quickly adjust things in the computer. He printed out another set of tickets for Kedar and handed them to him. "Now sir, you may want to arrive at least one hour early," he said. Kedar snatched the tickets from the clerk's hands and walked out.

Lady J sat on the trunk of her car as she waited for K to return. A smile was plastered on her face when she spotted him coming towards her. All she could think of was, how in the hell she had gotten here. This nigga had warned her of everything, but just like that, he had slipped behind the wall that she had built up for years. J looked in Kedar's face and noticed that his demeanor had changed. K walked right up to her, and stood between her legs. She cupped his face and looked him in the eyes, "What's wrong?" she asked.

Kedar shook his head, "Mannnn, my bus already left."

"So what that mean?" she replied.

"Well, good news is that it means I can spend another day with you."

J's clit jumped for joy at just the thought of it.

"So, what's wrong with that?" J stared at Kedar.

Kedar looked at her as if she'd lost her mind. "I'm supposed to report to my P.O. on time tomorrow. Even though there was a legitimate reason why I missed the bus, it'll still count as a technical violation. Them muhfuckas gon wanna put me back in the cell for at least two years. This judicial system is fucked up."

J's heart skipped a beat listening to the words that Kedar spoke. "They can't do that," she said.

"Shittin' me. They can and they damn sho will. Fuck it! I'm not even gonna go check in 'cause I already know how they rock," Kedar said.

J began to shake her head. "No, no, no look I'll take you," she said.

"Stop playing," he responded.

"I said I'll take you. Look, I already got a week off and I'm not doing shit anyway, so I'll take you," J replied.

Kedar liked the idea. "But look, I don't have no gas money or nothing to get there, but once I situate myself...."

"I know, I know, you got me," J said as she cut Kedar off. "K, I didn't ask you for nothing but your company. So, if you do, then you do. If not, then at least I got a slight vacation out of it. Now get your black ass in the car, before I change my mind!"

"Can I drive?" Kedar asked J.

"Pssst… nigga please, now you pushing it," she laughed.

CHAPTER 6

They both hopped in the car to take the four-hour trip from Pelham to Atlanta. K was up the entire ride to the city. He was enjoying the view riding up 75N. It felt good being out. As they got closer to the city, the tension began to build within him. They crossed over to 85N. Kedar could now see the King & Queen towers. The thought of how he had run these streets came back to him in a flood of memories.

J looked over at him, "Are you hungry?"

Kedar hadn't even thought about it until she asked. He pointed at the approaching exit and they pulled up to Varsity. He ordered two Varsity burgers, and some tater logs.

"God damn," said Lady J. "Who in the hell can eat these big ass burgers?"

"You will once you taste it," K replied. They sat outside of the restaurant, underneath one of the umbrellas and ate.

"Mmmmm," J moaned as she bit into the burger. She chewed a little more, then ate some of the potato logs.

"See, I told you so," said Kedar.

"Damn, this shit is bussin," J said. "This is gonna be a place I always hit when I come through," she said, while chewing.

Kedar looked at her and smiled. "Oh, so you already making plans to visit me?" he asked.

J rolled her eyes at Kedar and quickly replied, "Boy, don't flatter yourself!" She couldn't believe she had let that slip from her mouth. "I have to get a hold of myself around this man," she thought. After dinner, they jetted up to Gwinnett. They took Buford Hwy exit and pulled up into a Days Inn. Lady J was still exhausted, so once they checked in, she took a shower and put Kedar's tank top back on. J lotioned her body, then climbed into bed and fell fast asleep. Kedar sat on the edge of the bed smoking a Newport. The cigarette damn near took all of the air out of him, but after about two pulls his lungs were back in tune with one another. He gazed over at Lady J as the covers hugged around her curves. She looked so peaceful with her wrap around her head. He could finally see all of her facial features. She had high cheek bones, a full set of lips, and her eyes had a lil slant to them, which gave her an exotic, foreign look. As he looked closer, he noticed that she even had little freckles on her pretty pecan tan complexion. J had a very nice personality, and to top it all off, she had a body out of this world. Her uniform did nothing but injustice to her appearance. K leaned over and kissed her forehead, then climbed into bed behind her. From natural reflex, Lady J began to scoot back until their bodies formed the perfect letter C. He wrapped his arm around her and fell asleep.

The next morning J took Kedar to see his P.O. He sat patiently in the lobby area. "Kedar Simpson," called out a little petite white woman. K stood up and followed the lady to the back. He watched as her hips swayed from the little brunette woman. She had on a grey skirt, along with a white button up shirt. Her hair stopped just short of her ass, as she carried a folder to her side. "Mr. Simpson, have a seat," she directed as she took a seat behind the desk. She began to read out the stipulations of Kedar's parole. Right along with those guidelines, she read the fines and fees. She also explained about the random home visits and drug screenings. She explained to Kedar that she believes in second chances. The first mistake that he made, would be on her. The second mistake he made, she wouldn't hesitate to send his ass back into a six by eight cell. He took the out to inform Mrs. Jackson that his living conditions had changed, but he assured her that when he came back in, he would have a new address as well as his first pay stub. Mrs. Jackson made some notes in his folder. She ultimately agreed to it. She arose from behind her desk and leaned on the corner of it with her arms crossed. She eyed Kedar up and down. "Now one last thing," she said as she sat a clear cup on her desk. "Follow the officer and fill this up. Please, Mr. Simpson, don't let this be the first one against me because you will be back before you know it."

Kedar smile and asked if she had another one. "I always said No to drugs," he said as he grabbed the cup and followed the officer to the restroom. As Kedar walked out, it troubled him. How could you have a job watching another man's penis, day in and out? Ain't no way in hell I could do that, Kedar thought. Once K was done, he met J at the car.

"Is everything okay?" she asked.

"Yeah, it's fine. Can I use your phone?" He asked her.

"Sure," she replied as she pulled her iPhone from her purse. He quickly dialed Escobar's number as J started the car up and pulled out of the parking lot. About 15 minutes later, they pulled into the parking lot of Days Inn. Lady J dug around in her purse, looking for the key as they walked towards the room. Once she got the key out, she leaned on the handle as she was about to place the key into the slot.

"Hmmm. That's strange," she spoke.

"What?" K asked.

"The door looks open," she said.

Kedar stepped in front of her and pushed the door open.

"Hola, my friend," said Escobar from inside. K stepped in and took a look around the room. There were two Hispanic guards standing by the door. Escobar sat at the table, in the room, smoking a cigar and watching the news. He stood up to greet Kedar, as he approached him.

The two men exchanged handshakes and a hug. Escobar sized K up then spoke, "I see you haven't stopped training my friend."

"Well, you know, I was at least able to stay fit while I was in there," K replied.

"Indeed. Well I, for one, am glad to see you home in one piece. Oh, my goodness, where are my manners?" Escobar said, as he blew smoke from his cigar. "How are you, Senorita?" he said as he extended his hand. J placed her hand in his and Escobar kissed the back of it. "It is a pleasure to meet you."

"Thank you. Likewise," J replied as she stepped to the side. Escobar smiled then signaled for K to take a seat, while his security guards stood outside to guard the door.

Escobar gazed over at J. Kedar spoke up, "She good," then he told J to have a seat on the bed. K pulled out a cigarette. Escobar leaned over to light it for him with a silver Zippo lighter, decorated with the Mexican flags crossing on it. "I want you to know, Kedar, that I appreciated everything you did for me." Not being the one to go into detail, Escobar opened his jacket and pulled an envelope out of his inside pocket. He passed the envelope across the table to Kedar. K opened and examined the contents of the envelope. He thumbed through and saw nothing but blue-faced hundreds.

"Sweeeeeet…..," he whistled, then placed the envelope back onto the table. Escobar slid a small black bag over to Kedar with his left foot. K looked down and noticed the bag. He leaned over and unzipped it. The bag contained a brick and five pounds of gas. He zipped it back up and sat back.

"That's for you to situate yourself. Take it as a welcome home gift. But my friend, I really need you to get back on… how do you say it ehhh, THAT RALO." Kedar and Escobar both burst into laughter. "I'm glad to see you home, my friend," Escobar stated as he rose up from where he was sitting. The two men embraced once again, "Nice to meet you, Senorita," Escobar said to J. He then tapped on the table twice, the door swung open and just like that one of the guards was in the room. Escobar told K that he was only a phone call away. With that, he grabbed his hat and walked out.

Lady J crossed the room, still in shock of what had just taken place. "How in the hell did he get in here, K? Better yet, how in the fuck did he know we were here? I heard your conversation and all you said was that you were home. I highly doubt you lived in hotels, or do I even need to know?" she said frantically. Kedar looked on as she paced the floor.

"Come here, J," he said as he pulled her down onto his lap. He thumbed through the envelope that Escobar had given him. He pulled out $5k, then gave it to J.

"What's this?" she asked, holding the money in her left hand.

"Well," K started to respond. "While I was cleaning up your living room, I saw that you had a couple of overdue bills and shit. Plus, you fucked with me enough to make sure that I made it here on time. So, let's just say that this is my appreciation." J looked at him for a while in silence, then she replied, "Five grand is way more than what my bills come up to, so what's really up?"

"Yeah, well ok, how about you do a couple more things for me then we'll be square," K said as he smiled.

J hit K on the shoulder. "And what the hell you want me to do for this money, Kedar?" she asked.

Kedar laughed. "Nothing hell-lacious, chill…. Didn't I say I got yo bubble lip ass," he said playfully.

"You like my bubble lips too," J replied.

"Ummm hmm," Kedar said as he leaned in and sucked on her bottom lip. She dropped the money on the table, then pulled her shirt off. J straddled K as he palmed her ass. She kissed him passionately. They went at it for the next hour or so.

CHAPTER 7

After they were done, Kedar had J take him to Satellite Blvd. Once there, Kedar had J sign a six-month lease on a two-bedroom townhouse for him, which he paid the security and six months up on. J placed all of the bills in her name for him. She took him to a furniture wholesale spot off of Jimmy Carter Blvd. After his crib was situated, they went to Candler Rd in Dekalb County to a wholesale car lot, where Kedar bought himself a used all black Charger. It had to be a repo because the car was equipped with rims, a hell of a sound system, tints, the whole nine yards. I'll be damned if I let someone take something that I put all of my money into, he thought. With that, he went ahead and bought the car in full, $8,500 cash and carry. J trailed him back to the apartment, then began to make dinner. While he was waiting, Kedar took the time out to call his angels and his mother.

"Hello," a soft voice responded on the other end of the phone.

"Hey Ma," replied Kedar.

"Is this you Semahj?" His mother had always called him by his middle name.

"Yes, ma'am, it's me."

She yelled out to the girls, informing them that their father was on the phone. Kedar could hear them screaming for joy. He placed his phone on speaker and sat it down next to him.

"Daddy, daddy!" the girls called out. "What are you doing?" they said in unison.

"Thinking about my angels, as always. I miss y'all the most and love you with my all. You two do know you're my world, right?" Kedar asked.

"Yes, daddy," the twins responded. "When are you coming home? We miss you."

Anastasia, the oldest by fifteen minutes, and the most outspoken one of the two, blurted out, "Grandma be making us eat them nasty beans, and we don't like them."

"I sure do, and the same way I make y'all eat them, I made your daddy eat them too. Besides, what is y'all telling him supposed to mean to me?" His mother called out.

Asia nudged her sister, for her to be quiet. "She just means that grandma makes us eat healthy, but sometimes it's too much. Anyway, daddy when will we be able to visit you again?" she asked.

"How about daddy does you two one better and come see y'all?" Kedar asked.

The twins screamed and Kedar's mother spit out her tea. "Semahj what are you saying?" his mother asked.

"Calm down, calm down Elizabeth. Are the girls still scheduled for cheerleading camp this summer?" Kedar asked.

"What the hell I told you about calling me by my first name boy? Yes, they are," Liz said. "Matter of fact, they leave out tomorrow."

Kedar laughed. "Okay. Okay. Girls can you hear me?"

"Yes sir," the girls said.

"Alright y'all will go to cheerleading camp this summer, and I will be there for your first competition," Kedar informed them.

"Really daddy," the twins screamed excitedly.

"Y'all make me proud," he said. "Now don't give your grandmother any more problems, eat your beans, and mind yourselves. I promise I will be there soon."

"Yes daddy, we love you," the girls said.

"I love you too, now put your grandmother back on."

Liz returned to the phone, and took it off speaker. "Semahj, do you want to tell me what's really going on?"

Kedar informed his mother that he had been released, and that he was in the process of getting things in order for himself. "By the time cheerleading camp is over, I will have a house and everything situated. You and the girls will be moving from Florida to Georgia, so have your bags packed and ready, mama."

Elizabeth looked at the phone in deep thought at what Kedar had just said to her. "We'll talk more about it when they leave for camp," she responded, as she hung up the phone, and said a prayer for her only child.

When the line clicked, Kedar looked up and saw J staring at him. She walked over and sat his plate in front of him. "Your family sounds sincerely happy to hear from you. I can tell that they love you very much," she said.

"Thank you. Yea, those are my 3 queens," he replied.

J and Kedar enjoyed each other's company over the next few days. He took her shopping, and introduced her to upscale designer labels. The next morning, Kedar sat at the table in his new crib about to have breakfast, J had done her thing in the kitchen again. He sat pondering over his thoughts as she walked in and sat the plate down in front of him. J had cooked some grits, cheese and pepper omelets, turkey bacon, hash browns, and toast. She kissed him on the cheek as she sat down his glass of orange juice.

"What you thinking about?" she asked as she took a seat across from him.

"Nothing much," he replied. He began to eat his food. "Can you pass me the salt, please?" he asked.

"Sure!" She said as she handed him the salt and pepper shakers. "But yo' ass is thinking about something, so what is it?" J asked once more.

"Since you must know, I've run out of the money that Escobar gave to me and I was just thinking on what I plan to do next." J got up and grabbed her purse off of the bar, then started rumbling through it. She came back with the five grand he had given her a couple of days ago.

"Here," she said, as she handed him the money. Kedar grabbed her wrist and pulled her to his lap.

"Thanks, but no thanks," he said as he kissed her cheek. "That money is for you to handle your business. I'm good."

"You sure?" J asked, her hand still out with the money in it.

"I'm sure." Kedar laughs. "I still got the black bag he gave me. I just need to call my mans, Nike."

"Nike?" J asked.

"Yes, Nike," K replies.

"Who names their child after a shoe?" she laughs.

"Ha, real funny. His real name is Nicholas, we just call him Nike or sometime Nik for short," Kedar says to her.

"Well, I still got this money on standby if you need it."

Kedar smirked. That's sweet of you," he thought to himself. Then Kedar pulled out his phone and started dialing Nike's number.

"YO!" The voice said on the other end.

"What up my dude?" Said K.

"Who the fuck is this?"

"Nigga, it's me...K."

"Oh shit!! What's poppin' my guy? Long time no hear," Nike says.

"True, true. You know I had to do the time and not let it do me."

"Right! Right!" Nike says as he takes a long pull from the spliff he rolled. "What up tho', you need a G-dot?" He asked K.

"Naw shawty. I'm 'bout to pull up," Kedar replied.

"Nigga stop playin'.... I got like 3 bitches here now, I can send one of them to the store to get you a green dot," Nike exclaims.

"Nigga, I'm serious. I'm out!"

Nike fumbled the phone. "Hello? Hello?"

"I'm still here," Kedar says.

"Yo! We got some serious catching up to do bro," Nike says excitedly.

"Right, right! But look, you still in tuned?" K asked.

"I got a couple of numbers, but you know since you been gone, the migos ain't been fucking with a nigga. That's the real reason why I wasn't able to fuck with you how I wanted to while you was gone," Nike explains.

"It's all good. Ima pull up in bout 30. We'll rap then."

"Aight dawg, I'm waiting," Nike responds.

"Say less."

"Bet."

K hung up the phone. "See, problem solved." He finished up his breakfast then put on his clothes.

CHAPTER 8

He let J drive him around in his car, as he sat on the passenger side. He hadn't gotten around to getting his license yet. They pulled into The Falls apartment complex off of Satellite Blvd to Nike's spot. He was sitting on the steps, smoking a cigarillo. He stood up as the car came to a halt. K stepped out of the passenger side of his car to greet his friend. "Damn nigga," said Nike. "I see you got yo' swoll on." Nike and K began to play box. Lady J stepped out of the car, shaking her head. Nike stopped dead in his tracks, "Damn! Who dis?" he asked.

"None ya! Nigga come on, damn," laughed K. The two men and J went into the apartment.

"Excuse the spot," said Nike. "I had a party going on last night." Nike claps his hands together. "Let me get y'all something to drink."

Lady J looks around and scans the apartment, thinking to herself, "Oh no the hell you won't." Nike goes to the refrigerator and grabs Kedar a cold beer. K cleans off the barstool so that J could have a seat. "I don't like it here or him," J whispered in Kedar's ear. "Just chill," K said very softly, then he gently kissed her lips.

"What you got for me?" Nike asked.

Kedar placed the bag on the table and dumped the contents out. He neatly stacked each Ziploc bag one on top of the other, then he slid one over to

Nike. "Look bruh, I need 25 for each one of these four. You can keep that one," K said pointing to the bag he had slid over to his friend. Nike immediately bussed the bag open and inhales the scent.

"Ahhhhh........Now THAT'S some gas," he stated. "Cara!" He yelled out. Cara came out of the back room with nothing on but some red boy shorts and a matching sports bra. Half of her head was shaved bald, and she had a tattoo covering the entire right side of her body. She sashayed her way into the kitchen. "What's up boo," she answered Nike. She gazed at Kedar, looking him over as if he were a fresh piece of meat. Cara knew that chain gang glow from anywhere. He had to be just getting out, she thought to herself. As if on cue, Nike spoke up. "My mans, Kedar here, just got out. Here, roll this up, and bring me my phone." Cara switched her way to the back.

"And put some fuckin clothes on," he yelled. She stopped and looked back.

"For what?" she said as she popped herself on the ass. "You paid for them to be seen, right?" She was referring to her butt shots and breast implants. When no one answered her, Cara blurted out, "That's what I thought." Then she cut her eyes over at Lady J.

"Yo K, man how you want me to handle this?" Nike asked, interrupting the tension that was obviously building in the room.

Kedar picked up the kilogram of cocaine. "I need 30 for it," he said.

At that time Cara returned with Nike's phone. She had put on some sweatpants but there was no hiding them big ass titts in that sports bra. "Here you go," she said as she handed Nike his phone. Cara gazed over Lady J. "You cute," she said, speaking to J. "Who did your work?"

Lady J cocked one of her eyebrows up, mimicking the wrestler The Rock. "Huh......excuse me," J replied.

Cara smiled. "I can help get you in if you need a job."

Lady J looked at Cara strangely, "In where? K what the fuck is she talking 'bout," she fiercely stated at Kedar.

Cara but in before K could answer, "Girl, I can get you in at Strokers."

"Who?" J asked

"The strip club....," Cara replied.

She looked at K before asking, "Where did y'all find this one at?" Cara was examining Kedar, wondering what he would feel like inside of her.

J pulled herself from her thoughts. "Excuse me, but did you just fuckin say 'found me'?.....FOUND ME!!!!??? First off BITCH I wasn't lost in order to be muthafuckin found. Second, hoe, this shit right here......," J said signaling to the curves on her body, "is all Na-tur-allllll. Fuck you think this is....hoe yo' best bet is to find you somebody to play with. Third, I respect dancers but I got a job. And fourth, them eyes in your damn head, you keep wondering with them shits and YOU gonna be found some fuckin' where else....try me."

"LADY J......," chimed in Kedar, because the tension had gotten thick quick. Nike was still on the phone making calls. When he finished, he signaled for Cara to taste the product. She swiftly pulled out a pocket knife, while looking at Lady J as she flipped it open. She dug into the powdery contents and came out with a little ant hill on the tip of the knife. She placed it up to her nose, and in one quick sniff, it was all gone. Cara rubbed her finger over the knife, then rubbed her gums. "That's it," she finally stated to Nike. Cara licked the knife, while making eye contact with J, then flipped it closed.

J was about to stand up, but Kedar grabbed her by the wrist. Nike walked over to the cabinet, popped it open and pulled out a thing of Miami Ice. That was K's cue to leave.

"Look bruh, I gotta go. Is everything going to one person?" He asked Nike.

"Naw, buddy gonna grab two of the bags. I let them go for three a piece, and he gonna give me 32 for the whole thing. But you know I gots to get me, me," Nike replied with a chuckle.

"It don't matter to me how you move that shit, just have that 40 for me," said K.

"Say less. This shit will be done in 'bout a hour," replied Nike.

"Aight, bet that up. Well, I'm 'bout to grab a bite to eat. Just hit me up when it's done," K said.

As the 2 men embraced, a blond head white girl came from the back with nothing but a robe covering her naked body. "I didn't know we had company," she stated. She walked right up and kissed Nike, then she turned and kissed Cara. Cara handed her the pocket knife and she repeated the same process that Cara had done not too long ago.

Kedar shook his head. "Bruh Ima be around, just hit me up."

Kedar and J pulled into T.G.I.Friday's to have lunch. Good thing it wasn't crowded. They were escorted to a table as soon as they walked in.

"How you guys doing? My name is Lynn, I will be your waitress this afternoon." The young lady said, as she handed them two menus. Kedar opened the menu, then just as quickly closed it.

"Well, I'm ready if you are Lynn," he said.

"Go ahead, sir."

"Let me get the pepper steak and potatoes with macaroni and cheese...," Kedar started to order as J cut him off.

"Why so much starch?" she asked.

"Would you like anything to drink sir?" the waitress asked.

"Yes, may I have a Hennessey & Coke?" K replied.

"Are you ready too, ma'am?" she asked J.

"Yes, may I have.....," J quickly scanned over the menu and then set her eyes on what she wanted. "Can I have the Chicken Alfredo with a side of steamed broccoli & cheese?"

"And for your drink, ma'am?" Lynn asked.

"Uhhhh, I would like a.......Sex on the Beach."

"You got it," Lynn said as she gathered the menus and informed them that she would be right back with their drinks.

Kedar sat back in the booth, looking at J.

"What?" she asked.

"I'm tryna figure out how Cara looked you all over, and then you ask for sex out of this scrawny girl (referring to the waitress) mind you, on the beach might I add."

"First off......," J started. "Fuck you, and fuck Cara. I don't even swing that way." Kedar started to laugh. "Boy I'm serious. That bitch almost got her shit rearranged. Sizing me like that, hell. I don't mean to be in your business but you brought me there and put me in it, so I think I'm justified in what I'm about to say. I don't like yo' mans. He just gives me a bad vibe. Then on top of that, I always thought people was supposed to bless you when you come home, not the other way around. Your crib is bigger than his. You gave him some shit that he is gonna at least make 'bout ten bands." She stopped to take a breath.

"Is that so?" Kedar asked.

"Nigga, I may be a female, and from the country, but I'm not green. I know what the fuck Miami Ice is used for. And the way them hoes hit that shit, they got a everyday habit. Look, all I'm saying is, be mindful of your situation while you out here." Then she reached across the table and grabbed his hand. Kedar looked across the table, staring into J's brown eyes. He wondered how he could tell her about her two-timing roommate and what she did.

"What's up?" J asked, pulling Kedar from his thoughts.

"What is it that's on your mind?" she asked.

"I feel you on what you're saying, but I'm gonna tell you the same thing about your company, you keep," Kedar replied.

"Who?" J asked

"Your roommate," K said.

"Nesheya?!......well, the girl been through a lot, I was only trying to help her get her shit together. But the shit with her is only bringing me down. She supposed to have helped me with the bills and shit. But you see for yourself how that's turning out."

Ring.....ring......ring......ring. J's phone belted out.

"Mmm, speaking of the devil," she said.

"Who dat?" K asked.

"It's her. Fuck that, I'm not gonna answer, she probably don't want shit anyway."

"You might need to answer."

"For what? Whatever it is can wait 'til tomorrow. I already gotta go back home anyway and ain't no telling when I'm gonna see yo' black ass again," J said before she realized it.

Kedar rubbed her wrists. "Naw, don't act like that," he said.

"What? I'm gonna at least enjoy the rest of my lil vacation, while it lasts," J stated. Lynn came back with their drinks and food. She placed the food on the table in front of them.

"Thank you," they both said as they prepped themselves to eat.

"So, what are you gonna do about a job?" J asked Kedar.

"I was thinking about opening me up a detail shop," K answered.

Lady J began to smile from ear to ear, as she took a bite of her food.

"What you smiling like that for? I know that food ain't that damn good," Kedar shot at J.

"In fact, it is......," J replied as she twisted her fork around some more noodles then poked a piece of chicken at the end. She blew it to cool it off, then fed it to Kedar. "But for your information, I was imagining how you would look in a suit, sitting behind a desk."

"I would look professional with a suit on, huh?" he smiled.

"Nawww, a suit would look professional with you in it," J quoted. At that moment K's phone rang. It was Nike, telling him that everything was all good. Kedar hung up and they finished enjoying their meal. Before they pulled back up to Nike's place, J did tell him that she thought the detailing shop would be a good idea for him to do. Plus, it wouldn't be that much to just draw up a proposal, then he would get the bank's support.

"If not then, hell, you know how to get the money. Just try the legit way first," she finished saying, as she pulled into the parking lot. She didn't turn the car off.

"You ain't coming in?" Kedar asked her.

"For what? Me to go jail? I probably would tear that bitch up. So go handle your business, I'll be waiting. If your ass take too long, you will be walking," she laughed.

"You would leave me in my own shit?" K asked as he got out of the car.

"Is you black?" she responded.

"Yea!" K rebutted.

"Well, you know what that mean." J stuck her tongue out, as Kedar closed the door. He laughed to himself, she was goofy as hell. He was going to miss her company. He knocked on the door and was met by Cara. She had removed the sweatpants that she had on. "Good thing J stayed in the car," he thought to himself. Cara walked over to the table to have a seat. She could feel Kedar's eyes watching her ass bounce with every step she took. She had a seat with her legs spread. Kedar eyed the room, he could see that the back-room door was closed. It had to be at least two ounces of coke in the sandwich bag that sat on the table. Then there was about ten grams in lines on the glasstop, with a pile of money by it.

"Where is your friend?" asked Cara.

"She in the car," replied K.

A smile spread across Cara's face. "Then we got time," she said as she stood up and stepped up to him. She started to massage his crotch. She could tell he was already turned on while she walked. She couldn't wait to release the pound of flesh she was feeling.

"Thanks, but no thanks. Where the fuck is Nike?!" Kedar spit out. "The nerve of this nigga," Cara thought to herself.

"Nike!!" she yelled.

Nike emerged from the back room, fixing his pants with the white girl in tow, still wearing that damn robe. She took a seat by Cara and did one of the lines that lay on the table.

"My nigga, you straight?" Nike asked K while looking at Cara, who was pouting. Nike inhaled from a blunt and offered it to Kedar.

"Naw, I'm good homie. You know I'm on papers and shit," K informed Nike.

"My bad, my bad.....," Nike said as he passed the blunt to Cara. "Jessica give Kedar that money." The white girl reached across the table to grab the two stacks of money. Her robe fell open, she didn't seem to mind that it was all hanging out. She had a perfect set of breasts and her box was smooth shaved. She handed the two stacks to Kedar. Jessica then sat back down, crossed her legs, and began to roll a blunt out of the pound of weed that sat on the table.

"My bad dog, about Cara and the blunt," Nike said to K.

"No pressha homie," Kedar began to thumb through the money. He counted the first stack, then he waved the second stack like a fan. "Bruh, this shit feel light."

"Man look, the nigga didn't have all the money for the soft, right.....," Nike began explaining.

"Huh.....," Kedar blurted out as he looked back at the table where the two women were just snorting Peru with no cut.

Nike started back to get Kedar's attention, "Look K, I can give you the lil bit I made off the play to balance everything out, if you want."

Kedar looked back in his hand at the money. "How much is this?" he asked, waving the money.

".....like 38," responded Nike.

"Like or is?"

"Well, it is 38 bands. But like I said, I'll give you......,"

Kedar cut him off before he could finish. "No pressha homie," K said.

"Look tho', K....." Nike threw his arm around Kedar's shoulders, "We need to get back on that dog food 'cause its jumping right now. Niggas ain't got no plug and they been getting some bullshit."

Kedar looked at Nike. "Damn nigga, slow down. I just got home. You starting to sound like that nigga, E," he replied.

Nike stopped in his tracks with a look of discernment on his face. "E gave you this coke?" he asked K.

"Just chill homie," said K.

"Man, that's some bullshit! When you feel the nigga stop answering my fuckin calls and all! He acting like a nigga didn't take a bullet for his ass," said Nike, as he lifted his shirt revealing a zig zag line going from his navel to his chest. "This shit is cause of his ass," an angry Nike pointed out.

"Calm down my nigga," replied Kedar, in a firm voice. "I'ma holla at the nigga...."

"But you both gotta see where I'm coming from," exclaimed Nike.

"I ain't going back, I just got the fuck home. And I said Ima holla at the nigga and see what's what," Kedar shot back.

"It's all love fam.....," replied Nike. "You right, you just came home. Look, it's time to celebrate! I'm gonna take you out this weekend and I'm not accepting no for an answer. So, gon' ahead and tend to your folks that's waiting on you and Ima hit you up later in the week."

"Aight my dude," said Kedar, then he stepped out.

CHAPTER 9

Kedar and J drove back to his place, where J spent the next couple of hours submitting loan applications, and drawing up proposals for Kedar's car wash. She sat in his bed with her legs crossed, putting the finishing touches on everything. K came in the room with a plate of food that he had cooked. It carried baked chicken, rice with a creamy chicken and mushroom sauce, string beans, and garlic bread. He kissed J on her cheek.

"Thank you for everything," he stated to her. Kedar sat beside her on the bed. "I didn't know you wore glasses."

J looked over and glanced at him over the rim of her glasses. "What do that supposed to mean?" she asked as she turned back and continued typing.

"I'm just saying, they cute on you."

"Whatever," J replied as she rolled her eyes. "There, now everything is done. All you have to do is be patient, and wait on their response. Oh, and you need to quickly locate a building or a lot where you're gonna open up this establishment. Mmm....mmmm...mmm damn boy who taught you how to cook?" J had finally stopped talking long enough to take a bite of her food. She took another bite from her meal.

"Is it ok?" Kedar asked.

"I tell you what, you keep cooking like this and I'm taking you back with me," J replied, while pointing at her plate.

"I don't mind going," he said.

J placed the plate on the nightstand and crawled on top of him. She fucked him so good that night, he passed out immediately afterwards. J woke up around 3am that night to get herself situated to make the trip back home, and make it to work on time.

Her first day back at work seemed to drag. Kedar had been the only thing that she could think about, all day. She could not wait to get home. As she entered the building, Ginger came running out.

"Hey girl, you missed me? How did you get out?" J asked the happy dog.

Mrs. Jenkins met her at the stairs, "I'm glad you made it back. I thought the boy had kidnapped you." They both shared a laugh.

"Where is he anyway?"

"He had to go home, but Mrs. Jenkins, how did you get Ginger?" J asked.

"That nothing ass roommate of yours allowed the folks to come get her. She was saying that you left and all types of crazy stuff. So, I went ahead and kept her. I knew you would never leave this angel for the world." Mrs. Jenkins patted Ginger on the head as she wagged her tail.

"What?!" a confused J responded.

"Yes child, and the heffa felt some type of way after I stopped the animal control man. I had to pay him $150 not to take this precious baby."

"I'm so sorry Mrs. Jenkins.....," J started rumbling through her bag.

"Baby NO, it's ok. I didn't do it for you to pay me back child. I know that you are a good wholesome young lady, and you work hard baby. But you know, I also been seeing her taking her things out slowly. One day at a time, she'll ease some stuff out. She been having some dudes there too. Talking about they her cousin, but I know better. Hell, I know that child whole family," Mrs. Jenkins informed J.

Lady J opened the door to her apartment. The front room was empty. The living room set was gone. Nesheya had picked up all of her belongings and left nothing but her mat on the floor. The bills were sprawled out on the table. J shook her head as she sat down at the dining room table. Mrs. Jenkins rubbed her back, "It's gonna be ok baby, it'll be alllllright." She wanted to desperately call Kedar, but she opted not to. Mrs. Jenkins offered to keep Ginger while she worked. Jay thanked her and began cleaning up her apartment.

Kedar awoke the next morning. J had been helpful enough as to putting a list together of some potential spots he could buy or rent. He got up and out to start on the list. Kedar placed a couple of calls, and visited a couple of the spots. It wasn't until three that afternoon, that he received a call back. He arrived at the location on Buford Hwy, and sat down with the owner to discuss business plans. The place had actually been a carwash, but the owner explained that business had gotten so slow that he wanted to move on. The owner went on to say that he would give Kedar the business as is, with the equipment and all for 85 grand. He could put down a 50% deposit and retrieve the key. The remainder of the balance, Kedar could make monthly payments. They agreed and sealed the deal. To top it all off, the bank had approved Kedar for a $150K business loan. So, he faxed the information over to them, and made an appointment to finalize it tomorrow. Just like that, Kedar was in business. He got a phone call later from Nike.

"What up, my guy?"

"Chilling.....," replied Kedar. "I just got my business situated, what's good?"

"Even better, it's time to celebrate on another level now," said Nike. "Meet me at Strokers."

"Strokers?!" yelled Kedar.

"Yea nigga! And no is not an answer. You got yo' lil girlfriend wit' you?" asked Nike.

"Naw, nigga that ain't my girlfriend," Kedar replied.

"Well pull up, I'm gonna make sure shit set up. I'll be waiting."

Kedar replied to Nike, "Aight I'll be there."

He pulled up bout 30 minutes later, turning in off of Rockbridge Rd. Once he found a parking spot, he went inside the club. "This shit was jumping," he thought to himself. Kedar glanced at his watch. It was so early in the afternoon. It seemed like a whole other world once he walked through the doors. The lights danced across his face as he slowly walked through the club. Topless women walked around everywhere. He could hear the sounds of Migo's, "Bad & Boujee," blasting through the speakers. As soon as Kedar saw his mans, Nike in the VIP section the song changed to Yo Gotti & Nicki, "Rack It Up." Kedar scanned his surrounding, he rested his eyes on the main pole and saw Cara sliding down that bitch upside, down. Then she flipped off of the pole into a full split. The crowd went wild. Two more girls in little 'fits began to rack it up. Kedar made his way to Nike.

"Boy you got you one then!" Kedar yelled over the music to Nike, he signaled towards Cara. It seems as if she heard him. Cara looked back and had her cheeks jumping like an African beating a drum. The whole club smelled like liquor, pussy, and weed. Kedar ordered a double shot of Hennessy, as Nike started telling him that Cara was just his partner. There were three girls in the booth of the VIP with Nike.

"Glad to have you home, my boy," Nike stated.

Two of the women sat down beside Kedar as he tipped his glass to Nike. Nike pulled on the spliff that he had been smoking and nodded his head in approval. "Now this is how you celebrate," he said out loud. When the song was over, Cara came off of the stage and straight to the VIP booth. The women cleared way for her. She strolled right over and sat in Kedar's lap. Cara began to grind back and forth.

"I'm sorry miss lady, but you're gonna have to stop. I didn't bring no paper with me," Kedar informed Cara.

"It's ok......," she replied. "This is on the house." Cara bent all the way over and made her ass cheeks jump up and down. She turned around and straddled Kedar.

"That's what I'm talking 'bout," yelled Nike. "Loosen up some my dude."

Cara spun around and arched her back while on him. As Kedar began to get aroused, it seemed she was enjoying this more than he was. At that moment, two guys approached the booth.

"God damn Nike, you gon' cuff all the bad ones?" laughed Tank.

The two girls that had been racking it up, waltzed in with the two bags.

"See what I mean?" said Tank, sizing up the eye candies.

"Cara, handle this money," shouted Nike. Cara was in her own world, trying to please her damn self while riding on Kedar. She leaned back and whispered, "We'll finish this back at the house or I can get a room if you want."
To the least of her knowledge, Kedar's dick had gone soft the minute the niggas approached.

Nike instructed Cara to take the money and the women with her as they exited the booth. Nike offered the two gentlemen a drink. They gladly accepted the offer. Then he passed them the blunt. "Yo Tank, this my mans Kedar, he just came home. Kedar, Tank...Tank, Kedar." K raised his glass in acknowledgment of the man. Then they had a seat around the booth. Something didn't sit well with Kedar. The more he looked at Tank, the more he looked familiar. Kedar's street senses told him that the other nigga was probably just a shooter, the way he was dressed in all black with a hoodie. K felt awkward not having a gun. But being the outspoken individual that he is, he couldn't contain his suspicions.

"Do I know you from somewhere?" he asked the man. Tank took another long pull from the weed, as he exhaled, he allowed the smoke to dance around his head.

Then he answered. "I'm sorry to disappoint you and no disrespect but, I never been down the road before."

"None taken," Kedar replied.

"Say Nike, I need some of this shit you blowing on," Tank stated.

"I got you, just let me hit my folks and I'm gonna see what they talking about," Nike responded.

Tank passed the blunt to Kedar. "Naw, I'm good. I don't smoke." K then lifted his glass up.

"Aight, say less," then Tank passes the blunt to his partner. "I was just coming over to speak, that's all......," said Tank. "I didn't mean to intrude. But look Nike bruh, shit drying up on me. I need some dog food."

"I'll look into that too, once I call him," Nike replied.

"I don't need that stepped on shit. I'm willing to pay 65 a piece," Nike damn near spit his drink out.

"Man come on Tank wit' the games. Shit round here drying up fast. Once I call my folks, he probably gonna have some of that Afghanistan Brown or that China White dope. Shit easy on the market raw, 85 to 100 bands a pop."

"Well if it's what you say it is, then tell him I'm willing to try two of them for 150, and I'll grab a couple of bags from him too. Just once I get to spending, drop the ticket," Tank informed Nike.

"Aight bet. If you agree to pay a initial 80 a piece and cop 50 bags, I can get him to drop the ticket to 70 a piece and we'll go from there. But I need at least five bags for my hassle and five grand," Nike responded.

"Done......just make it happen."

"Say less......," Nike said as he tossed Tank an ounce of the weed that he was smoking. Tank left the VIP with his homie in tow. Kedar immediately looked at Nike.

"Mannnn, what the fuck was that?!" he spat.

"What? The nigga just pulled up," Nike explained.

"Ummhmm," Kedar replied.

"Real nigga shit, but you see the demand for the shit. I even got the nigga up to 80. Bruh shit is really real out here."

"Man... I know that nigga from somewhere," Kedar said as he thought hard about his statement.

"Fine....if you don't wanna fuck wit' the nigga then that's cool. It's more niggas out there, but homes really moving weight," Nike said.

"Chill....," Kedar replied as he thought to himself that it would be good start up money. "Look I'm gonna call E and make it happen, but I'm not doing the transaction. You are."

"Aight my dude," Nike responded.

"No shorts neither nigga."

"I got you," Nike said as he signaled for the girls to come back in. Kedar took another sip from his cup, then stood up to leave. "Damn, you not staying to finish celebrating?" Nike asked him.

"Naw, I'm good. Ima hit you tomorrow or in a couple days. Just answer nigga."

"Aight bet"

Kedar wanted to tell J everything that had happened. He knew she would be happy about some of it and pissed about Nike. So, he opted to wait until he finalized everything with the bank tomorrow, then he'd tell her. He went ahead and texted her, "goodnight bubble lips."

CHAPTER 10

J rolled over that morning and saw the text from Kedar. It brought a smile to her face to hear from him. It had been well into the night before she had finished cleaning and settling in, so she had not gotten much sleep. She got up and got dressed for work. On her way to work, she called Kedar's phone twice. Knowing that he was probably still asleep, she texted him. "I know you want to blow a bubble wit these lips tho." She thought to herself, "Damn.... How in the fuck did we get here?" She could only shake her head. She waited a few more minutes before turning off her phone. She went into briefing with nothing but Kedar on her mind. She was placed back on duty in F building. Right after count, Lt. Taylor brought the same cadet, Tangela, to her dorm. After Lt. left, the women began to speak.

Tangela started off, "Girl, how 'bout I didn't know I was entitled to have time off."

"Huh? They didn't tell you?" J asked.

"Hell naw.... I found out a week later and I took that week's pay." The two women burst into laughter. Jay went on to tell her about her downtime but was careful not to mention anything about being out of town, Kedar, or any other male for that matter. She really just told her that she enjoyed the much-needed break. As she was speaking, she spotted Divine about to cut some hair. J went into the restroom and quickly wrote Kedar's number on a small piece of paper. When she came out of the restroom, she grabbed a few razors. J then hit the glass and signaled for Divine. He approached the window and saw that it was her, "Hey Ms. Jones... I appreciate the lookout," he said to J.

"No problem Divine, I saw your partner Kedar on my way out."

"Word?" he replied. "I hope my mans holding it down out there."

"He told me to make sure that I keep you with some razors, so that you can handle your business."

"No doubt, 'cause I need them."

J passed him about six razors with the number in the middle.

"'Preciate it," he responded as he grabbed the razors. He didn't notice the paper until he made it back to the table. When he unfolded the paper, he saw Kedar's name and number. He folded the paper back up, then turned and gave J a head nod. He was definitely going to hit his homie up first chance he got.

Kedar awoke the next morning, and began to get dressed. He grabbed his phone and noticed J's text. She always had some kind of slick ass response. He laughed and wrote back, "Call me when you get a chance." He clipped his phone on his hip, then made his way to his appointment at the bank. At the bank, he finalized his paperwork and headed over to his new detail shop. He met up with Greg Owens, the former owner to give him the remainder of his money. The two men exchanged a handshake, then parted ways. Kedar began to clean up the place. He looked around and thought about how he was going to change it up and drip some sauce into the place. He started to clean up the outside, removing some of the trash and debris. His phone began to ring, he pulled it out and didn't recognize the number calling. He answered anyway.

"Hello," he called out.

"Damn Houdini, you cut out before I did my last act," the voice said back.

"Who dis?" K asked, noticing that the voice sounded familiar.

"Oh you got jokes now. Nigga, this Cara."

"Oh. What up? What can I do for you, seeing that I'm busy," he asked.

"I don't mean to take up much of your time, but I got your number out of Nike's phone. I wanted to see if we could kick it?" Cara stated.

"I mean.....that would be cool, but like I said I'm kinda busy. Just check wit' me later, aight?"

"I don't mean to be all up in yours, but what can a man possibly be doing this time of morning? Being that you just came home," Cara asked.

Kedar began to laugh. "Working! I just copped this new detail shop off of Buford and right now I'm trying to shop around for some interior decorators that can add some flavor to my shit."

"Ohhh.... A man with a plan. Well, a man that have a plan when he come home, I salute you on that. Look, I got a couple of friends that owe me some favors. I can holla at them, and get you a good quote for some quality work."

"That's wassup. I appreciate it," Kedar replied.

"No problem."

"What's the catch?" K asked.

"No catch ..... I'm just looking out, that's all. Don't get me wrong now, a bitch gon need her shit polished from time to time though." They both burst into laughter.

"I got you," K assured her.

"Listen Kedar. Don't take this the wrong way but, you come off as good people, and Nike hasn't stopped praising you since you got home. I respect the fact of you having a girl and all, I won't do anything to jeopardize that. But I really would appreciate if we could be friends. Not just me and you, but I want to associate with your girl too."

Kedar pondered for a minute. "You did come off strong, but you good peeps. I know J may not be so heartfelt and she live down south. But I'll run it by her."

"Cool, I respect that. Hey, seeing that it's going to take me 'bout 30 minutes to make these calls, how about I buy you lunch today?" Cara asked.

"I appreciate that, but I'ma have to take you up on that offer later. Make the calls for me and hit me back to let me know wassup."

Cara laughed, "Aight. I'll be your secretary. I'll call you later with the quotes."

Kedar laughed at Cara's response, then hung up the phone. "Damn," he thought to himself, "let me handle this lil bit with Nike, 'cause I know this interior decorator might knock me down a little." He continued to pick up the debris in the lot.

When Kedar had picked up majority of the trash outside, he stopped for a quick break. He pulled his phone out and quickly dialed Escobar's number. "Holá my friend," said Kedar into his phone.

"Holá"

"I'm gonna go ahead and open up the kennel we were talking about."

"Sí, Sí."

"I'm gonna need two boys & two girls. I'm looking for about 150 square feet of property to put them on," Kedar stated.

"Sí, well I know a spot that will cost about 500 per yard. Top of the line lawn care and all. But my boys are gonna cost about uhhhhh....... for you my friend, 4,200 and the girls, 1,500," Escobar informed K.

"So, 4,200 for each boy and 1,500 per girl? Well, I can start breeding with that."

While Kedar was on the phone, a white Chevy Lumina had pulled up on the side. A lady had stepped out of the car and was walking towards him from behind.

"Well, that's doable," Kedar said into the phone.

"What kind of dogs are you breeding?" the woman asked him from behind.

Startled, Kedar grabbed his chest. "Damn lady, why you sneaking up like that? Give me a minute. Hello? Cool...... Understood. But please allow me to speak to you later about the animals. I must entertain my PO right now."

Escobar understood and hung up.

Kedar turned to the lady, "What can I do for you today?" he asked.

"Nothing much....," she said. "I was actually passing by and noticed you picking up trash, so I figured I'd stop."

Kedar lifted the trash bag and walked it over to the dumpster. "Well, ya know, I'm just trying to tidy up the place. This is my new business and work-place. I can't tell you how much I'm making as of right now, but I can solidify the fact that I have a job. Take my word though, I will be on time to make my monthly payment."

"I see.....," replied Ms. Jackson. "And you're into breeding dogs, but I hope not for fighting purposes."

Kedar frowned, "I truly love animals too much for me to place them in a situation like that. I'm only trying to do something productive to keep myself from going back and besides.... they will be show dogs."

"I see....," she said, "especially at that price."

"Yes but, it is a thing of patience, because you have to wait until the girls go into heat in order to breed them. So, technically I'm on a woman's sched-ule."

They both laughed.

"You got a sense of humor," Ms. Jackson smiled.

"Would you like a tour of the place?" he signaled towards the shop.

"Naww, I'm good maybe some other time, but I will be checking on you from time to time."

"Well hey, you're always welcome to."

"Keep up the good work, because many men that come out don't know what their next step will be, but you came out with a plan, just stay clean and I won't be down your back. By the way did you get your living arrangement situated?"

"In fact, I did." He asked to see her notebook, then he quickly wrote his address down. "Come by at will. Official or unofficial," Kedar informed her.

She smiled, then raised the book. "I'm going to keep it official."

Kedar grabbed her car door for her, and closed it as she sat down and buckled up. "Have a nice day." He waved to her as she pulled off. Kedar made his way back to the entrance and began walking through the building as he dialed Escobar's number. Just as the phone began to ring, he was approaching his office door. He stopped in his tracks as he heard the receiving phone began to ring as well. He looked around and asked, "How did you get in here?"

Escobar was sitting at Kedar's desk with the remote, watching the news. It was actually on breaking news about a man and his entire household, wife, and two kids were found dead. Escobar just shook his head as he turned the television off. "So much violence in the world," he said.

Kedar walk behind his desk and had a seat. Escobar's guard handed him a cigar. He sniffed the cigar from front to back, then pulled out his cutter.

"Do you mind my friend?" he asked Kedar.

"Naw....," he replied. "Go ahead." Kedar pulled an ashtray from his desk. Kedar leaned over and lit the tip of the cigar, while Escobar puffed on it. When the cigar developed a nice cherry, Kedar sat down and lit a Newport. Escobar allowed the smoke to linger around his head. Kedar knew that Escobar always did that when he was contemplating what to say. He was always a man that watched his words because he meant everything that preceded out of his mouth. After a relevant silence Escobar spoke.

"My friend..... I like you." He said as he pointed his cigar at Kedar. Then he signaled at Kedar's feet. Kedar placed the bag onto the table, and quickly unzipped it. He glanced over it and realized it was twice the amount that he had asked for. Escobar chimed in on the end of the thought. "No need to call me right back. Bring me back 280. I like you Señor Kedar." Escobar stood, straightened his jacket, and grabbed his hat.

"Oh yeah me and my man Nike gonna be able to handle this lil bit." Kedar said out loud.

Escobar turned back to face Kedar, "My friend, I gave him the same thing I'm giving you, plus what I originally gave him like I gave you. But some kind of way he brought me back only 175. He called a couple days later and said he needed more time. I just didn't answer him no more because for that little ounce of disrespect... I would kill him. He is only alive because of you. I don't know but maybe you want to look into his habits.... but I will be expecting your call, oh and get you some cameras for the place. Anybody could just waltz in....," the security guard closed the door behind him.

Kedar put half of the package in his safe, and went home with the other half to cut it up. He quickly got the two of the dog food and turned it into two and a half then hit the Coke in the same manner two into two and a half. He had to completely ignore Jay while he was in the lab. When he finished, he called Nike to let him know to make the calls.Nike said everything was everything. Kedar then went to drop the finished product off to Nike. When he made it there, he was at least halfway hoping to see Cara, but Nike told him that she had just been there that night he had come with Jay.

"She got her own shit. I told you she my partna." Nike looked over the product like 'hell yea,' "And you got a blessing with a lil extra on top."

"Hell yeah that's wassup."

Kedar responded, "Yeah but look this how this shit got to go, seeing you charged ol' boy 80 a piece, you go ahead and take 20 of that. Then with the half you get 9, I get 9. For the soft I got to have 30 a piece, then we split the half and for my 9, just give me back 7. The 30 bags is all you, but that's gonna be 40k. So that's going to be 155 for the first one, 67 for the soft and 40 for the trees. That totals out at 262."

"Look I'm just going to give you 265 'cause this definitely puts me back on, and more paper for my pocket," Nike said.

"Oh yeah?.... did you short E one time?" Kedar asked sarcastically.

"Kinda, sorta," Nike responded then he started to think off "......it was like I gave him the bread right, but it wasn't all of it. Some shit was going on, but I hit him back later and he just didn't answer the phone.... but I tried to pay him."

"Aight, but look bruh I need all the paper on this," Kedar said.

"I said I got you....265," Nike said as he really examined the contents in the bag. "It will be all there. You my nigga. I will probably have it done by the a.m."

"Aight let me slide out," said Kedar.

"You ain't staying?"

"Naww you got it, cause I just came home and besides they don't need a new face. So just handle your business, hit me when you get the 265."

"Aight but did these come from E?" Nike asked.

"Bro it could have come from the pope, chill my nigga just have the bread." They laugh and Kedar walked out. As he was driving out of the complex, a red E-class Benz pulled up beside him. The driver let down their window, "I got that info for you," Cara called out.

He turned down his music, "What you say?"

"I said I got that info for you, and that I get paid by the hour sir.... since I'm your new secretary," Cara stated.

He laughed, "Alright what's the info?"

She looks at him crazy like, "You want me to give it to you like this. Alright where you on your way to?"

"I was just about to slide around for a while."

"Good then, since you turned down my offer you can pay for lunch now and I'm still getting paid by the hour while I'm giving you dis info while we at lunch, that you paying for."

Kedar looked at the cherry red E Class Benz, then he looked at the small diamonds she had on, it wasn't that bling-bling-bullshit that's all bulky and stands out. It was that I'm-plain-but-my-earrings-cost-more-than-your-car type shit, and that bracelet had to have set her back 50k easy. "It looks to me you need to be paying," he said.

"I tried so now you're going to pay," she joked, "So follow me." She backed up and put her car in front of his. Cara went to this little hole-in-the-wall Jamaican restaurant. It was tight in the inside but the food smelled delicious. The reggae filled your ears as you entered and there was a greeting at the door by a chubby Jamaican woman. Kedar liked the little place, and the fresh smell of the food was intoxicating, you felt like you were actually in Jamaica. They had a seat, and were given some menus.

J pulled up home. She greeted Mrs. Jenkins as she got Ginger. Mrs. Jenkins told her she might want to go to her apartment first because that girl was up there with a friend or something. J went upstairs to her apartment, the remainder of Nesheya's stuff was by the door. J went to the back and a guy was putting on his pants, then Nesheya came out saying that she was ready to go before J made it home. She stopped as her eyes met J's like, "Oh never mind." J looked at her as if she had gone crazy.

"I know you just ain't walk in my shit and fuck, knowing damn well you ain't put shit on them bills on the table," she yelled.

"Girl, I put your keys on the bar, and I got the rest of my stuff, you don't have to worry about seeing me again."

"I know that's damn right," J said with her hands on her hips.

Nesheya looked at her, "Umph.... anyway, at least somebody fuckin in this bitch."

"Make sure you don't bring your dog ass back," said J.

"Dog.....dog?! Bitch you got me fucked up, that's your problem now you worry about my dog ass and not paying attention to that dog ass nigga you fuckin wit."

"Bitch shut the fuck up, I don't know what you talkin' about!"

"Aight, that nigga that just got out. Kedar dog ass, who got your nose wide open, you ain't watching him. Did his dog ass tell you I sucked his dick when you wouldn't?"

J's face began to get red.

Nesheya liked how she had just got up under her soft ass. "Did he tell you?" she asked again.

J spat back, "Fuck you, dog ass hoe!"

"Don't fuck me, 'cause your nigga did that too," as she turned around and pat her ass. J had heard enough, she rushed Nesheya and pushed her into a door. Nesheya hit the wall with a thump. She grabbed her forehead that had a knot starting to form. It was quickly growing out like a unicorn. She turned and rushed J, screaming. She quickly overpowered J because she was only about 5'2" and Nesheya was a firm 5'9", 160 pounds. She began to grab J by the hair and knocked her head against the wall. J swung a right uppercut that drew blood from Nesheya's nose instantly. Nesheya's hands went from J's hair to holding her own nose. J popped her with a quick two-piece. Nesheya let out a loud cry. J then doubled her over with a body shot.

As quick as Nesheya hit the hallway floor, J was on her ass, kicking her. The male came out of the back and snatched J up from behind screaming, "You stupid bitch!" He had J in a bear hug from behind. He felt like an average 6-footer. He swung her around while squeezing her. J head-butted him from behind. He squinted his eyes, as he bent over. As soon as J's feet touched the floor, she kicked back striking him in the nuts. He hurried and let her go, she scrambled to her room and got her mace and taser. J ran back into the living room and sprayed both of them. J went back over to the male and bent over in his face shouting, "I got your stupid bitch," and she kicked him in the gut.

J kicked him about six times then she tazed him in the nuts.

"Learn to take a bitch to your house next time," she spat.

J then walked over to Nesheya and grabbed her by the hair. She began to punch her and talk to her at the same time. But she was having a one-way conversation with her fist to Nesheya's face about five times before Mrs. Jenkins came and pulled her off of Nesheya.

"Baby chill, please stop....," cried Mrs. Jenkins.

J ran over and kicked the man in the abdomen then walked over to Nesheya and kicked her. "Now you better not bring your ass back and make sure you get this shit out of my house," she screamed.

With that Mrs. Jenkins pushed J out of the door. J was in Mrs. Jenkins' apartment just crying, "How could he do this?" She truly felt heartbroken. She had trusted another man and again her heart was broken. She knew he was too good to be true. She cried through tears and rage.

"Calm down baby," said Miss Jenkins. "You haven't given the young man a chance. You just running off of what this heffa saying. Now the boy looks like a fine young man. I like him and so does the dog. So go by his house and talk to the man like adults do."

"It's not that simple. He doesn't live close," said J.

"Well, I'm pretty sure he got a phone," said Mrs. Jenkins.

J began to angrily dial Kedar's number. The phone rang about four times then it went to the voicemail. She hung up and dialed again. This time he picked up on the second ring.

Kedar answered, "Hello beautiful."

Any other time that would have put a smile on her face, but she wanted to know if he had slept with her roommate. "Where the fuck are you?!" she barked.

"Hold up, hold up lil one...what's the matter?"

"We will deal with that matter next, but answer the first question," J replied.

"Whatever....but I'm actually eating lunch at this Caribbean restaurant."

"Well your lunch can wait. Did you fuck Nesheya?"

"J let me explain."

"See this the problem with niggas.....they always wanna explain," J yelled.

"J it's not like that....."

"Not like what....yo' dick jumped in her mouth and pussy?"

"J if you let me explain....."

"Explain what?!" There was a long silence. "Kedar, just answer me yes or no," J asked calmly, while squeezing her fist. Kedar thought on it for a minute if he told the truth he would lose her, if he lied and she found out he was fucked royally with her.

"So.......," he started, "..... I want you to know that I really care for you, and I have been nothing but 100 with you because I respect your mind, right or wrong. So, to answer your question....." He took a long deep breath. ".....Yes, I did." He didn't give an explanation. He sat listening for something to come back from the other end of the phone.

"Kedar," J said calmly. ".....Please lose my number. Don't call me or come see me.... goodbye." Kedar didn't put up a fight. J hung up and his screen lit up, "Call ended." Cara looked at the once smiling man.

"Kedar, you alright?" she asked. Cara reached her hands across the table. Kedar looked off and responded.

"Nah, I'm good."

Cara pulled her hand back. "Alright. For a minute it looked like somebody took your best friend away."

The waitress pulled up with the curry goat and rice meal. The food was steaming hot. Cara dug her fork into her food. She began to blow to cool it down then she put a fork full in her mouth. "Mmmmm.... Now this is done right," she said as she pointed her fork at her meal. "What about yours?" she asked.

Kedar snapped out of his daze. "Huh? Oh yeah, yeah let me check this out." He began rubbing his hands together.

Cara looked at him. "You sure you okay, because I can get this to go and I'll just fax you everything."

Kedar was trying to hide the truth and what she said about how he looked when he truly felt like he'd just lost someone close. "So....," he joked, "... For what? For me to have to pay you overtime for faxing?"

She laughed. "Oh, you got jokes?" They both laughed and began to eat their meals. Cara gave him quotes and checks on the people. They even made a couple of calls before he settled in on one. And she did well too, quality work inside and out, for reasonable hook up price, all legal.

"I told you so," was all Cara said smiling, while having another taste of her food. They kicked it for a while at the restaurant. Cara finally looked at her watch, and said it was time to go, unless he was serious about her overtime. They hugged and he paid. They got in their separate cars and went in different directions.

CHAPTER 11

When K made it home, he tried giving J some time to cool down. He called about three times but no answer. About 30 minutes had passed when his phone vibrated. It was a text from Cara saying that she appreciated the dinner, and that she, along with the decorator, would be there bright and early the next day. He tossed the phone to the side, frustrated. He grabbed it back and tried one more time calling J. She sent him to voicemail.

"Fuck!" he yelled out, then flopped down on the bed. He tossed and turned all night. He may have gotten about two hours of sleep. He was up early the next morning due to the fact that he was up all night. He didn't want to look like a train wreck, so he took a hot bath and rejuvenated himself. Kedar met up with Cara and Rhonda, the decorator. She gave him the ideas as they walked in and around the place. He just nodded and agreed. Most of it sounded fly. Cara had good style in decorating. His phone rang and it was Nike calling about him having the money. When he hung up, he excused himself from around them. Cara asked him if everything was okay.

"Yeah. I just have to handle something."

"I know you are not about to leave," she questioned.

"Well yeah, I got something to handle," Kedar replied. Kedar didn't want the ladies to keep looking at him like something was on his mind. He told

Cara that he liked her taste, then playfully popped her on the ass. "Make sure everything looks good, secretary."

That put a smile on Cara's face. Rhonda looked at her. "Girl, I wish he was my boss. He can pop this ass all day!"

"Girl stop playing, he couldn't afford me as a secretary. Now let me see those blue and white designs." The women stood at the table talking about the patterns and colors.

As Kedar walked out, he had nothing on his mind but J, so he tried her number again and it had been changed. He thought 'damn.' "Fuck," he yelled. He hit the steering wheel, his car swerved, a horn blew. "Damn, I got to get myself together."

Kedar checked his mirror and looked at himself. "K, pull your fuckin' self together." He had to do a self-check. "Man, I am." He said to himself. He spent the whole drive over to Nike's place, convincing himself of who he was. He looked and felt confused as hell when he made it to Nike's house. Nike met him at the door.

"What's good my nigga?" The two men gave each other a pound. Kedar followed him into the apartment and Nike locked the door behind him. "What up my nigga, you good?" asked Nike.

"Yea...I'm good," Kedar replied.

"Kim!" yelled Nike. "......Bring me the envelope!" Kim was a cute petite Asian that came sashaying out of the back. She got on her tiptoes to kiss Nike on the cheek before taking the blunt and handing him the envelope. She curled her tiny lips around the blunt and pulled deep. As she hit it again, she looked over at Kedar and offered him the cigar. He casually declined and she shrugged her shoulders. Nike told her to take it to the back and with that, she left just as she had come in, without a word. She went and sat on the bed, cross legged and watched TV.

Nike handed Kedar the sealed envelope. "It's all there just like I said. 265 my dude. Plus, I came up big on that," he smiled. He began to break some weed down into a blunt. "What you think about that?" Nike asked.

"She fine," K replied.

"Huh....nigga I'm talking about the money," Nike seals the blunt. "My nigga...you sure you ok?"

"Yea....yea I'm good."

"Well, the money counter in the closet. I'm about to head back in the back."

"I'm good," replied Kedar. "I'm just 'bout to slide."

Nike looked back. "Now I know something wrong! You ain't 'bout to count that money?" he laughs.

"Is it all here?" Kedar asked.

"Yep," replied Nike before he lit his blunt. "......Plus, I didn't get around to ol' boy. I caught that break elsewhere, 'cause I figured you needed the paper."

"Nah, nah.... hit the nigga and tell him you got him, and I'll drop that off. Just make sure everything straight with the paper. I'll be back in 'bout an hour."

"If you say so," Nike said as he whipped out his phone and told Tank it's all good and that he'd call him once he got it in hand. They hung up. "You sure you good?" Nike asked again.

"Yeah bro, it's just that I might need some extra paper for my interior decorator that's all."

"Yeah whatever," said Nike shaking his head. "You need to go get your dick sucked or something." Nike hit the blunt again. "Now I'm waiting on you, seeing that you made me make that phone call."

"Shut up," Kedar called back. "That money better be good."

"The money good," replied Nike, walking back to his room. "Your nuts ain't good though," he laughed. "They need some attention."

Kedar shook his head at his friend and left out. He went by his home and counted the money. It was 265 like Nike said. So, he quickly counted, he owed 42k for each brick of dog food. It was four of them and 15k for each brick of coke, then 15k for the thirty bags, plus, a front cost. Kedar took out 15k of the money and dropped the 250 off to Escobar. Escobar nodded his head in approval. Kedar told him he'd be in touch. Once he finished, he went back to the detail shop. The women were gone. He called Cara. She was out having lunch and told him the designs were on the desk, along with the cost, and that they were going to start tomorrow.

"Look Kedar, your secretary, I can be, but your bank I can't," Cara had said. She was referring to the eight grand she had paid so that Rhonda could start. "I'm going to need my paper back."

Kedar laughed. "I got you, no pressure."

"Shiiiiid, no pressure my ass!"

"I thought we was friends," he joked.

'Nigga, you peeling me like I'm an Idaho Potato."

Kedar had to laugh again. "I got you."

"This my last time asking, are you good?" Cara asked.

"Couldn't be better," he replied.

"Well, I'm about to finish up my lunch and if you need me before tomorrow just call me. I'll be by there in a day or two to make sure everything is on schedule."

"Appreciate the look out."

"Huh..... you funny. Call me later, okay?"

"Aight." Kedar hung up the phone. He bought the material he needed and put the work together making the two go to two and a half on both products. Kedar remembered what Escobar said, so he made a call to the Brink's company for some security cameras. After he concluded that, he slid over to Nike's to drop the product off. Kedar told him the same thing went for this package as the last. He informed Nike that if he wanted, he could put up 50 next time and get his own dog food.

"Hell yeah," was Nike's reply. Kedar peaced his mans up and went home.

The next day was busy for Kedar. The decorators were there starting their work on the inside, as well as the out. Cara pulled up on the second day, like she said she would. She was wearing a business two-piece skirt suit and strutting in some heels. She gave Kedar a hug.

"What's up?" she asked. Before he could respond she was on one of the decorator's asses about where they were placing something. She kissed his cheek and said she'd be back and that her money better be in that office.

Kedar signed off on some paperwork that the security company had given him, then he went into his office. He sat behind his desk drinking cognac and smoking cigarettes. Cara knocked on the door.

"Oooouu.....," she frowned up her nose. "Boy, it smells like the strip club up in here. Nothing but ass, cigarettes, and beer." Cara then looked around and started picking stuff up off of the floor. "Kedar, it looks like you've been staying here."

"I have," he replied.

Then she saw the pillow and blanket on his new leather couch. She started to have a genuine concern for him. She sucked her teeth. "Now I asked you, was everything straight? Look Kedar, I'm good on that little paper."

Kedar responded, "Nah, nah, nah." He reached in his desk and tossed ten bands on the desk. Cara walked over while folding up the blanket. She saw the three empty bottles and the half full one on his desk.

Kedar took another gulp and walked around the desk to where Cara was thumbing through the money. He crept up behind her then wrapped his arms around her and started grinding on her butt. He bent over and kissed her neck. "Stop," she whispered

He whispered in her ear, "You don't want me no more?" He spun her around and planted his tongue in her mouth. She begins kissing him back, as he went under her skirt and realized she had on thongs. He picked her up and placed her on his desk.

Cara kissed him passionately and stopped. "We can't be doing this," she cried out. Kedar began kissing her neck while easing his hand between her legs. He pulled her thongs to the side and slid two fingers in, he could feel her juices instantly running down his wrist. She grabbed his hand. "No! Not like this." She moved his hand and slid down off of the desk. Cara tilted her head back to catch her breath, because it had instantly gotten hot in there. She knew that she was about to go against how she truly felt.

"Now Kedar, I like you. Trust me I do. But something is on your mind and I can't do it like this. God knows I would. But something here is wrong." She kissed him on the cheek. "Pull yourself together because this ain't you. Go home and clear your head, I'll wrap this stuff up here."

Kedar couldn't look Cara in the face. "My bad yo', I'm sorry." He began to fix his buckle. "You right. I need to clear my head. Things have been tough since I came home. I do need a lil time alone."

Cara walked back up to him and placed her hands on both his cheeks, "You do," she said smiling.

"Thanks Cara," Kedar replied. Cara kissed him then turned to exit.

She stopped and looked back. "If I didn't stop you, we would be fucking right now, huh?"

Kedar smiled. "Yeah."

Cara shook her head. "Damn." She bit her lip. "I'll call you and keep you posted. Go home and get yourself together."

"Thank you," he called back to her.

She walked out and closed the door behind her, because she knew if she stayed another minute, whatever he was going through she would have surely let him take it out on her back. Her pussy got wet instantly, thinking of him fucking her while she stared into his brown eyes.

Rhonda walked up on her with the design book, "Girl, you okay?" she asked.

"I'm good, why? What's up?" asked Cara.

"Your damn skirt!"

"Huh?" Cara looked down and slightly adjusted her skirt, then smoothed out her shirt. "How's that look?" she asked.

"Like you just been fucking your boss, girl!"

"Stop playing," replied Cara. "I was talking about the designs in your hands."

"I was too, do he have any part-time workers?" Both women laugh and began walking through the place directing.

Kedar went home and laid up a couple more days. He had to get himself together.

Nike was walking through the Gwinnett Place Mall, when he spotted Cara and Rhonda having lunch together. He had his little Asian sensation in tow as he made his way through the food court.

"You think he going to want his name above the building?" asked Rhonda.

"His ass might want it dead center,'" responded Cara. The women burst into laughter. Nike pulled up and caught an eye full of the designs.

"What's up stranger," spoke Nike. Cara looked back.

"What up Nike?" She rose up and gave him a hug. "This is my co-worker, Rhonda." Cara waved at the little Asian woman, "Hi." She then sat back down.

"What you got going? I haven't seen or heard from you in a while," he stated.

"Uhhhh a little this, little that, just working mostly."

"I see," he said trying to get a better glance at the folders that lie on the table. He knew for sure he saw Kedar's name at the top of the business.

"We really got some work to do for the client, so we can do a catch up later or something," Cara said.

"Client," he thought. Why was she referring to Kedar in that manner? "Aight, then," Nike smiled and shook Rhonda's hand, "Nice to meet you." The Asian girl grabbed his arm, obviously wanting him to him to hurry up.

"You know how the line gets for the new MK bags," she cried.

"Imma catch up with you later," he told them. Rhonda looked at Cara like, "Who the fuck is he?"

"Huhh," responded Cara.

"I mean, he ain't your boss fine, but I will let him work this. Girl where you know all these fine-ass men from!?"

"If you knew where they came from you would scream."

"You right I probably would scream, fuck me daddy! Fuck me daddy!" The women share the laugh and finished up their lunch.

Nike's mind was in a daze for the remainder of the day. He ended up buying four of the new high-end bags, two for his Asian, and two for her twin, that he met and brought back to the house. He fucked the lining out of the two women. They were only good for rounds 1&2. Nike sat on the corner of his bed saturated in sweat and began to dial Cara's number. His dick began to harden while imagining Cara's lips wrapped around his manhood. For some odd reason she would never sleep with him. In the three years of knowing her, she never even attempted to. Cara would get another female to tend to his needs, her voice pulled him out of thought.

"Hello?"

"What's up love?"

"Love? Who is this?" she questioned.

"Oh, you got jokes. This me, Nike!"

"Oh, what up Nike?! What can I do for you?"

He began to smile, imagining how she can come and bend that fat ass over in his face, so he could eat it from the back. "I'm checking to see if you're going to come by tonight," he stated.

"I can't tonight," she yawned.

"Why not?" he questioned.

"'Cause I got work to do. If you want, I can call my friend Angelica. She is Dominican and black, beautiful as fuck, if you need company."

"Naw.....," he growled. ".....I don't need no high-end hookers. I got two of them in my bed now, bitch I want to fuck you!"

"Man you trippin'," she stated. "Why would you talk about my friends like that, you don't even know her."

"All you stripper bitches are the same."

"First off I'm not no stripper bitch! I started dancing once I met you because your ass liked the club, and I liked your company. For two, I got two de-grees, so don't think the club makes me. Have you not noticed that I barely even dance? My car cost more than yours, and not to mention, my shit was already together before I met you. I don't know what type of trip you on, but I'm not the one," she snapped.

"Fuck you bitch," he spat. "I know what this is. Your ass don' hooked up with that nigga Kedar."

"Huh?"

"I know you fucking him, so he can get the pussy and I can't?!" Nike took a sniff of the substance on the mirror, laying on the table beside him.

"You know what Nike," she calmly stated. "You probably got a lot on your plate right now, coz I do too. So, I'm going to act like this conversation didn't happen and I'm going to get me some rest. Good night, Nike," then she hung up.

Nike threw his phone across the room, breaking it into three or four pieces. The two women woke up startled, asking him if everything was okay. He placed the mirror, and the rolled-up bill in front of them, both of the women were instantly rejuvenated. They began taking turns sucking on Nike's manhood.

Cara hung up and quickly dialed Kedar's number, but he didn't answer. She started to go by his house, but chose not to seeing that she was never formally invited there, and she was pretty sure that his girl had a key and could pop up anytime. So, she figured she'd tell him in the a.m. The next morning, she tried again twice. Since he didn't answer, she went by the shop to let the crew in.

CHAPTER 12

knock... knock... knock....

Kedar rolled over in his bed.

knock.... knock.... knock...

He rolled over and looked at the clock. 11 a.m. stared back at him in big red numbers. His head was throbbing, especially with every knock. He slung himself out of the bed to answer the door. When he got there it was three sexy ass French maids at the door.

"Molly Maids," one of the women said in a strong French accent. His morning hard had gotten even stiffer in his pajamas.

"Ohhh........," the women said as they came in.

"No, no, no," he said then the first woman handed him a phone.

"Hello, good morning sleepy-head," said Cara.

"What you send these women over here for?" he questioned.

"Because your house probably looks like your office, a pigsty. You do know you got a business to run. And jokes on you, because if I do anything else or pay for anything else, this shit is mine! You do have a grand opening in

72

a few days."

"Shit," he spat.

"Nah, nah, nah man," she answered. "I got everything on track. You're going to scream once you see my bill."

Kedar laughed. "I bet." Which reminded him, he needed to pick the money up from Nike.

"Oh yeah....."

"What's up, secretary?" He looked around for his lighter. One of the women struck a lighter and told him she was about to start vacuuming. He pulled on the cigarette and watched The Three Little Bees tighten up his place. Kedar walked into the bathroom to get from around the noise. "Go ahead Cara."

"Your mans Nike is beginning to act funny lately. You might need to talk to him or something."

"What do you mean?" Kedar asked while taking another drag of his cigarette.

"I can't really say but you know you niggas get in your bags too, just like women. Just check up on him."

"Aight," replied Kedar.

"Oh yeah, one more thing....."

"What is it?" he asked.

"You need to let one of them French things drain that pressure."

"How about you do it," he shot back.

"Don't tempt me, coz I will pull up. Anyway, I will expect to see you here tomorrow sir," she said.

"Damn you starting to sound like you my boss," he stated.

"Kedar, I'm not playing. Bring your ass in tomorrow!"

"Yes ma'am." He hung up the phone. The women cleaning his house look too tempting, so he went ahead and jumped into the shower. When he came out, they were putting the finishing touches down. One of them started on the bathroom as he exited. He went into his room to dry himself off. Kedar began to check his missed calls and texts. Afterwards he dried his head off, and put on some lotion. He reached into the drawer and paid the women a tip. The third woman was taking the trash out when he had tipped the other two.

"You sure you don't want a happy ending?" the women asked as they rubbed his chest.

"I'm good," K replied.

The maids blew kisses as they exited. They had laid out an outfit for him. He dropped his towel and placed on the tank top.

knock .....knock .....knock ...

"Shit," he thought as he grabbed some more money, knowing that it was the third woman. "Here you go I don't have change," he said as he was passing two one-hundred dollar bills out of the door.

"Excuse me," responded Ms. Jackson.

"I'm sorry," he said. "Damn." He was still in his briefs and a tank top. She eyed him over with the pen in her mouth.

"This personal or professional?" he asked.

"Strictly business," she said as she brushed past him, copping a feel of the place. She looked around and asked, "Your place always smell this way?"

"What way?" he asks. "Like I just got out of the shower? Do you mind if I put on some pants?"

"This is your house," she responded. She walked around looking into the trash can and the guest room. She followed behind him and watched him as he put clothes on. She walked around to his closet and checked it, then opened a few drawers. Kedar was thankful Cara had sent the Molly Maids through to tighten up the place.

"Anything else ma'am?" he asked as he was jumping into his Timberlands. He stood and grabbed his car keys.

"In fact, there is," she handed him a cup. "Fill this up," she said as she leaned on the bathroom door.

Kedar examined the cup. "You serious?" he questioned. She flipped open her notebook.

"Chill lady." He unzipped his pants and pulled out his penis.

Ms. Jackson was caught in a trance. Staring at Kedar's penis she thought to herself, "Oh my God". Her mouth began to water. That thing was big, black, and pretty. She could barely contain herself, so she crossed her legs at the ankles as he filled up the cup. She watched in awe as he squeezed the remaining urine out, he wiped off the sides of the cup before handing it to her. Kedar washed his hands as she placed a stick in it.

"Ok, you good." She handed him the cup back.

Kedar poured the contents into the toilet and flushed. He tossed the cup into the trash as he escorted her out. Before she got into her car, she looked back at him. "It might be the same time next week."

"Aight, I'll be home," he responded.

Kedar slid over to Nike's spot. It wasn't even after one and Nike was hammered. Kedar looked around the house. It looked like a tornado hit it. He asked Nike, was everything cool, because his mans was drinking cognac straight so early.

"Nah fool, but it's all good," Nike said in a slurred voice and raised his cup. "I got that paper for you." Nike yelled to the back. A red bone came out of the back.

"Yes daddy?" she said.

"Bring me that bag in the back." She then turned on her heels and headed back to retrieve the items.

Kedar shook his head as he tapped the chair that Nike sat in. "Look homie, if you don't slow down nigga, your ass going to end up like Eazy-E," he joked.

"Shawty, who?....if I was going to end up like Eazy, that would have been 50 bitches ago." Kedar laughed and shook his head.

"One thing I can say, you keep some bad ones with you." Giving his mans his props.

"Oh you like that? I can put you on if you like."

"Nah, bro, that ain't my speed," said Kedar. "She bad and all but I really got to stay focused, my nigga. I just came home."

"Uhmm," responded Nike. Kedar looked at him.

"What uhmm mean nigga?"

"Uhmm nigga! Like you don't know what that mean. Nigga, you know what you fucking Cara mean, right? .....the same uhmmmm!"

"Homes, you trippin', ain't nobody fuckin' Cara. Besides, I thought you and her were just friends.....uhmmm," Kedar hit him back with it.

Nike's expression begins to slightly change then the red bone came back with the bag. He looked all over her, like a lion on a zebra's ass, then he popped her on it. I'll be back there in a minute. Kedar saw the slight change in his mans, so he never took his eyes off of him. Even when the fine ass woman came in he was still looking at Nike.

Nike turned around and saw him looking at him. "What, nigga? I got it all." He had mistaken Kedar's look for something else. So, he opened the bag and went into the kitchen to grab the money counter. Kedar sat there and counted it all as Nike poured drink after drink, while watching ESPN. The money was all there. He had begun to neatly place the stacks back into the bag when Nike spoke.

"My nigga that wasn't enough... buddy wanted like five... he had the bread, but I told him that was all I had left but I'll touch basis if things change. By the way...," Nike went to the closet and grabbed something out of it. He returned and dropped 50 grand on the table. Kedar picked it up, and thumbed through it, then he waved the money in the air. Nike understood. "That's a whole 50 from me. And yea, it's all there. Cuz, bro, you been looking at me like I only been fuckin off and I haven't. Granted I fuck alot." He laughs at himself. "But I'm on my shit." Then Nike pulled out 25 more bands. "That's 75k. Make sure you fuck with me. 'Cause listen, if you got buddy 5 then I'll use mine to serve the other two niggas." That made Kedar lighten up a little, then he gave his man dap and told him to be patient.

"I'll call with the info." Kedar walked out with the bag over his shoulder and hopped into his car. He thought about what Cara had said and true enough he had seen a little bit of what she was talking about, but he saw bruh on his grind handling business. And besides he hadn't fucked Cara, so he just wrote that shit off. He made it home, and ordered something to eat. He caught him a movie or two and passed out.

Two weeks later everything was in tip-top shape. Cara's homegirl had come through on the remodeling. She truly turned the place into something desirable. "Special K Detailing" covered the top and the windows of the place. Kedar was ready for the grand opening. She even helped him with the advertising and marketing. This place was way far more fabulous than he had planned to do it. Kedar walked outside and saw foreign cars pull up. It was a crowd of folks. People danced to the music that came from his building. Balloons everywhere. He walked through the waiting room where some ladies were enjoying their refreshments while their kids played in the play area. Kedar walked to the side and spoke to a couple of the new VIPs. One of them gave him his props and assured him that this was their new spot for their toys from here on out. Kedar then walked up on the Migos, the rappers out of Georgia, who had matching Lambos outside. While he walked around and looked at the progress from such a short trip, he began to thank Yahweh. As he finished up his walk through, he spotted Cara looking professional as hell, talking to some Caucasian fellas. She waved Kedar over and introduced him to the men. She explained that they were from Miami and felt like Kedar's business and brand would thrive in South Beach. So, they were wondering if he would keep them in tune if the business ever wanted to expand. Kedar respected the businessmen and would consider their offer. The men shook hands with Kedar and departed as the Bentley they were in, pulled up..... spotless.

"I like," said one of the men. They both acknowledged with a head nod as they entered the vehicle.

Kedar looked over at Cara like I appreciate everything you've done for me. They both bask in the success as Cara gave him a hug. He laughed. Cara was funny as fuck.

"Oh yea, don't let me forget. Don't let me forget....." As he pats himself then opened the inside of his suit jacket. He pulled out a Manila envelope.

"What's this?" Cara asked as he handed it to her. It was a check and about 20K cash.

"Thank you for your services," Kedar said to her.

Cara looked at him and whistled, "This check, it better not bounce."

Kedar smiled. "Naw... it ain't gonna bounce."

Cara took the 20 grand. "Now this, a woman can love....," she play smiled and stuck her tongue out, "....Hey." she laughed. The two shared a bottle of wine and had a toast to not only new business, but good business.

"Now, you can call me boss man from here on out," Kedar joked.

"I'll call you anything as long as this check don't bounce," Cara joked back, then she excused herself to go back and start mingling with, meeting, and greeting some of the customers.

Kedar walked into his office he looked around at the decor in the place. It was plush. He had only a couple of black paintings on the wall, a leather sofa, and an oak desk. There was a leather chair to match the sofa. He even had carpet so soft that he could walk around with no shoes on. The 60-inch screen, parallel to his desk, showed all 15 cameras on the property at one time. Whenever he didn't have it on cable TV, he made sure to keep his surroundings on point. He strolls over to his desk and begins to go through some of the papers, he signed and place them back into the folders. He also saw some invoices, he signed, and dated them, then went to place them into his safe. Kedar peered at the money. He had around five hundred grand including the money he had gotten from Nike, his profit, and some of the loan money that was remainder. Kedar couldn't help but think that after this flip he will be knocking at a million, with only having been out a little less than two months.

His business took off, and everything was all good, which reminded him he needed to call Nike. He had been totally engulfed in getting his detail company situated, that he had his mans on pause. As he shut the safe, he pulled out his phone to dial Nike's number. He sat down, enjoying how the soft leather felt, as the phone rang.

"Yo," answered Nike.

"What up my dude?"

"Man where you been nigga?" Nike asked.

"Shiiiit, caught up in this lil business," Kedar replied.

"So you making moves without me?" questioned Nike.

"Naw nigga, not like that but I got that lil none on none for you, and a lil something I need you to handle for me."

"Check, check," Nike responded.

"But, look," Kedar said as he scanned the paperwork on his desk. "I was just letting you know everything is everything and that I'll call once it's in hand."

"Say less," said Nike.

After he closed out the call with Nike, he dialed up Escobar.

"Buenos Dias," answered Escobar.

"Buenos Dias to you too señor," responded Kedar. "I was calling to let you know that breeding was a success, and I will probably be expecting about five girls, and five boys with the same square feet and I have that 30 feet that wasn't paid for. He could sense Escobar thinking about something then he heard him blow the smoke out from the cigar.

"Sí, sí..... How about you double down on everything, and I get my lawn care service to handle the cages and all, but you got to tip at least 100 bucks."

Kedar didn't know whether he was asking him or telling him due to how it came out, then Escobar spoke. "Well, my friend that will put you at about 630 total for my bill."

Kedar took a split-second. "Hell fuck it, time to get ready for a puppy talent show. I have half on the registry to put them in motion. I should have the rest in a few but sooner than later, if we want to catch the pageant around the corner."

Then he heard a loud shout like some Indian calls or something. "You all right?" Kedar asked.

"Sí, sí, my friend. Mexico scored a goal."

"I understood. Well Escobar, give me a minute and Ima grab the registration fees, then pull up on you."

"No, no, no need, hold on to it. Go to screen three." Kedar looked at the phone awkward, then he flipped the full screen on three.

"I'm on three," Kedar responded.

"Make sure the laundry gets taken care of then." Kedar squinted his eyes and noticed a blue tub labeled 'Laundry'.

"You still got a couple of blind spots, my friend," said Escobar, taking notice to the awkward silence on the other end of the phone.

"I'm going to get on them about it tomorrow."

"Oh yeah, you do that. I'll get the other things when your company leaves."

Kedar thought E was tripping, seeing that he was in his office alone. "What you talkin' about? I'm in my office......." before he could get it out, there was a knock at the door.

Knock....Knock

"Speak to you later, Senor." Not waiting on a response Escobar hung up. Kedar looked at the door as it open, and in came Nike.

"What up my nigga," he called out, smiling from ear-to-ear, walking with a dip in his step with Tank and his mans in tow. Kedar raised up out of his seat and stared directly at Nike, for if looks could kill, Kedar had committed mass murder six times over and was still wanting his nerves to stop twitching, so that he could mark something again.

"Damn my nigga," called out Nike, as he was making his way toward Kedar. Nike was looking around, taking in the place. He complimented Kedar about how grand his office looked, as he made it to the desk and took a seat. Kedar straightened up his tie, and changed the channel from three to all the cameras in the place.

"What do I owe this unexpected visit?" he asked.

"Come on bro, didn't you say you have a little bit for me? I just so happened to be around, homes, when you called." (Signaling at Tank).

Something didn't feel right to Kedar and his gut was shouting it to him. As he eyed all the men in the room, he could see through Nike's glasses. He looked like he was skied out of his mind, but the other two looked sober as hell. Nike cut in, breaking him from his train of thought.

"Look Bro, I know this ain't protocol and all, but homes got the paperwork on him now."

Kedar looked at the bag that the henchman was carrying and thought, "Who the fuck ride around with damn near a half a mil in cash on them?"

Tank, seeing his opportunity, spoke up. "Look my dude we just came to handle business. If you not the man we need to be talking to.......," he said as he patted the bag in his security's hand. ".......Then point us in the direction coz my man, time is money."

"How dare this nigga speak to me like I'm some second-rate peon," Kedar thought as he opened his desk drawer.

Tap....tap.....tap

The door swung open. It was Cara. She stopped in mid-stride as she entered. "Damn, excuse me," she stated, as she brushed past the men to make it over to Kedar, who was standing straight up making him seem taller than life. She could also sense some tension in the air. As she made it to him, she noticed he had his hand on the desk drawer, then she spotted the pocket .45 that sat in there.

"What the fuck did I just walk into," she thought, seeing that K didn't break his stance of looking at Tank. She leaned into him to tell him that she had tried to call and let him know they were in the building. Kedar glanced at his phone and picked it up, he had several missed calls and texts from Cara, stating such. This had been while he was on the phone with Escobar. Cara then reached out and grabbed his cigarettes and pulled one out. "May I have a light please?" Kedar went into the drawer and pulled out his lighter, then lit the cigarette. Cara pulled on it, then handed it to him. "Sir when you finish, there's still a few more people that would like to speak to you."

"Aight, tell them I'll be right there."

"What up Cara?" called out Nike.

Cara spoke back to him and kept walking. The men watched as her ass bounce in the tan two-piece skirt suit that hugged every curve on her body. Tank reached out and grabbed her wrist.

"Aye ain't you the same stripper bitch that was at the club that night?" he asked.

Cara snatched away from him. She looked him face-to-face before she answered. "Yeah, and I'm the same bitch that got your mama stripping on oldie goldie night, and I'm going to be the same bitch that's gonna cut your tongue and hands off, if you ever called me a bitch again, OR if you ever touch me again."

She let it settle in on him for a minute, then she spent on her heels and walked out.

Nike begin to boil on the inside. Tank licked his lips. He liked the feisty type. But something in her eyes said she meant everything she said, and that made his dick get rock hard. He knew the sex with her had to be crazy.

Kedar pulled on his cigarettes twice, and thought before he spoke. "Tank!" he snapped. The man turned around, seeing that this was the first time Kedar had spoken directly to him. Kedar was calm in all of his words, "Drop the bag."

Tank tapped his henchman, and he did as instructed. Kedar then turned his attention to Nike, "Now I'm going to make the call like I said I would, and everything will be everything. But I want you to truly listen Nike, don't you ever bring your ass to my place of business under NO circumstance!" Kedar adjusted his eyes on Tank, "Don't you ever bring your ass to my place of business again, and if you disrespect any one of my employees again.......well, it will be what it be. Now get the fuck out of my office!"

Tank put a smirk on his face, and told the other two, "Let's bounce." Nike got up and just walked out. Tank was the last to leave, he calls back to Kedar, "I apologize for any disrespect I may have caused you, your workers, or your fine establishment, but if you don't come through for your mans, take that bag and go ahead and pay for your business insurance, workers compensation and your funeral arrangements," then he gently closed the door.

Kedar's blood began to boil. What the fuck is wrong with Nike?! How could he bring this nigga around me and, even worse, to my place of business. Nike done got sloppy as fuck, then the nerve of this nigga Tank. Who the fuck he think he is?! Kedar begins to massage the trigger of the pocket rocket that sat in his desk drawer, as he let out a loud growl.

Kedar stormed out of his office and headed to the back, he brushed past Cara, she turned and began to walk with him. She could see he was pissed about something. She noticed a big ass vein in the side of his neck, just above his collar.

"Is everything all right?" she asked.

Kedar stopped and looked her in the face, "Look, I got to handle something, so I need for you to wrap everything up for me if I'm not back in time."

Cara seeing that he wasn't asking her, simply agreed. "I will."

"Thanks Cara," he said then he kissed her cheek and headed toward the back exit.

He walked out, and noticed his workers in the back taking a smoke break. One of them was smoking a joint, that he quickly tossed. Everyone began to scatter. "Wait!" Kedar commanded. All three of the workers stopped, he walked over and picked up the joint. He could smell the gas coming off of it. If he had to guess, it smelt like some Hawaiian Haze of some sort. He looked at the three young men.

"Man up, whose is it?"

They looked at each other in confusion, then the one to the left said, "It's mine."

Kedar studied the clear-eyed boy, then shook his head. "I said man up, not stand up!"

The other two dropped their heads, and both said in unison, "It's mine."

Kedar looked at the three boys, they seemed like some good kids, plus Cara had hired them, so they had to be straight.

"This......," he held up the joint. "This is extra-curricular, and extra-curricular is designed for after work, not during work. Plus, I'm on parole. Do you know what would happen if my PO pulled up on my business property and found this? She would lock my black ass up! So, if anything, even if you don't respect yourself, respect my shit and please respect my freedom!"

"Yes sir," the three boys answered.

Kedar then pulled out his lighter and lit the blunt. He had been wrong. It was some rapper weed. He handed it back to them, as he blew out the smoke. "Now if you smoke this in your car, she would only lock your asses up." The boys respected it and went into their car to smoke.

CHAPTER 13

Kedar grabbed the laundry bin and went to the back room. The joint had done little to ease his mind, as he put the blocks through the press. He couldn't do anything but constantly think of how sloppy Nike had gotten. How could he uncover his hand like that, and plus expose him, after he specifically gave him one direction, which was to not include him in the business. Kedar made the decision to cut his right hand off in order to save the body. So, he left one of the dog foods uncut and two of the softs raw. That would be the last thing he would do for Nike. He would have to find his own route after this. He placed Nike's work in a small bag, then placed the rest into a bigger gym bag. He was in the back room so long, that by the time he came out, everyone was gone.

Kedar made it through his establishment. His nerves were still shot. When he made it to his office, he dropped the bag into his closet. Kedar went next door to Walgreens and grabbed some Dutches. He made it back to his office, pulled out one of the bags and began to roll up out of it. As he pulled on the Dutch filled with weed, he sat back in his chair and blew smoke into the air. Kedar had smoked half of the blunt, and to no avail, he was still heated. He was so blowed, he didn't even notice Cara as she walked in.

"What the fuck are you doing?" she asked him.

He turned around in his seat, not even responding. Cara looked at the pound of weed that sat on his desk. She smelled the weed from her office when he first lit it. Kedar took another long drag pondering what to say. "Nike fucking up," he murmured.

Cara could only shake her head. She walked over and grabbed the blunt then pulled on it before putting it out. She sealed the bag up as she spoke through the smoke that came from her lips. "Don't beat yourself up because of Nike. Just look around you. You got so much positive shit going on, and you 'bout to throw it all away because you're pissed with Nike."

Reality set in on Kedar. He knew she was right, and that made him even madder. What the fuck was he doing smoking, knowing he was on papers, and could have a piss test at any time.

Cara rubbed his head and felt how hot it was. "Damn this nigga is literally heated," she thought to herself.

"But why?" Kedar asked. "Why would he bring homes around me knowing better?"

Cara looked for the words to say, but quickly decided with what came to mind. "When niggas hand you shit, you just make cherry pie."

Kedar looked up at her like, 'huh?' Cara began to laugh and he did too.

"You silly as hell," he responded.

"Hey, got you smiling again though."

"Thanks, I appreciate everything you've done for me," Kedar said to Cara.

Cara mushed him playfully in the face. "Okay now, I see the weed done set in." With that, Cara turned to leave.

Kedar caught her by the hand and turned her around without getting out of his seat. Cara stood in front of him with her arms crossed, "What K?"

Kedar took in her stance, then flashes of her words and past actions came across his mind. "What is it that you're looking for?" Kedar asked.

"Huh?" Cara responded.

"Seriously. What is it that you're doing here, helping me and all. Not that I'm not appreciative of it but help me understand your angle."

Cara sat back on his desk and pondered the question. "I just want to help. I like helping a person come out of a bad situation. Something like a Feed the Children Foundation or Breast Cancer Awareness. Only thing is that I know where my money is going and if I see potential in something I try to help them reach their peak. I mean, or at least help them see the fact that they have potential within themselves. If I can accomplish that then all of my efforts were worth it."

Kedar raised up from his seat. "So, you lowkey a Martha for the hood?" They both laugh, then he got into her personal space, and looked her directly in her eyes. "Now is that all you're trying to do or all that you want?"

Cara was beginning to breathe heavy. "Aye man, back up please."

"What's wrong? You don't want me this close?" he asked looking into her eyes.

"Okay, please?" she struggled to say.

"When was the last time someone has done something for you?" he asked. Cara tried to come up with an answer, but could find none. Kedar leaned in and kissed her lips. He kissed her two more times and asked her, "Do you want me to stop?" Cara slowly shook her head 'no'.

Kedar spread her legs and stepped in between them, then he began to passionately kiss her. He started sucking on her neck as she let out a loud gasp. He was on one of her spots. Cara began fumbling with his buckle to free him up. As soon as his pants hit the floor, he tore open her shirt, popping all of the buttons that held it together. He was in awe at how sexy she looked in the violet and lace bra. She had a flat stomach, like she was constantly in the gym. He massaged her breasts as she massaged his manhood. Kedar popped her bra from the back exposing her bare breasts. He took the left one into his mouth, sucking and licking.

Cara could feel her body tensing up and Kedar, not being selfish, gave both of her breasts equal attention and affection. He placed his hand in the swell of her chest, as her body began to recline. He placed each one of her legs on the arms of his chair. Kedar pulled her panties off gently then rolled her skirt up to her hips. He then sat back in his chair admiring how clean shaved her vagina was. As he leaned in to kiss the slit, some of her juices fell on his lips. He spread her lips apart exposing her swollen clitoris. Kedar took it into his mouth, as she began to moan loud. He started to make figure eights around her clit, her body went into a frenzy. She was unaware of what she was asking for. "Yeah, I want him but shit," she thought to herself.

At that moment Kedar slid two fingers into her pussy. He began to slide them in and out, as she rocked back and forth. Cara let out a loud moan again. He could feel the juices flowing down his wrist, as she reached down, and begin to palm his head like a basketball. Kedar could see her stomach sink in as he felt the vibration of her body. He removed his fingers and slid his wide tongue into her.

Cara placed both her hands on his face and began to slide his tongue in and out of her. She couldn't believe how she could just have her way with his face. She held his stiff tongue inside of her as she came. "Ahhhhhh....ahhhh shiiiit," she dropped her hands, knocking things off of his desk. Kedar begins to lick all of her juices up, he kissed her clit one time and she immediately begins to twitch as she lay flat on his desk.

"What did I just do?" she thought to herself. Then..... "Ohhhh shitttt," she screamed. She moaned as he slid the head of his penis inside of her. "Oh my Goddd," was all she could say.

Kedar gracefully moved in and out of her, as she moaned and went crazy.

"Deeper, deeper," Cara cried, and she spread her legs wide, so he could gain all access to her vagina. As he drove deep into her, she realized he was too big. She placed her hand on his abdomen, and he grabbed a hold of it.

"Nah, I'm giving you what you asked for, so don't even try to push me out or else." He moved her hand out of the way.

"Oh shit," Cara cried out, as he hit her back wall. With every stroke she could feel her insides clinging to the size of him. She wanted more, with pain came pleasure. "Yes, yes, yes," she screamed as she came all over him. Her juices filled his abs. Cara was exhausted. He pulled her up off of the desk as she dropped to her knees. She was amazed at how much she had cum. She slowly took his head into her mouth. Cara loved the way he tasted with her juices all over him. She sucked on the head of his dick, then licked the vein that protruded at the base of him. She tried to take in all of him, but she could only go down halfway. Cara gagged as she tried, she massaged his balls and stroked him up and down at the same time. She pulled his dick from her mouth and just stroked it. She was just in awe. His penis was so beautiful to her. She spit on it to lube it up good. Cara grabbed his hands and placed them on each side of her head. She lubed it up really good for what she was about to do. She allowed him to fuck her throat, she could tell by his rhythm that her head game was on point. She felt his head hit the back of her throat. The size of him was amazing. Cara felt the head throbbing in her throat, signaling that he was about to cum, she jumped up off her knees.

"Noooo," he moaned.

Cara shook her head, "Not so fast, I want it from the back." She walked over to his couch, he watched her perfect red apple bottom just shake, as she went and bent over the arm of his couch. Kedar stroked himself up and down, while admiring her sexy body. Cara looked back at him, then popped herself on the ass. "What you waiting on?"

Kedar stood up and walked over to her and slapped her ass hard. He loved the way it jiggled. With her heels on, she was the perfect height. So, he guided himself into her with ease. As he stroked, she looked back at him. Slap my ass!"

With the first pop, he left a handprint on her. He smacked her ass again, then rubbed it. The pleasure and pain of what he was doing, she loved. Kedar could feel her getting wetter, so he did it again. Cara's legs began to shake. He gripped her hips, and began to bang her hard.

"Yes, yes," she cried. "Fuck me, fuck me," she screamed.

Kedar balled her skirt up in his hand and began to hit it even harder. So, it shocked him that she began to throw it back, to match his rhythm. The fucking they were doing was intense. With every stroke she threw it back, making her ass hit his abs. He could see his dick change colors from her nutting on him, so he knew he was hitting the right spot. He spread her cheeks so that she could take more of him. She stretched out and allowed him to do it. It drove her crazy how his balls slapped her clit every time he went deep.

"Cum for me Daddy." Now that turned Kedar up a notch. He began to sweat hard while he was fucking. Cara looked back at him moaning, "Can you cum for me Daddy?" His legs began to shake he could feel it coming from the sole of his feet. He stood straight up, then she began to drive, throwing that ass back. She was looking to get her one more good nut. "Yes, yes," she screamed as she came. Her legs shook like crazy, and she couldn't stop them.

Kedar just smiled, enjoying the pleasure she was receiving. She could feel him throbbing inside of her again. Cara quickly pushed him back, and dove face first into his lap. She wanted to see what they both taste like together. It threw him off how warm her mouth was. Her throat was tight like her pussy.

"Yes," he moaned. She sucked just the head and massaged his balls. Cara sucked and stroked and sucked and stroked. She could feel the pressure coming up.

"Yes, yes don't stop," he cried. Faster and faster, she went. "Oh shit!" Cara could feel his warm semen going down her throat. He tasted delicious, she stroked, and he kept coming. She swallowed every drop of him, then she pulled his penis from her mouth and placed kisses up and down the sides of it.

DOUGLAS THOMPSON

Click.....Clack

CHAPTER 14

There was a masked man standing behind K with a 9 mm barrel pointed at the top of his skull. The man looked down at Cara, "If you scream, you will be next."

Crack!

The man hit K in the back of the neck with the butt of the gun. K couldn't see anything but the room spinning before he went out.

MOMENTS LATER............

"Wake that bitch ass nigga up," the heavy guy barked. The slim figured man came from out of the shadows and walked up on K, striking him with an open hand slap.

Pop!

Then a backhand.

Pop!

Blood began to trickle from K's lip. The man cocked back again.

"If you slap me again, I won't just stop at killing you, but I promise you I will erase your whole bloodline," mumbled K.

Slim laughed then hit K with a cross left. K maintained his composure, as he tried to quickly process what the fuck was going on. He could see Cara still half naked, with her hands tied, and her mouth gagged, in a chair to his left. There was a man standing behind her. There was also two of them in front of him, his hands were tied behind his back, and he was strapped to a chair. "What the fuck did these niggas want?" he thought.

Just like that one of the men read his thoughts. "You know what we here for, so come on with it, and we can be out!" Kedar's vision was blurry because of the cut that had formed above his eye. It was leaking blood into his sight. The slim guy ran up on him, and gave him two quick body blows, then another cross right. "Where the fuck the work at?!" he barked.

Kedar spit the blood that was forming in his mouth onto the floor. "So that's how you feel Nike?" he asked. Nike paced back and forth in front of him, then he took off the mask.

"Fuck this shit," he barked, then he grabbed K by the back of the head and place the barrel of his gun into his eye. "Where the fuck is the dope?!"

Kedar looked up at Nike and began to laugh.

"Oh, you think this is funny? You think this shit funny," quoted Nike, as he reached behind his vest to retrieve a silencer. He twisted it onto the barrel of the gun. Kedar just kept laughing. Nike raised the gun and sent one straight through Kedar's right leg.

"Ahhhh....you bitch ass, snake ass nigga! Fuck," hollered K.

Nike stared at Kedar. "All you got to do is tell us where the shit at and we can go."

Kedar wanted to laugh again, but the bullet was still burning hot inside of him. "If I could, I would, but I can't and you know why." Then he spit blood onto the floor.

Nike kneeled down by K. "If you don't tell me where the dope at, I'm going to kill your little bitch." Nike looked over at the gunman standing over Cara. He quickly drew his gun and cocked it. He didn't give a fuck about shooting Cara in the head, but they had just watched the sex escapade between her and Kedar, and he wanted to tap that ass from the back too. He had a bulge in his pants that he kept at her eye level, letting her know that he was going to get some of that pussy. Then the way her breasts sat so perfectly, her nipples had been hard the entire time, and still was. He just shook his head, 'there goes some good pussy,' he thought as he began to tighten his grip on the trigger.

Kedar looked at Nike, "What's that supposed to do for me 'cause you want to kill her? You and I know that shit don't matter, 'cause Escobar would have a fuckin soccer game with my head……. Literally!"

"Escobar!? Escobar!?" barked Nike. "Fuck Escobar!" Nike lifted up his vest, exposing his stomach, showing where he had, had surgery. "This shit is from Escobar!" Remembering that night that got his front blowed out, and it was actually the same night Kedar went to jail. "This shit is your fault too!" An enraged Nike spat at Kedar, "I told you…. I told you to stay in the car, or let's go but nawwwww… K want to go check on Escobar dog ass!"

Boom…

A shot rang out as Nike sent a bullet ripping through K's left shoulder. "Aahhh," K hollered.

"I bet you listen to me this time, Kedar!"

Kedar saw his life flash before his eyes, as that moment time came into view. Kedar had told Nike to ride with him, to make sure he made it home safe. Kedar had a little too much to drink. Nike jumped into the driver's seat and pulled off. Along the way, Kedar had Nike make an unscheduled stop. It wasn't until they hit the Avenue that Nike questioned him.

"Don't E live around here?"

"Yeah nigga, I'm about to holla at him 'bout something," Kedar replied.

Nike was against the unscheduled stop and told K that he might want to call first or wait until tomorrow because it was late as hell. Kedar silenced him and told him to pull around back. As they pulled around back, there was no one to greet them. "That's strange," K thought, as they drove down the winding driveway. When they came to a stop around back, Kedar called Escobar's phone but got no answer. Nike looked over at Kedar.

"Man let's go!" he exclaimed.

"Hold up," K called back. He could see the back door open, and someone was lying on the floor. He pulled the 40 off of his waist. "Look Nike, you stay here and keep the car on. Matter of fact, turn it around in case we got to peel."

"I don't think you should go in there," Nike started to say.

"Shhhh, just stay put," K repeated as he got out of the car. Kedar crept up to the back door. He could see Ruiz, one of Escobar's personal bodyguards, laid out on the floor. He eased up on him and checked his pulse. He was dead, in a pool of his own blood. K quickly grabbed Ruiz's gun and began navigating

through the house. He heard some talking coming from one of the bedrooms upstairs. Kedar could hear a man asking Escobar where the shipment was and if he
didn't comply there would be consequences. He could also hear Escobar respond
in Spanish saying something to the effect of, "You better kill me or else."

K peeked around the corner and saw about four of Escobar's bodyguards face down, dead. Jose, Escobar's right-hand man, was tied up on his
knees. He could only spot the gunman that stood over Escobar. Kedar scanned
the room, as he crept up behind the assailant. Kedar could see the butt of a gun
where Escobar lay on the floor, still cursing in Spanish. Kedar eased within six
feet of the intruder, "Drop it!" he commanded.

The man began to ease his weapon down.

CLICK.....

"No, you drop it!" a voice demanded from behind Kedar.

Nike bent the corner, and saw the scene. "What the fuck is going on?!"

The split-second was all that was needed, Jose got to his feet and
rushed the gunman that was behind Kedar. The man fired a shot, sending a bullet
whizzing past Kedar's ear. K shot, sending two bullets ripping through the gunman standing over Escobar. Escobar had gotten hold of the Uzi that lie under the
bed, and sent about six rounds through the man's face, as K shot him in the back.
Escobar was now up from the floor, gunning at the other gunman. The gunman
began to shoot back, as he tried to make an exit. He spun Nike around. Escobar
sent bullets ripping through Nike, trying to hit the man. The gunman ran and
jumped out of the two-story window. Escobar was on his ass, still shooting until
the clip ran dry. He then returned to the house.

Kedar was over Nike, trying to stop the bleeding. Escobar quickly un-
tied Jose.

"Where is your car?" Escobar asked Kedar.

"It's out back."

Escobar instructed Jose to quickly get Nike to the car. "With the gun-
shots in this community, the police are on their way." As they made it downstairs,
Escobar looked around like he forgot something.

"You good?" K asked him.

"No, my friend, I got some drugs downstairs that need to be destroyed."

"I'll handle it. Just please take care of Nike."

Escobar nodded his head and pointed in the direction of the room. K made it downstairs to the basement. As he hit the door, he could smell the raw dope from the top of the stairs. He ran to the bottom, there was another door, he went in. There had to be at least three hundred blocks a piece of heroin and coke sitting on two separate tables, neatly stacked. There were about five bathtubs in the room, he also spotted barrels of acid. He began dumping the blocks into the tubs, while pouring acid and whatever other chemicals they had down there, onto the drugs. Kedar emptied his gun into the tub, then he tossed the gun into one of the barrels of acid, as he finished up.

Kedar made it up and out. Just as he was breaking through the hedges, an officer spotted him. Kedar took off like a bat out of hell, but the area was already blocked off and locked down. They got K in a matter of minutes. Then it hit K, as he looked over at the gunman.........

"It was you!" K yelled.

Tank walked over to K and placed the gun onto his temple. K knew that he knew him from somewhere. Tank was the gunman that Escobar had been trying to kill. Kedar had caught a glimpse of Tank as he had jumped out of the window.

"I'm not yo partna," Tank spat. "I don't have no bullets for pussy ass flesh wounds! They went back took my brother away from me!" He grinned, with his finger dancing on the trigger. "Now, I'm gonna take everything I can from him, starting with that dope I know you got in here, and that money you haven't left here with. Then and only then I might let you live, if you tell me where to find Escobar."

"HERE I AM!" Roared Escobar, as he entered the room.

BOOM.....BOOM

Escobar sent to bullets flying into the man that stood over Cara, dropping his brains across the desk.

"You won't be so lucky after all," Tank said to Kedar.

Boom....Boom....Boom....Boom.

Tank put four bullets into K, knocking the seat back, and onto the floor. Nike let out shots, to cover Tank, hitting nothing but the wall and pictures. Tank took a spot behind the couch. He and Escobar along with E's crew exchanged gunfire across the room.

Boom! Boom! Boom!......Tat! Tat! Tat!

Cara scrambled across the floor to K's side. "It's going to be alright!" She cried as she tried to stop the blood from spilling. She was still crying, as the men continued to shoot it out in the office. Kedar could see Nike, who had run out of bullets, steady dodging bullets coming his way. Then Nike made a break for the side exit of the office, he got hit in one of his legs, but still somehow made it out

Cara opens up Kedar's desk drawer and pulled out the mini .45. She had a clear shot of Tank. She looked back at K, and noticed his eyes were now closed. "Noooooo," she screams as she squeezed the small cannon.

Boom! Boom! Boom! Boom! Boom!

She struck Tank every time. Cara tossed the gun and ran to K's side, crying hysterically. "Don't die! Please don't die!"

Escobar and his men approached a wounded Tank with their guns drawn on him. Tank was now with his back pressed against the couch. Escobar walked up on him.

"No, no, no, my friend it's not your time yet. I got a lot of plans for you," he said to Tank.

"Fuck you!" spat Tank, then he placed his gun in his mouth and pulled the trigger.

Shanice James walked into the control booth, relieved that she was working with someone she could relate to. "What's up, Jayell Jones?" She called out, emphasizing J's full name.

Ms. Jones spun around to see her classmate, "Oh shit, what's up Shan?"

"Girl, I'm glad they didn't stick me with these self-centered bitches again, TONIGHT!" The women begin to laugh. "I'm dead serious," said Shanice. "These niggas don' gassed some of these hoes up, I mean fuck 87 or 93, these niggas got jet fuel in some of these bitches. You know Kema?"

J pondered for a minute. "Which one, new homes or Padget Circle?"

"Bitch, Padget Circle. Foot dragging ass Kema, no tennis shoes having Kema. Bitch who fucked the whole basketball team Kema. Dirty, nasty pussy, non-bathing ass Kema, bitch! Hair longer than a damn snap Kema." Shanice snapped her fingers then both women burst into laughter.

"That funky bitch tried to front on me, in front of these niggas! I let her have that little bit, but when we made it back inside the booth, I told that bitch, if she ever, ever, ever try me like that again, I will pull up with my sister, and we will begin a throwback party, and commence to whooping that ass!"

"No, you didn't girl! J looked up at her.

"Hell yeah, I did," responded Shanice.

"Did she go tell?" questioned J.

"You see me in here with your ass, right?" They laughed again. "And I told the warden, that if I can't work with someone on my understanding level then I'll leave and find me a new job."

"Girl, you ain't tell Barry no shit like that."

"Like hell I didn't, then I asked what building you was working in, and here I am," Shan said. J looked at Shanice like she was crazy.

"How your mama doing?" J asked.

"She fine," Shanice responded. "I even got some of her dressing you love so much on my plate. I'll just give you this plate and tell ma to bring me another one. 'Cause I only got a appetite to whoop some ass anyway." Then both women burst out laughing again.

J told her to pop the plate into the microwave. As the smell of the home cooked meal filled the booth, J's stomach began to turn. Shanice looked at J, "Girl are you okay?" J just nodded her head as the timer went off. When Shanice pulled the hot plate from the microwave, J beelined to the bathroom and began to vomit. She had beads of sweat around her head.

Shanice knocked on the door. "Girl you sure you okay?"

"I'm good," called back J. She got herself together, then came out. "I'm not feeling so good," she stated.

"No shit, Sherlock," quoted Shanice. Shanice took a look over J from head to toe, "I thought I was tripping, but bitch, yo' butt bigger."

J looked at Shanice. "Bitch, I always had ass!"

"You did I can't lie, but tell me this, yo' bra feel tight?" asked Shanice.

"Come to think about it, they have been a little tight to me."

"'Cause they bigger smartass," responded Shanice.

"Heffa I don' had the same size titties since I was 16, ain't shit changed."

"If you say so." Shanice went fumbling around in her purse, "I know I got it in here somewhere. Gum, Tic Tacs, Keys, chips......oh, here it is," she pulled out the stick and handed it to J.

J looked at the stick, then at Tamara with a what-the-fuck face.

"Look bitch," responded Shanice. "You the one with the big ass and big titts, and can't hold the smell of food down. If it's negative, then I'm glad to have it out my bag, and if it's positive then bitch you got some planning to do."

J looked at Shanice, "This is a waste of time! I haven't had sex in damn near a year!"

"Bitch, unless you an elephant you ain't walking around pregnant for no year."

"Well I had an episode about two or three months ago."

"Girl just go pee," Shanice said.

J thought about it. "Fuck it. I'ma do it." She went into the bathroom and set the stick on the sink. As she finished up using the bathroom, she looked over. She noticed two blue lines, so she grabbed the wrapper to see what it meant 'positive'. "Ain't no fuckin' way," she said as she fumbled around to check the expiration date on the test. It was good, so she came straight up out the bathroom and made her way to Shanice's pocketbook. She rummaged around and pulled out the box.

"Is everything okay?"

"When did you buy this?"

"Actually, I got it for my little cousin two weeks ago, but she already had taken one, so I just kept it in my bag. Hell, I would have taken it back, if I didn't lose the damn receipt. Why?"

"Can I take this?" J asked without really asking and went back into the restroom. Again, two lines popped up, signaling that she was pregnant. J began to sob in the bathroom. Shanice let her get herself together.

"J, girl we got to count. You okay?"

"I'm good," she called back. She opened the door. Her eyes were puffy and red.

"Damn girl," Shanice said as she hugged her classmate. "Here, put this Visine in so we can get through this count."

They breezed through the F2 dorms, then went over to F1 dorm. "Count time, count time," the men screamed. "Let them get in and out!" When J came in, she noticed that Divine wasn't cutting hair. He always kept him some heads to cut, and she used to allow other people from other dorms to get their haircut by him, granted that they would leave immediately when he was finished. She allowed it because for the most part Divine would notify her, that he was finished, and she'd let the man out with no problems. But today, he had been working out all day, punching on a punching bag, made up of a mat and a net bag hanging from the second range. He was off in his little corner, just punching away during count. "Warden coming down the walk," one of the men screamed out.

The warden came on in. The women were through counting by that time. Divine was off in his own zone, punching away. The warden walked up on him, "Smith! Smith!"

Divine stop punching and looked at the warden. "Yes, sir," he answered.

"Is everything alright?" the warden asked.

"Truth be told sir, no. He cut his eyes at officer Jones. My brother got shot, and he is on life support. They don't know if he is going to live or die, so I got a lot on my plate right now, sir. Can I please get back to venting?"

"Leave him be," said the warden then he turned and began walking and talking to Shanice about her new post.

Ms. Jones asked, "You good Divine?"

"Hell nawww, man, K got shot the fuck up."

J's heart had fallen to her stomach. She paused and was stuck in the moment. "What?....When?....Who?....How?" She could feel her eyes beginning to tear up.

"I really don't know but I think they said some tennis shoes nigga name."

"Nike," she chimed in.

"Yeah, that's it! The way they was talking is like he either did it or had something to do with it, but my man's is laid up dying and ain't nobody there with him. They say they got his phone and called his wife in Albany."

"Albany?" questioned J.

"Yeah. Albany. The number was like 229 348 or some shit but it had been changed. The nurse says that's the only number saved in his phone, and he called it daily."

J didn't know what to think. Her mind was moving a thousand miles a minute. Her stomach turned again. She shot past the warden and Shanice, and ran into the mop closet in the dorm. She began to throw up and cry at the same time, she couldn't control it. When she couldn't give up anything else from her stomach, she passed out. J woke up in the medical room at the prison.

"What happened?" she rubbed her head.

"Girl, you passed out. The warden not too long ago left, and said to us that, when you wake, we needed to call a ride home for you. He also said for you to take a few days off until you get well. He's noticed that you've been dedicated pulling doubles. So, he said for you to take some time off since you gave us a scare. What if you were in the dorm by yourself? God forbid."

Realizing the scare of if she had been any other woman, she could see the terror in the situation. But she had a full understanding in her dorm, plus there were some, like Divine, that would ride with her if a nigga tried a stunt. She grabbed her bag, and headed to the front gate. 'Damn waiting on a ride, she jumped on 16 to 75 North to Atlanta.

CHAPTER 15

Kedar's eyes began to crack open. He could see God's light shining upon him. An angel appeared before him with all white on, blue eyes, and blonde hair. He thought, "Where the fuck is the black angels?..... Can I say fuck in heaven?" Then he smelled cigar smoke and immediately felt pain throughout his whole body.

The nurse looked over, "He's beginning to wake!"

"Owww," Kedar moaned. He literally felt like an elephant was sitting on his chest, after a truck had hit him. The nurse thumped a needle and began to inject the pain meds into his IV. All at once, the pain began to subside, as the high was about to take off. "Where am I?" he thought, struggling to see. He got his eyes open, and his head scanned the room. He was home, in his own bed. Escobar sat at the foot of the bed, while the nurse propped some pillows behind K's head. Afterwards, she collected her pay from Jose, Escobar's head bodyguard, and headed out.

Escobar never turned around. He just continued to puff his cigar while watching the news. He pulled on his cigar long and hard, then he allowed the smoke to fill up around his head. "You are one lucky motherfucker, my friend, he said to Kedar. Escobar snapped his fingers towards Jose, who then retrieved the chart from the foot of K's bed. Jose handed the chart to E and began to read, "SIX gunshot wounds, a fractured jaw, two broken ribs, two fractured ribs, a bullet removed from right shoulder and left leg, two bullets removed from abdomen, one bullet pierced the right lung, and one bullet an inch from your heart. Not to mention, you died on the operating table twice."

"He's one tough cookie, Boss," Jose said, as he took the chart form Escobar, and placed it back at the foot of the bed.

K's head begins to spin. "What the fuck?!" he thought. At that moment, realization struck him, oh shit! What about Cara?'

Listening to the heart monitor speed up, Escobar looked back. "Calm down my friend, you just fought through several surgeries, now you're going to kill yourself with a heart attack. What's wrong?"

Kedar mumbled through a fractured jaw, "Cara."

"Oh, the young woman.....," he paused for a second. "She is fine. A little shaken up, but fine. She is stronger than most women I know, and trust I know some tough mommies. She's been coming by checking on you every day. Who do you think has been washing and changing your clothes? Not Jose, or myself." Escobar glanced at his watch. "She should be here in a few. By the way your P.O. came by, she drew some blood from you. Did you know you had THC in your system? Of course, you did, that's why I called my people, and had the test results changed to negative."

"I'm sorry, Escobar," mumbled Kedar.

"No, no, no, my friend. Not sorry but be more careful."

K tried to straighten up but the pain was overbearing. "I promise to get all the money back up for you, and that's my word."

"No worries my friend, I know you will." Jose dropped the duffle bag by the bed, it contained all of the work and money that Kedar had in the safe at the shop. "I would rather you pay me when you're well, my friend." Escobar took another pull from his cigar.

"Can you answer something for me, E?" questioned K.

"Sure, my friend, anything."

"Why do you constantly watch the news, it's not like much changes on it?"

Escobar looked back at K and took a long pull from his cigar, then he glanced back at the television. Jose handed him his coat and hat as he stood up. Escobar walked over to K. "My friend, for one the news is entertaining, for two it is sadness," he said as he rolled the covers up to Kedar's neck, and sat the remote on his chest. "But most of all, I watch it because it is very informative, my friend."

On the TV. **News Flash** "Breaking news: An autopsy report has discovered that the decapitated body, that was found today, belongs to Nicholas 'Nike' Daniels. Daniels was the last known survivor of his family, whom just in the passing week were mysteriously murdered in random fashion. Local police stated that Nicholas' death was taken over the top. His head and hands had been taken from his body. He had several bruises covering his body that indicated him being tortured repeatedly. All his main organs were found in jars that sat around the table, which he was found on. Talk about gruesome. Now, in other news......"

Kedar clicked the TV off. "Damn, Nike," was all he could say. Kedar did feel as if he deserved to die (fuck that nigga), but damn don't take your family with you. Not to mention, your whole family. Literally. "That's crazy," he thought.

"You up?"

Kedar turn his head to the lovely sound of Cara's voice. She stood over him with her arms folded. He had not even noticed that Escobar and Jose had left, let alone that Cara was now standing over him. "How long you been standing there?" he asked.

"Long enough to know that Nike is gone, and he let his people get fucked up royally. Kedar, I got a confession to make, I truly thought that this was what I wanted. You know, this thing with you. God knows I would love to suck, fuck, and ride you all day long, but a bitch could lose they life fuckin' with you! I'm not glad that you got hurt, but it was definitely the wakeup call that I needed. I'm thankful for the time though because now, I can fully think straight. I will say that you warned a bitch, but my grown ass wouldn't listen. Ohhhh but trust me babyyyyyy, I'm all ears now!"

K tried to laugh, but the pain in his ribs kicked hard. He stopped immediately. "You stay with jokes," he grunted.

'But I'm glad to see you're recovering well."

"Thank you for being there for me, seriously," mumbled K.

Cara leaned in and kissed him passionately, "No thank you for allowing me in your life." She rubbed her nose against his. "I'm always in your corner when you need me K."

"Thanks," he replied. Cara leaned away from the bed.

"Get well soon," she replied.

"I'm trying," Kedar stated.

"No for real, for real, get well soon. 'Cause a bitch need to be paid for cleaning up your shit.......literally. Then getting your shop back up and running and maintaining your bills. Not to even count the trauma I saw and went through! Oh, and we ain't fucking ever, ever, ever, again! I truly need to be compensated!"

They both burst into laughter.

Kedar quickly grabbed his side, and Cara almost tripped over the bed trying to reach him. She looked down and realized that she had tripped over the duffle bag, which was partially open.

"Oh, hell yeah," she shouted, and pulled out a wad of cash. She popped the rubber band off and thumbed through nothing but one-hundred-dollar bills. "Yea, this is a good start," she laughed. Cara grabbed the bag from the floor, and placed it in Kedar's closet.

At that moment they both heard the front door close, as someone stepped quickly towards the room. Cara was a little nervous because she knew that she locked the door when Escobar left. A puffy eyed J stood in the doorway of the bedroom. She had a mixture of emotions on her face, sorrow, and disturbed, once she saw Cara coming out of Kedar's closet.

Cara could read the emotions on J's face, so she quickly grabbed a hold of the situation. "I'm only here to collect my paycheck." She showed the money in her hand. She was headed for the door when she stopped to reassure Kedar that everything with the shop would be on point, back up, and running at the top again. She then looked at J, "Now he is your responsibility." Cara patted K on the hand and left out.

J had an ocean of questions that she wanted to ask, until Kedar grabbed her wrist. From there it seemed like all negativity went out the window, as she began to break down and cry. She was completely at a loss for words, seeing him bandaged up, and with the IV running in his arm. J didn't know what to say or do, so she just cried. Kedar placed his hand up to her face, and wiped away the tears.

"I'm okay. Just chill," he said.

She sat back and gave him a look that questioned what he had just said. She hit him in his left shoulder.

"Ahhhhhh......," he cried out.

"You muthafucka.....you got me up here worried about you, and you been playing house with that bitch!? You fucked all up, laying here like you barely making it, then you have the nerve to tell me to just chill! I don' passed out at work, from working so many fuckin hours, trying to keep my mind off of you. Then this damn baby got me throwing up everything BUT it, 90 going north........."

"Baby!!????" Kedar said, interrupting J's tantrum.

J stopped talking a mile a minute, and realized that she had just broke the news to him. "Yes, baby," she responded as she dropped her head.

Kedar tilted her head up gently, by her chin. "Is it mine?" he asked.

"Yes K, it's yours. How could you ask me something like that?" She began to get emotional all over again, with tears running down her face.

"Calm down little grasshopper, I'm not questioning you like that."

"So, you ain't mad?" she asked.

That million-dollar smile spread across his face. "Mad? No. Why would I be?" Kedar pulled her down as she kicked off her shoes and snuggled up close to him. He placed one hand on her belly, and his other arm around her neck. "We got some serious talking and planning to do," he stated, then he kissed her forehead. "I thought you were done wit' a nigga. What made you come back?" he asked.

"Well first, I need to thank your nurse, for trying to constantly reach me. Where is she anyway?"

Kedar looked around, "You just watched her leave."

"Cara was your nurse?" J said in total shock.

"Yeah, why do you ask?"

"Because that's who's been constantly trying to reach me! I'm so sorry. I truly owe her an apology. She spoke with Divine about what had happened to you, and he gave me the message. Matter of fact, you really need to call him, because he is taking this shit very hard." J reached over Kedar, and grabbed his phone off of the dresser. She was about to call Divine but not before looking through Kedar's call log. She noticed that Cara had been calling her continuously, and she also noticed her number and picture were saved under "wifey." She stared at K.

"What?" he questioned, as he looked at her scroll through his phone. "His number is saved under Divine, little nosey ass girl."

J exited out and went to the contacts, she located his number and pressed 'call'. Divine answered on the first ring.

"Hello?"

"Divine? Yea, hold on, here is Kedar."

"What up tho?" called out K.

"Everything good?" questioned Divine.

"A little bump here, and bruise there, but all in all I'm gon' pull through aight," replied K.

"So, what's the nigga resume?" questioned Divine.

Kedar just layed there in the bed and nodded his head in approval. Divine was ready to straighten out the situation from behind the wall. "All is all. Everything..... Everything. It's been taken care of already."

"Check, check. But what happened? I mean how you end up in this predicament bro?"

"Well, my supposed right-hand man and them was helping me put this dog food away."

"Why you ain't just call me bro? You know I'm in tune. My people in PA dropping like $100 a piece. I would have lined that up for you, no problem bro. Don't do no shit like that no more, and you know I barely curse, so I mean exactly what I said."

"I feel you my dude," responded K. "But look, I was touching bases, to let you know that I'm good. Ima do that other thing with you, and I'll kick back to you for making that happen."

"Look at God," responded Divine. "I'm doing that on the strength, but who am I to turn down a look out, while being in my current situation. I'm going to get on that, and I want you watch how they fly."

That put a smile on Kedar's face, because he was speaking to a genuine friend.

"Oh yeah, I got one in the oven bro. So now I got to guard all movements better." He begins to rub on J's belly in a circular motion.

"Whaaatt? That's what's up my guy. But you know old girl slick pregnant too."

J raised up and looked at K. There was an awkward and telling silence on the line, between the two men.

"Oooooooouuu!" Divine blurted out. "Boy, I know you ain't get...."

"Hey, hey got dammit," Kedar chimed in laughing. "Hold that volume down." Both men laughed.

"You know you good by me," responded Divine. "Besides, she is really good peoples, and plus y'all will make a nice couple. I got to admit it."

"Thanks Divine," J yelled, as she put a smile on her face, feeling secure in Divine's comment.

"That's her?" he asked.

"Yea man, she right here by nigga side in my time of need. Plus, she put on point to hit my true right hand up. Thanks for looking out for a nigga bro."

"Check, check," responded Divine. "I'm going to let you catch up with your peeps, 'cause she been working hella overtime. I'm going to get on that other situation, and I'll be waiting for your call. Love bro, take care of yourself."

"Love," then K hung up the phone.

CHAPTER 16

Over the next couple of months, Kedar healed his wounds. He had plenty of time to focus, and to put things back on track, especially with the people that he had surrounding him now. Cara had the shop up and swinging. She had him all on the radio station. K's Detail became the after spot to be at, where everybody that was somebody, was there. You could meet anybody there, from the entertainment world to Wallstreet business. The parking lot was always full of money, power, and respect, and K's Detail was the center of it all.

Kedar had adopted a bond with one of his detail workers, ever since he had caught them smoking at his shop. Lil Jesse was the only one to tighten up, but Swift is what Kedar called him. He had sat down, and taught him the ropes, partly because he liked the way that Swift rocked. He had been willing to take the hit for his friends that day. He had not even been smoking the weed, but knowing his friends had two strikes at the job, and with the law, when he had none, made him take blame. He was quick on his toes, as well as in response, at action towards Kedar that day.

K had pulled him to the side, and began to groom him, giving him the game step-by-step. He gave him the ups, and the downs of the game, but he only let him play with the weed. Kedar called him Swift because he got the product gone quick. True enough Swift was making a little money, profiting only about a hundred and fifty off of each bag. **You know the game is to be sold not told** Swift never changed his style up. He purchased himself a nice little Maxima. Swift never missed a day of work, nor did he slack off with doing his job. Kedar never showed him favoritism while at work either. He would ride Swift's ass like he would any of his other employees. In fact, he might ride Swift harder than the rest.

The arrangement with Divine helped Kedar out a lot. Big Joey, one of Divine's cousins, began coming down grabbing the bricks of heroin for 100k. The shit was so raw, that it could only be matched, or compared to 'Blue Magic.' Big Joey was on the come-up. He now had a steady connect with some raw work. Kedar later found out that bricks of the dog food go anywhere from 100 to 150 grand. It can even catch at 175K. Big Joey ran through the ones that Kedar had gotten from Escobar.

Things were running so smoothly, that he was taking 20, stretching it into 25 bricks. Kedar was charging Joey 1.5 million for the 20, if and only if he promised to give Divine 100K every time he re-up. Joey jumped on the deal, but he had to get off Kedar's 5 blocks for 100k a piece. Joey did the math, with spending 1.5 for 20, it would be like 75 a piece, plus K's 5. He could dump each one for 125K, and everyone would be happy around the board. He showed Kedar love, his cousin love, he showed PA love, and most importantly, he showed himself love. That was a good ass arrangement. Big Joey had been coming to Atlanta consistently for those 25 bricks, and then Kedar would slide in some blocks of the 'white girl' to get off. He couldn't go wrong.

Kedar would frequently go down and stay with J in Thomasville. He would leave the business in Cara's hands, and may be down there two to three weeks at a time. Cara always made good business decisions. She even purchased the old Walgreens that sat next to Kedar's shop. Cara placed one of her friends that was a five-star Chef, who was out of work, there. In no time at all, they whipped the place around, and right into a thriving restaurant. The place thrived off of K's shop, and his shop made more because of the restaurant.

Kedar pulled up to the restaurant to meet up with Cara. He spotted her at one of the tables, enjoying a glass of Southern Sweet Tea. Kedar hopped out of his Escalade, the Georgia heat was okay, but only because there was a cool breeze blowing. He entered the restaurant and smiled as he approached Cara. She got up and gave him a hug, he pulled out her chair for her and pushed her closer to the table. As soon as he sat down, the waitress placed a cup filled with sweet tea, sugar, and a dab of honey, in front of him. She informs him that his brunch would be out shortly. Cara thanked the waitress, as Kedar fixed the napkin in his lap.

"Now that's what I call customer service," he blurted out.

Cara giggled, as she went over some paperwork with him. Kedar was always Hands-On with his business, but today he was kind of in a rush. The truck had been detailed, and he was going down south to see J. He had really wanted to skip this conference, and wait until he returned. But Cara wasn't going to accept not having this routine meeting. She brought him up to speed, and let him know what the numbers were looking like. She also touched bases on some of the ups and downs, but mostly ups.

The young waitress returned with the turkey bacon, and egg white, toasted sandwich, seasoned fries, and Ranch dipping sauce. Everything was separated into three sections. Kedar never liked his food to touch. He was very pleased with the preparation, and presentation of his meal, as well as the services. He looked at the young lady's name tag. It read Kayla. "Kayla, I will definitely be tipping you big today, and I will place a good word in with management for your service." The young woman's face lit up as she gave Kedar and Cara a smile.

"Thank you," she said.

The young waitress, made her way over to her next table. Cara looked at K and smiled. "I see you made someone's day."

"She must be new here?"

"Yep," replied Cara.

"Well, I hope management decides to keep her. She has such a sweet personality."

Cara smiled again. "I think management will." She slid an envelope over to him. Kedar tore it open and examined the contents. It contained a check with the restaurant's name on it.

Kedar gave it back and told Cara to tell the owner that they owed him nothing. "I send people here because it's a nice place. Then, looking at the amount of this check, it gotta be their income. What's up with them?"

Cara laughed, "Hold on, let me check." She cleared her throat then looked at Kedar. "Excuse me sir, my friend can't accept your money. You owe him nothing. He sends people to your establishment simply because it's a nice place to eat. He also says..........."

Kedar cut her off. "Stop playing! That's the problem, yo' ass play so much," he said, while laughing.

"What?!" she questioned. "I'm doing what you told me."

Kedar looked at Cara, "So, let me get this straight. I own this spot?" he asked.

She signaled around the establishment. "Well," she stated. "It's a three-way split with me, you, and the chef. But ultimately, it is mostly yours."

Kedar leaned across the table and kissed Cara on the cheek. She began to blush. "Aight now, ain't you on your way to see your people? Fuck around and start some more shit. And we both know folks get fucked up behind your shenanigans."

Kedar fell out laughing, as he sat back down on his side of the table. He caught a glimpse of Escobar having lunch at another table with some dorky looking white boy. He watched the men converse, then the young guy got up, and left. He had hopped into a two-door Toyota Celica. Kedar ate part of his meal then excused himself from the table. He walked over and greeted Escobar.

Escobar pulled on his cigar before he signaled for Kedar to have a seat. K had planned on calling Escobar once he made it back from down south. Escobar talked to him about increasing his order, which is something that Big Joey always asked about. K would always reply, "We'll see." Kedar was actually content with how things were going, plus he had just found out about his new restaurant. He was good but, he knew with Escobar, a question wasn't a question. It was a statement. The only thing Kedar could do was tell Escobar, "No or that he was good." But that may not be good enough because he truly owed Escobar his life and vice-versa. Nevertheless, Kedar respected his place on the food chain, so he told Escobar that he would double up, or even triple up, on the weed. On the soft, and dog food, he would accept an increase of 1/3, but anything more, would be unsettling, or even slowing up business.

Escobar processed Kedar's response. Kedar lit a cigarette while Escobar thought it over. He agreed under one condition, if Kedar would handle what was in the case. Kedar had already peeped the case from across the room. It was sitting on the floor, next to the seat that the young white boy had been sitting in. Kedar truly didn't want to know what was in the case, but it's not like he was going to say no, because everything dealing with Escobar was dealing with money. Although Kedar knew that this had to be dealing with money, he was on his way to see his unborn seed, so he had made up his mind to kindly refuse the offer. Just when he was about to respond, two police cars pulled up. Neither one of the men even attempted to panic, they just continued to smoke at the table, while having casual conversation.

Kedar looked over at Escobar, "Do I really want to know what's in this briefcase?" he asked.

Escobar casually stated that there was about 23 pounds or ten kilos of meth in the case, as well as some new shit that the chemist had put together. The new shit could go for approximately 10g's per key. Kedar swallowed hard. Four officers began to maneuver through the patio of the restaurant, in a formation that surrounded the two men. They began to move in on the men, with their hands positioned closely to their weapons. Kedar watched their movement out of his peripheral.

"So, I take it that the white boy set you up, E? Now you want me to take the fall?" questioned Kedar.

Escobar pulled on his cigar again. "No, my friend. Actually, I have been being followed since this morning. I was trying to get this case from around me. The guy, he refused, much like you are doing now."

Just before the officers stepped up to the table, Cara walked over. "Glad to see you, Mr. Escobar."

"The pleasure is all mine, Senorita," responded Escobar, as he kissed her hand. "Are you enjoying yourself this morning?" he asked.

"In fact, I am. Mr. Escobar sir, I apologize for the interruption, but would you mind if I took my supervisor back, for a second, we have some work to finish up?"

"No problem, ma'am." Escobar responded.

Just then, the officer placed his hand on Escobar's shoulder, "We would like a word with you, sir."

"Officer, what's the meaning of this?" questioned Kedar.

"Who are you?" the second officer asked, looking to put hands on Kedar.

Cara shot her hand out. "He's the owner of this fine, PRIVATE establishment, and I'm his attorney, LaCara Polk. Pleased to meet you."

The officer uneasily shook Cara's hand. "Well ma'am, we were looking to speak to Mr. Santiago, downtown. I know you or your client aren't going to hinder officers of doing their duty, are you?"

"In fact, sir," responded Cara. "We are always open to cooperate with the law, but may I have just one word with Mr. Santiago?"

"Escobar, is there anyone you need for me to contact on your behalf? I'm asking because, I am open for retainer," she boldly stated.

"There's no reason to lawyer up, we would only like for Mr. Santiago to follow us to the station for a few questions," the officer replied.

"It's okay," stated Escobar. "I will accompany these young men to the station. Kedar, tell Maria that I went ahead and separated the clothes already, they're in the laundry room in the back. It's like 50 pieces of white and dark clothing. Since I got behind from the soccer event last week, there's also about 300 uniforms full of grass stains that need to be bleached really good. Tell her to start on them now, so that they'll be ready in time."

"Will do," replied Kedar.

Cara eyed the case. As Escobar began to move away from the table, one of the officers picked it up. Cara immediately grabbed it, and placed her hand on top of it. "Thank you, sir."

"Is this yours?" questioned the officer.

"Actually, it belongs to a patron that was here prior to Mr. Escobar. He called and stated that he had left it, being in a rush, so I promised I would retrieve it," she stated with a smile. The officer released the briefcase.

Escobar tipped his hat, "Since they only would like to speak to me. Tell Marta, I will be home before 10. Tell her to look for me around 6."

Kedar nodded his head, knowing Escobar had just dropped the price of the meth to $6,000 a piece, and had left him with 50 kilos of heroin and coke. There was also 300lbs of green.

Escobar walked over to his car, then the officers escorted him in the direction they wanted him to go. They drove away with a police car in the front, and one in the back.

Kedar and Cara walked off. Cara eyed K before she spoke. "Do I even want to know what's in this case?" she asked.

Kedar smiled, "Probably not, just place it in the safe in my office." He kissed Cara on the cheek then walked her to her car. Kedar hopped in his truck, and pulled up behind his shop. Just as sure as the sky is blue, and the grass is green, he spotted three tubes that were labeled 'Laundry.' Kedar placed them in the back room of his shop.

"What the fuck am I going to do with some shit to this extent?!" he yelled out to himself. "Fuck it," he thought. He'd just try to push it off on Big Joey. Little did Big Joey know, Kedar was about to give him the upgrade he had asked for and more. Kedar figured he'd kill two birds with one stone. Once Kedar had situated everything, and made sure it was secured, he then jumped on the road and went to Thomasville to spend time with J.

Kedar had battled through a storm to get to Thomasville. Rain was dropping hard onto his Escalade. The raindrops were sounding like little Pebbles tapping on the windshield. He only imagined what it was doing to his paint job. He had a beautiful black and silver truck with 28-inch rims on it and a system that was top-notch. The V12 engine in it was all the way good. He could pull a mobile home with ease. The only thing that Kedar hated was that the windshield wipers were not worth a fuck. He placed his arm outside, to clear some of the rain, so that he could see. He quickly stopped that, as some of the water hit his peanut butter interior. Kedar made a mental note to grab some new windshield wipers, once the weather decided to die down. As for right now, his mind was set on making it to J and the baby in one piece.

When he made it to the apartment, the bottom had fallen all the way out of the sky and, he was drenched once he made it inside. J wasn't home yet, so he dried off, prepped dinner, and sat back on the couch with Ginger watching the news. Ginger had taken a real liking to Kedar, he would sometimes bring the dog back with him to Atlanta. She was very protective, but she was glad when he was there, because she no longer had to live in the cage. She was able to roam the house.

Sometime later when Kedar was in the kitchen, Ginger stood up on the couch, facing the door while growling, signaling that someone had entered the building, and was headed for the door. A few seconds later, there was rattling at the door, Ginger hopped off of the couch with a loud thud, and faced the door, looking to take the intruder head on. When the door swung open, Ginger's tail begins to shake from side to side, seeing Jay walk through the door with Angel.

"Hey mama's baby," responded J as she rubbed her dog's forehead. "Hey baby," she yells out, while balancing behind the couch. Kedar was barely able to catch her wrists.

"What's up love. Why the rush?" he asked her.

"Stop K, I got to pee bad! You know, sometimes your baby just sits on my bladder and refuses to damn move."

"Don't talk about my baby like that," he said to her as he dropped down to his knees to kiss her stomach. The child in her womb immediately reacted on the sound of his voice, as he rubbed her belly delightfully.

J had her hand settled on Kedar's head. "Oh shit! Move baby, I got to shit now," she shouted.

Kedar grabbed her by the hand, "Why you moving so fast?"

She snatched away, "Unless you want to hand wash some shitty drawers, I suggest you let me use the restroom," she playfully joked.

"I'll hand wash, smell them, and eat them, if you like," he responded.

"Now you know you nasty as hell." She tiptoed to kiss him. "Now move!" She pushed him to the side, to go into the bathroom, locking the door behind her as it closed.

Angel could do nothing but look, and smile at the couple. Angel was one of the few friends that Jay had at the job. She had been with Jay every step of the way, seeing that she was a mother as well, she knew firsthand what being pregnant was like. She volunteered to pick Jay up, and drive her to and from work.

Ginger went and found herself a seat outside of the bathroom door.

"Oh shit! Bae, put some water on that shit," Kedar joked. He could hear the toilet flush.

"Eat my ass," yelled J.

"Not smelling like that," he replied.

Angel burst out laughing. "You two are silly as hell."

Kedar smiled knowing that she was telling the truth. He loved the relationship that he and Jay shared. "Would you like something to drink?" Kedar asked Angel as he made his way to the kitchen.

"Let me get a shot 'cause shit is stressful," Angel replied.

Kedar could clearly see that something was on her mind, so he gave her a double shot of yak. She immediately tossed it back. She did not give the strong drink time to settle down on her tongue before she told K to hit her again. Kedar lifted up one eyebrow, "Girl you better slow down, you got to drive," he joked. Angel let out a soft giggle.

"Boy, stop! I just left work dealing with some grown ass kids, now I got to go home to deal with my two boys who think they some grown ass men. My world is completely upside down and I don't know whether I'm coming or going. Pour the damn drink!"

Kedar laughs, knowing how the men in prison act like big ass babies. He poured her one last shot, then he went into his pockets and handed her 300 dollars. "Thanks for taking your time out to make sure my woman and seed make it to and from work safely." Angel stood in shock and almost dropped a tear as she took the money.

"Thank you! You just don't know how much help this is to me. I know it's wrong, but thank you for not telling J about this."

Kedar finally poured himself a drink, "No problem." He went back to the living room to finish watching the news. He whistled for ginger to come.

She came running and hopped onto the couch, then placed her head into his lap.

Angel came in the living room and took a seat in the chair. "Kedar?"

"Wassup?"

"Do you mind if I ask you a question?"

"Sure, go ahead!"

Angel pondered over it for a second. "Well, it's this guy at the prison that I'm feeling right.....and I can't help but to wonder if he's worth it. I truly would like to have what you and my girl got 'cause she actually found true love. I mean even when a jail wall was separating you two."

Kedar responded, "We both found love for each other."

"That's what I'm saying," she replied. "I think dude is genuine in the things he telling me. Like, he is not over the top with it, but it's enough to have me thinking about him while I'm at home. I can't help but imagine what it would be like with him in the house."

Kedar took in everything that Angel was saying. "Look Angel, what my baby and I have is real, uncut, no bullshit. And I take to you like family, so I can be nothing but raw with you. Some dudes in prison want nothing more than to just get in your drawers, get the pack in, or have this quote-unquote chain gang reputation of fucking with officers, but you do have some good cats in there."

"That's what I'm saying......," she chimed in. "So, it is good ones."

"True, true," he responded. "But you need to be careful while assessing a situation like this."

Angel placed her head down. "I know, and don't get me wrong, I appreciate everything you do for me and mines, but I want to help him out so that I can help myself as well."

Kedar sat up in his seat, "So you want to bring the pack in, is that what you asking me?" he inquired.

"Shush! Damn nigga, not so loud!"

Kedar leaned back and began to laugh. "You cool over here. Did he put that thought in your head?" he questioned.

"Boy, stop! I'm born and bred here, it ain't nothing but two jobs you can get here. That's the chicken plant or the prison and everybody know that the prison is a come up. But who really want to make a career of babysitting grown ass men. I done looked up a couple of people before and saw their backgrounds, especially their financials."

Kedar burst into laughter hearing this. "Angel, in prison looks can be deceiving. It's a place where you can be who you want to be. I met a dude who said he was an astronaut, but hell, who was I to question what or who he was. Some of them flamboyant ass niggas probably junkies on the street, you just don't know. Prison saved their lives. They be talkin' like they move bricks and shit, yeah, they move boulders alright. Right into a glass dick."

She tossed a pillow at him, "Stop playing! I'm serious!"

K caught it while laughing. "Hell, I am too. But on a serious note you need to think about your boys first, then weigh the pros and cons to that shit."

"I know," she mumbles. ".........and I have, that's why I'm talking to you now."

K took a deep breath, "I don't think you are asking for my approval. At this point, it seems like your mind is made up, so look......," he reluctantly spoke. "I'll see." Angel jumps up excitedly. "Hold on, hold on. I said I'll see. But you don't do nothing till I get back with you. Oh, and if I help, and this is a big ass IF, you must do it my way. Alright?"

"I'm okay with that," Angel replied with a smile on her face. She got up and gave him a hug before leaving out. "Thanks, K."

Once he locked the door, he looked back. Ginger was sitting up looking at him with her head cocked sideways. "What?" he questioned the dog. She hopped off the seat looking like, 'oh you know' then made her way back by the bathroom door. A few minutes later, J came out the restroom.

"Where is Angel?"

"Hell, she went to get the baby some clothes. We figured that you were having the baby, how long you took."

"Shut up," she replied. "What you cooking?" she asked as she made it to the couch.

"Well, I'm making something healthy for you and our baby to eat. I got some baked chicken, dinner rolls, string beans and rice. I also got a healthy salad to the side for you to eat."

"It sounds yummy," she replied before placing a big kiss on his face. She had grown fond of Kedar cooking, cleaning, and babysitting Ginger. She was very appreciative of all the wonderful things that they had partook in, most of all she grew fond of their relationship's communication. Ever since the incident with her roommate, he was always being straight forward with her in everything. He even told her about Cara. At first, she felt some type of way, and he didn't get none of that good wet pregnant sex for about two weeks. After that, she did reason within herself that everything was all good. She even knew that he was giving Angel money for transporting her to and from work. He made her promise to not say anything about it to her, though. She was all right with him doing so, because hell she was a good friend, and she would have given her the money too for nothing. She figured an even swap is a fair exchange, Angel worked by driving and got paid for it. Plus, the girl drives like Miss Daisy, not even so much as going through a yellow light. She would slow down damn near a block away from an intersection.

J looked into his eyes. "What's on your mind?"

"Your girl was telling me about this dude she like at the prison."

J laughed. "Oh, she like this dude named Rico."

Kedar leaned back. "How you know? She told you?" he questioned.

"No, but I can see and I'm not dumb. Hell she's an ass with everybody but him. He's a real laid back kinda guy. He reminds me of someone I know."

"Alright now! Make me pop off in this bitch. Can't no nigga compare to me. I'm in a league of my own," Kedar said playfully, while feeling himself.

She playfully hit him. "Not like that sir, but he sticks to himself. But it's this new loud ass Blood nigga, that recently moved in, and Rico is the only cat, it seems to keep the nigga in his place. But anywho why would that make you look how you looking?"

"Well because she probably going to try a stunt or something like that."

"Let me guess, she asked for your approval, huh? Ya know, she does look up to you like a big brother."

"Shit, it seemed like her mind was made up. I told her I'll see, but don't do nothing drastic that would get her in any trouble."

"So, you gonna help her?"

"I'll let her know. I also told her that if I do, and that was a big ass if then it would be on my terms or I'm out."

J wanders off into space, "Well to each its own, but don't include me in that. Aye while you trying to come up with something, get that ass in the kitchen and make me a plate! I'm starving."

Kedar kissed her on the cheek. "Your ass is always eating."

"Well, somebody forgot to pull out. Now you going to be my personal everything for the remainder of your life. Now, Alfred make me a plate."

Kedar got up off of the couch and J popped him on the ass. "Get to it, Daddy."

"Don't start nothing," he responded.

"Or what?" she questioned.

"You going to have your thumb in your mouth, curled up like a baby."

J stuck her tongue out.

Kedar tossed the remote to her, because he felt like he had seen enough of the news. He spent the next two weeks in Thomasville tending to all of J's needs and wants. It rained most of the time while he was there, but with rain comes sweet love making. As the weather cleared up, he was reminded that he did have a business to run. So, after having some good morning loving, he made J some breakfast. Kedar then dropped her off at work, before heading back to Atlanta.

CHAPTER 17

Kedar had made it to Macon when he realized that he needed some gas. He had barely drove around while in Thomasville, so he hadn't paid much attention to it. He jumped off the interstate to gas up. While pumping gas, he noticed the mud and dust that had built up on his truck because of the weather. He shook his head. Luckily, the gas station that he was at was a link to a small car wash. He pulled up around back. There was an old man sitting there with a dirty bucket of water and a sign that read, "Will wash for food." Kedar respected the hustle so he allowed the man to do his thing. He offered to get some clean soap and water, or for the man to use the machine, but on Kedar's dollar of course. The old man had kindly refused, stating that the stuff was watered down.

"This is the real deal," he said holding up his bucket and towel.

Kedar laughs at the man's sense of humor and took a seat. He sat back and watched the man bring his truck back to life with just a bucket of water. His rims shined like new, as the man finished up. Kedar had to ask him what he put on the rims, because they now looked like they came right off of the assembly line. The old man stated it was a secret but that Kedar wouldn't believe him if he told him. Kedar looked over the man.

"I have no choice but to believe you, if you tell me," he said as he reached into his pocket handing him one of his business cards. "I own a detail shop. I would like to know the secret."

The old man analyzed the business card. "Well, if you give me a couple of those Lucy's with my pay then I'll tell you."

Kedar told the man that he would do better. "Old School, here is a honcho and you can keep the pack of cigarettes." The man grabbed the money and the cigarettes, as his eyes lit up. He began to smile from ear-to-ear revealing his three missing teeth, one from the top, and two from the bottom.

"Jesus, you can have my last tube of it!" He handed the tube over to Kedar.

K looks over the tube. "Is this what I think it is?"

"If you ever been around them parts before then, yeah." replied Old School.

Kedar had to smile, "State toothpaste! I can't get you for your last one, Old School."

"Son it's fine, I spend the weekend in jail, so I'm about to re-up anyway."

The old man was really making Kedar's day, so he placed the toothpaste in his pocket. Before he drove off, he informed Old School if he was ever in Atlanta to call the number and he'd have a job for him at his detailing shop. The old man jumped up and clicked his heels like the peanut man.

"I'm going to call, Young Blood. Oh yeah, you may want to check on your wipers."

As soon as he said it, Kedar looked up at the sky. There was a chance of rain, seeing how dark the clouds were. He had spotted an AutoZone down the street.

"Good looking out, Old School. Damn, I got to hurry up." He didn't want the man's work to go to waste. He pulled up to AutoZone, quaking. Kedar hopped out of his truck, wearing a short sleeve white Polo shirt, a pair of short khaki pants, a pair of mid Air Force Ones, and a plain Jane band presidential watch. Kedar was a real watch fanatic. The one he was wearing ran about 40 bands. He went into the store. The bell chimed signaling that a customer had entered the building. Kedar located the windshield wiper section, he looked over the items trying to figure out which one to select.

"Can I help you?" a familiar voice called out.

Kedar turned around. "Oh shit. Sarge that's you?" It was Sergeant Wilson, Kedar's old detail officer. "Man, what's up?" The two men gave each other dap.

"Special muh-tha-fuckin K!" quoted Wilson. "Man, what's up?" Wilson was one of the few laid-back officers at Macon State Prison. "What you doing this way?" Wilson questioned.

"Trying to find some wipers for my truck Sarge."

"Well, it's Lieutenant now," Wilson corrected.

"That's what's up! Congratulations!"

"Is that your truck right there?"

"Yeah, that's me."

"Damn when did you get out?"

"I've been out for a couple of months now."

The two men began walking toward the exit. Wilson stared out at Kedar's truck.

"I can't flex, this bitch clean for real, for real," he commented.

K opens the door, so that Wilson can see the interior.

"I got a little something for that," said Wilson, looking at the water that had hit the peanut butter interior.

"I appreciate it," Kedar replied.

"You got the manual in there?"

"Yeah, I do," K said as he leaned over to the glove compartment to retrieve it.

"Let me check it out to make sure I have the right wipers. I can put them on for you too."

"That's what's up Lieutenant!"

"Man stop with the formalities and shit, my name Tony!"

"I got you, T," smiled Kedar.

"Man, you used to be the talk of every motherfuckin briefing. They used to roast ass saying you was manipulating people and shit! The first time I spoke up for you, telling them you was alright, they damn near put my ass under investigation!"

"Manipulating???!!....shiiiit! I was getting manipulated, FUCK manipuIaTING! I was getting extorted by officers, paying them $250 for a damn can of Bugler that was only $40 to $50 on the street. Hell, I would have to buy the motherfucker sometimes too," joked Kedar. "But any who man, since you made lieutenant, what you doing still working here?"

"Don't get it twisted, K. They don't pay like that, even for Lieutenants. I still got mouths to feed. You know how that go. But shiiiiiit, I'm glad to see you're doing all right for yourself. Let's go and grab those wipers."

"Give me a second, I'll be in after I smoke this 'Port."

"Alright, I'll have it ready at the register."

Kedar leaned over to reach in his console for his lighter. As he peered out of the passenger side window, he noticed a white '96 Honda Accord pulling up. He thought nothing of it as he closed his door, and leaned back on it to light his cigarette. He inhaled then blew the smoke into the air. He looked again at the sky to make sure he had time to get the windshield wipers on so that he could get up out of South Georgia.

"Mr. K Simpson, tell me that ain't you."

Kedar looked back. "Oh Shit, what's up Ms. James?" He leaned over to give the small woman a hug. Ms. James was an officer that also worked at Macon State while he was there. She looked totally different from the way she did in uniform. She was a pretty lady while he was locked up, but now she looked basically average. She kept her hair and nails done, but the way it looks right now, she should have been spending that money on a new muffler. Her car was smoking like hell.

"Damn stranger," she said as she stepped back eyeing the man from head to toe. She was admiring his cologne, right along with his looks. She had always had a silent crush on him, but he was talking to a co-worker that she didn't like to share the same booth with. "I see that you're doing good for yourself. Is this your truck?"

Kedar smiled, "Yes, this is mine. Do it stand out that much?"

Ms. James started peeking in the window, putting fingerprints on his glass. "Stand out? Shit, boy it's only two Escalades in this area, and both of them belong to the pastor. How I see it, God has not even blessed him like this, to be riding with the shit you got. Wait till I tell your old running partner, Rolax that I saw you."

"Damn my nigga still there?"

"Hell yeah, still doing him. He stays talking about you and shit. Talking about how you got a shop and everything. He always says that he's proud of you for doing your thing once you touched down. Most people were saying that he was capping and shit like that."

"Well tell them haters to stop holding their nuts." Kedar opened the door and gave her a business card. "Tell bro' shit is official and to hit me up. I got some paper for him, anything he needs to tell him to call me." He turned the card over, "If he can't catch me in the office, like now," he began to write his number on the back. "Tell him to hit me on this number. I'm going to pick up every time."

Ms. James grabbed the card and read the front, then the back. She had a sly grin on her face. "Do you mind if I call?"

"With all due respect, I am spoken for, but look if you are in the city, I will detail you up for free. Oh, and I got a restaurant right beside it, you and whoever you're with, your bill is on me." Kedar peeled off a hundred-dollar bill, and gave it to her. Her eyes lit up at the neatly crisp bill. "Make sure you take care of that for me."

"I got you. I go back to work in a couple of days, so I promise I will pull up on him."

Tony came outside. "Special K, your wipers are at the counter, you need to come pay for them before I can bring them out. Hey, what's up Ms. James."

"Hey Tony," she smiled.

"You came to put something down on your muffler?" Tony questioned.

"Yes, I did," she said humbly.

"Look T, just total her the whole Muffler out on my receipt."

"You want me to total out the muffler or her lay-a-way plan?"

"T!!!" Ms. James yelled.

"What?" he questioned.

"How much is the total?" Kedar questioned.

"Well with all the parts she needs, it's about $670 plus labor."

"Can you handle the labor?"

"Sure but....."

"Well total it out then," Kedar said cutting Tony off as he peeled off $300. "That should cover the labor." He handed the money over to Tony.

Tony's smile spread, full of appreciation. "Thanks man, you don't know how good you just looked out for me. My bills were due and everything."

"Just chill," smiled Kedar. "It's all good." He dapped up T, and gave James a hug. "Y'all be easy, and take care," he called back as he exited the store.

"Alright," they said at the same time.

Kedar got into his truck and strapped on his seatbelt for the trip back to the A.

Cara was in her office with her homegirl, Erica, who was a successful entrepreneur. Cara's assistant, Stephanie, who was a slim pretty girl, and a graduate from Spellman University, was closing out a business call from some wine vendors in California. Erica was babysitting the bar inside of Cara's office, as she poured three drinks, one for each woman. Cara sat behind her desk as she took a sip of the strong drink.

"Damn! I needed that," Cara said out loud.

Erica sat across from her, "What your ass need isn't a damn strong drink, but some strong dick," she joked.

"Child boo! I need to figure out how to ask Kedar to help me with this wine vendor. You know it is the one thing that I really have been trying to get on with, and it's been hard to get. Cara allowed the tension to ease off of her face.

"Girl don't worry, you'll get it done some kind of way."

Cara just glanced out her window that overlooked the view of the parking lot, and part of the detail shop. She had picked the office with the view, so she could see what was coming and going, and who was working and who was not.

"Are we still on for lunch today?" Erica asked.

"We are, but I wanted to be here when Kedar brought his ass in here today."

"Yeah, on that note, when am I going to meet the man that be having my friend cooped up in this office? Which, by the way, is a nice ass office. Girl this leather here is soft as hell." Erica rubbed her hands across the seat of the chair, she then stood up. "I don't see why you just don't break it down on his old ass, in order to get what you want," she said that as she placed her hands up in the air and dropped her ass down, like she was bouncing on a dick. "......and make his old ass tear it off!" The women laughed.

Cara looked at her friend. "Girl you stupid! First of all, he is not old. and for two......."

Erica cut her off, "You run this shit like it's yours. And whether he is young, old, or got damn maturing, the power of the pussy can make any man act right." Erica started to demonstrate the motion of hula hooping. "Ayyyyyyye," she said amping herself up.

Stephanie sat beside Cara's desk smiling and enjoying the way Erica acted. Erica was very strong and outspoken. Stephanie could only wish that she had been born with the same type of personality. Cara looked over at Stephanie, and could tell that she was deep in thought about something that Erica had said.

"Stephanie, chyle pay this fool no mind. She never knows what to say out of her mouth, and furthermore she never knows how to act."

"What!?" Erica yelled. "Look lil mama.....," she said as she signaled Stephanie over to her. "Yo' boss is tripping. In all honesty, my girl has lost her edge. Do you see those men out there? They are ripe for the picking. You've got to only become what they want, or make them want you." Stephanie stood there like a little girl, getting lessons from her big sister. "You see him?" Erica pointed.

A soft voice Stephanie questioned, "Who, him? The one with the ball cap on?"

"Yeah, him. He looks like he's married with children, but he would pay nice to keep his family."

"What about him?" Stephanie pointed.

"Yeah, he is cute, but look at his shoes, Reebok Classics. Cheap, but clean. He broke."

Cara burst out laughing. "But look Step, that doesn't mean that he won't dip deep into them pockets to deal with you, because baby girl you got 'Sunshine' between your legs!"

"Why you filling that child head up with that nonsense?" Cara said.

"What? I'm just calling it like I see it."

"Stephanie keep your eyes on your career, get yourself situated first, then you worry about a relationship. Don't get me wrong nothing beats a good fuck, but if you fuck him too good, and he becomes a stalker, then you have problems."

"Oh yeah, that part," responded Erica. "I've got plenty of those." She stood looking out of the window, staring at the men. "You'll just have to get a 50b, they'll leave you alone for the most part."

"A 50b?" Stephanie's eyes shot up in questioning.

"Yeah, a restraining order," Cara called out. "But that isn't the worst, you got some out there, but very fucking few, that will put that dick on you."

"Cara don't fill the girl head up with bullshit like that," Erica yelled as she rolled her eyes.

"I'm dead ass serious!"

Erica looks at Stephanie and rolls her eyes upwards in a long slow manner.

Cara grabbed Stephanie's hands, then began to speak. "These are real facts Stephanie. I came across one like that, right? I had to call up my mama, and ask her how she had managed to tell and teach me everything but somehow, she happened to leave that out. She was like, "Girl, if I would have told you then I would have had to keep you away from your father."

Erica burst out laughing. "Now girl you shot out!"

"I'm serious," joked Cara.

"Like look.............." Erica pointed at the black truck that had just pulled up. "See men like that, with big trucks, and big rims, have them because they have big egos and small dicks," she emphasized with her thumb and pointer finger. "But, because there is a but........BUT even with that, that's why you learn how to hula hoop. Eeeeoooowwww," she said finishing off with her tongue out. Erica poured herself another shot and took a seat back on the couch.

Stephanie smiled. "Cara, do you want me to reschedule the appointment that's scheduled for tomorrow and push it back till Friday?"

"Which appointment is that?"

"The one with Ms. Susan Connors," Stephanie responded.

"No, just move it to 4 o'clock today."

"Yes ma'am," Stephanie confirmed.

Erica had begun to multi-task with making calls and tapping on her laptop and tablet. "Girl, you know Susan Connors?"

"Yeah, why?"

"Isn't she like the Senator, or something?"

"I told you to broaden your horizons, Erica, and yes she is a Senator," Cara replied.

Erica snapped her fingers. "Babygirl, with those types of connects, you're supposed to be running for Mayor or something."

"You should, because you would definitely have my vote." said Kedar, who was standing in the doorway, smiling. Erica tossed the drink back, while looking at the glow of Kedar's dark skinned complexion. She immediately thought to herself, "Damn he fine." "

"Hey how you doing Step?" He waved as he entered with Swift in tow. ".......and how are you Ms....."

"Oh, my name is Erica. I'm a friend of Cara's."

"Well, any friend of Cara's, is a friend of mine. Nice to meet you."

"The pleasure is all mine," she responded.

Cara loved the way Kedar's presence demanded attention. He walked over and sat on the corner of her desk, "Working hard or hardly working?"

"What do you think?" Cara asked.

"I don't know, because if you're running for Mayor, then I need to be on your promotion team," he joked. "So, what have you been doing all day, then, Ms. Cara?"

"Wouldn't you like to know?" she responded.

Kedar reached over, and tossed back her cup of yak. He then proceeded to pour himself another one. "Stephanie, would you mind giving me the schedule for today?" Stephanie looked over at Cara for confirmation.

"Are you questioning my employee?" she asked.

"Seeing that I pay you, and you pay her, that pretty much makes me her employer. So, Stephanie give me Cara's plans for today," he said as he swished the drink around in the cup.

Stephanie started from when Cara had her regular one-hour workout at 5 a.m. Moving into opening up the shop, to getting coffee ready for the workers, a couple of phone calls made including several to you then.....," she cleared her throat. "She has reservations with Erica."

Kedar stopped her. "What did you just skip?" Stephanie again looked at Cara.

"Tell him," Cara responded with the sinister smile.

"Well sir, she scheduled an appointment to, and I quote, 'cuss your ass out' for not answering." Swift dropped his head in laughter. Kedar joined in with a laugh.

"She actually placed that in her log for today?"

"Yes, sir."

Cara sat on the other side, grinning from ear-to-ear. "I damn sure did, and we can start that appointment right motherfucking now. Unless you trying to reschedule that shit."

"You funny," he laughed.

Erica got up to get herself another drink, Kedar poured it for her. "I was just talking to my girl about......"

"Shhhh....hush," Cara cut her off.

"About men and big trucks," Cara informed Kedar.

"What about men and big trucks?" he asked.

"Go ahead Erica, tell him."

"Well........," she rolled her eyes at Cara. "You act like I'm scared to speak my peace."

"Yea, you still haven't spit it out yet, have you?" joked Cara.

"Damn bitch! Give me a minute. Well, they say men with big trucks got big egos."

"Well, I can't speak about everyone else, but my ego is a pretty big size," Kedar replied.

"Oh yeah?" taunted Stephanie. "They also say that big egos come with a small penis," she emphasized the same way that Erica did earlier, with her pointer finger and thumb.

K looked around at the women. "Ya'll need help for your logics. What's truly on your mind Cara?" There was a pause, along with a long awkward silence.

"Well since she put me on blast, my girl needs some paper for a wine vendor."

"Erica!!!"

"What? You might as well spit it out, you know you've been grinding to get one, and yet you are at a standstill."

"Why didn't you say something?" K asked.

"Because it costs a lot and it is something that I wanted for me. So, I was trying to do it myself."

"So basically, you need me to finance this dream of yours, right?"

"Actually no, but the majority of it, yes," Cara stated.

"Well why didn't you say so? That's cool, no problem. If it's in my range, then that's what's up."

"You'd do that for me?"

"Sure, why wouldn't I?" asked Kedar.

"70/30 split, my way?"

"Hell naww, my way. I got to put up the most paper, and take the least cut?"

"Yea, because I got to do all the work," spat Cara.

"60/40, your way."

Cara pondered for a minute. "Fine."

"Say Swift, you want in on this? You can jump on my 40," Kedar said to Swift.

"You know I'm about money, so just tell me how much I got to put in."

"That's all it took?" questioned Erica. "Shit, I was looking to open up a lounge in the city. I need some help too."

"Why don't you jump in on the wine vendor with your friend, so you can come up with the money for your own lounge?"

"I consume alcohol, not make it. And hell, with the wildfire in California, you might lose the crop. At that point it would be cheaper to go overseas, but with the tricky weather, you may lose the crop there as well. Not including the tariff, Trump got Import and Export jacked up. That shit is like rolling dice right now. If I'm going to roll dice, I rather do it right, in a club, in Atlanta."

"What's your job by trade?" questioned Kedar.

"I'm a jack-of-all-trades, but I know people, that know people. We'll just keep it like that."

"Swift, we've heard the pros and cons of the wine business. Are you still in?"

"I'm in, if it's something Cara wants to do, then count me in."

"Thanks Swift, for your confidence in me," Cara replied.

"Now, this lounge thing does sound good, what you think about it, Cara?"

Stephanie chimed in, "Well there's one in Buckhead that's nice. Me and my friends frequent it a lot. Every Tuesday and Thursday to be honest.

Erica responded to Stephanie, "You talkin' about 'Blues'? It's nice, but uptight. I was thinking about that when I went looking. I found the old skating ring off of Jimmy Carter Blvd better......way better."

"Blues is still okay. It's a lovely choice," Stephanie spoke up. "It just needs better lighting and a makeover," she mumbled.

Swift spoke up, seeing that Stephanie felt intimidated. "If it's a group of women like you there, I will be in the place every night."

"Thanks Swift," Stephanie blushed.

"No problem."

"You see what I'm saying?" responded Erica.

"Come here Stephanie," Kedar demanded. Stephanie looked around as if it wasn't her name, that K had just called out. "Yeah you, come here," Kedar called her again. She placed the tablet down, and clutched her phone tight, as she walked up to him with her head down. When she got close, she couldn't help but breathe in the masculine scent of his Tom Ford cologne. She hadn't been this close up on a man in years. "Relax," he told her as he eased her hands down, and placed her phone on Cara's desk. He slowly slid her glasses off then tilted her face up to his. Stephanie looked Kedar eye-to-eye, and began to blush. She couldn't help but think of how gorgeous this chocolate man was.

Kedar straightened her hair out of her face, then he placed her in front of him. "What do you see?" he asked no one in particular. "Let me tell you then. One ....she is a beautiful petite woman. Two ....she is a beautiful working woman. Three ....she is a beautiful woman with a lot of class and poise about herself. Now she and her friends, whom, I would guess, all work too?"

"Yes, we all went to college together."

"Okay how many other groups like y'all are in there?"

"A Bunch from what I see, but then again, I only try to make it twice a week."

"Even though you work for me, I don't know your salary. Hell, I don't even know what Cara gets paid," he joked. "I just know we are never behind and the bills are always paid, so I'm guessing you're making about mid-to-high 5 figures with your degree."

Stephanie responded, "Well I make about 45K a year."

"Granted you are a working individual and your friends are too." Kedar leaned in and whispered in Stephanie's ear, "We going to see about getting you a raise. Now Swift, you said you'd be there every night, if women like this were there, right?"

"Right," he said as he rubbed his hands together.

"Stephanie, get me Blues, and Erica we partner into it, but you will be working with my man Swift."

"Huh?" responded Swift.

"Thanks, Kedar, but I was thinking more along the line of coming from the ground up, ya know, with something fresh and new," Erica said.

"Plus, K. Man, I don't know nothing 'bout no club. Hell, I barely even go out to clubs."

"Ok, bet. This is how we're going to solve this. Stephanie, get me Blues. I want you to help Swift run it. Erica, you can be the social life for me there, and I'll pay you for it. The minute we get that thing on the map, then we get right on the old skating rink. Now, your club will depend on your work to help with mine. One hand washes the other, but both hands wash the face. So, what's it gonna be Erica?"

"70/30, my way?" she questioned.

"Naw your leg work, and you put up half the money, then I would consider 60/40, your way," K responded.

"That'll work for me," Erica stated. Right then, Erica jumped onto Kedar for a hug. Her eyes grew big immediately, when she felt his girth through the slacks he had on. "Oh my God," she thought to herself.

"But K, what about my job here?" Swift asked.

"Swift, my boy, you can be responsible for training your replacement because you have just been promoted in a major way. I got faith in you."

Everybody was happy in this moment. Stephanie walked over to Swift, to thank him for having her back.

"Did you mean what you said?" she asked him.

Swift looked the pretty petite woman from head to toe. "Yea, I did. Listen, do you want to grab a bite to eat?"

"Sure! I would love that!"

"Well, let me clock out right quick. After that, then we can head out." Swift skipped out of the office like a kid who had just won a prize.

"Yo," Kedar called out to him. Swift stopped just short of the door. "Here," Kedar said, as he tossed Swift the Keys to his truck. "Make sure you drop my truck off at your house, I'm gonna ride with Cara."

Swift walked up on Stephanie, "Can you drive?"

"Yes."

"Well look, take my car and follow me to my apartment to drop off Kedar's truck there."

"You mean follow you to your place?" she asked shyly.

"I'm not saying you have to come in but you can if you like," Swift was fumbling over his words.

"Ok, I'll follow you," Stephanie responded. Swift then grabbed her laptop and her bags and carried them out with him.

"Girl, Ima get up with you. I got some moves to make, biiiitch I'm bout to get my own shit," Erica said smiling at Cara.

"What about lunch?" Cara asked.

"Bitch, you better eat a hot pocket or something. I gots to go," Erica said laughing.

Kedar waved bye to them all, then turned to face Cara, while pouring himself another drink. Erica was waving at Cara from behind Kedar's back and signaling with her mouth 'girl that thang ain't small.' Cara couldn't help but giggle.

"What?" Kedar asked.

"Oh nothing. You are really one for the people," she responded.

"Girl, stop! You the one for the people. You really should run for mayor or governor."

"Don't gas me now 'cause you know I don't mind trying a stunt," she replied.

"Governor Cara." They both tapped their glasses together, then burst into laughter.

CHAPTER 18

Kedar was sitting at his desk, signing some paperwork. He was half-way expecting a call from Big Joey with the beginning of that upgrade money. His phone began to vibrate on the desk. He had to shuffle some papers around to find it. When he grabbed the phone, the screen lit up. It was a number that was not saved in his contacts. Kedar paused before answering the call, then he swiped the phone button. "Hello?" he spoke into the receiver.

"What up, Black," the caller blurted out.

"Who dis?" K answered.

"So, you don' forgot bout a nigga now?"

"Mannnn....What up Rolax," Kedar said excitedly.

"Shiiiiit you, my nigga!"

Rolax and Kedar were running buddies when Kedar went to prison. Rolax had shown him the do's and don't's but he had already known that Kedar could hold his own. Rolax had given him the game anyway. Kedar paid back the appreciation once he got his first mule. He had put Rolax all the way on. Kedar stayed up for the most part and he felt that Rolax would be there to pick him up, if he ever fell. There was a mutual understanding between the two men. They had each other's backs. They respected that aspect of one another. Even in an environment full of robbers, killers, and thieves, there were still some real ones with morals, principles, and values. Truth be told, most of the men incarcerated were truly cut throat to the bone. They believed not in the double cross, but the triple cross, which meant that he would cross you first, so that he wouldn't have to worry about you later. That is a hell of a way to think.......that everybody is out to get you.

"What up my nigga, dis yo number?" Kedar asked Rolax.

"Naw bruh but......."

Kedar cut him off, "Well ask the nigga that owns this phone, what he want for it, because the bitch just been bought. He can't have this one back, sorry!"

Rolax laughed, "Bruh chill. They 'bout to have some in a day or two, I'll get one then."

"Aight, cool. Just hit me with the ticket and it's done. Do you need some Greendots? Damn, nevermind, that was a dumb ass question."

Both men burst into laughter because they both knew that a nigga was always in need when in prison.

"Well look, I'm grabbing my keys now. Can you stay on while I grab you three $500 dots, right quick? Tell buddy I'll get him a $25 card, just to let you grab this money. Aye bruh, that weed smoking?" Kedar said.

"Hell yea, he gon' get him a sack with that."

"Aight, bet. I'ma set up the account today. Text me your GDC# now. I'll go ahead and drop 500 on your books. You got any debts that need to be paid?"

"Naw bruh, I'm good. I just owe Rick a 50 spot."

"Say less. I'm gonna get a card for that, too. I can cashapp too if you prefer that, bruh."

"Boyyyy, you a life saver," responded Rolax.

"Man look Rolax, bruh, when you text me your GDC#, just go ahead and text me all the cashapps too. It doesn't matter the amount. You just call before you send the info and it's done."

Rolax looked at the phone that he had up to his ear. "Damn, my nigga! You really doing it like that? Shiiiit, then send a nigga a pack or something," he said.

"Aight, just tell me how much, when, where, then it's done. I got a couple bags of that Gushers left, but I can grab some more pressure, right quick," Kedar spat out. 'Oh shit,' he thought to himself, "I got some Iggy too, bruh."

"Nigga stop bullshitting," Rolax screamed.

"Hell yea, and it's this new shit. It's supposed to be three times stronger than regulation, too."

"Shit, put it together and it's done. You remember the old way you used to get it?" Rolax questioned.

"Which way, the lunchable or the can?" Kedar asked.

"Nigga both! And the ramen good this way."

Kedar thought quickly about where he could acquire everything. "Done. I can put that together as soon as you need it."

"Say bruh, I don't mean to put you under the gun, but do you think you could put it together for tomorrow?"

The line was silent for a moment. "Anything else?" questioned Kedar.

"Wowwww, my nigga," Rolax screamed.

Kedar laughed. "You stupid! Nigga, you know I got you."

"You really about to do what he asks?" A woman's voice said into the phone.

"Who that, bruh?" questioned Kedar

"That's Ms. James," Rolax responded.

"Oh, what up lil one?"

"I told you girl, that's my nigga," said Rolax.

"Shut up! So, Kedar you telling me, that you're gonna put this stuff together and have it ready by tomorrow?"

"Yes Tam-a-ra," responded Kedar, emphasizing Tamara James' first name.

"So, you're going to reimburse me for my gas and everything, for having to come up here?"

"You in Atlanta?"

"Yes."

"Then sweet, I'm going to come pick you up and take you to the restaurant. Where are you staying?"

"We 'bout 40 minutes out, me and my homegirl."

"No problem, I'll get you a room, and set a couple things up. That way, y'all can have a good time. It will all be on me. You in your car?"

"Naw, we in a black Dodge rental."

"Okay, look. Type 1438 Buford Hwy into your GPS. That's the address to the restaurant. I'm about to call them and make y'all a reservation. Once you make it there, call me so that I can pull up. But go ahead and order y'all food, they already know what I like. I'll see y'all then."

"Thanks, K," she responded.

"And bruh still text me your GDC, so I can put the money on there now, and what all did you want?"

"I need that Sour Diesel, and some of that White Widow. If you could get a hold of some of that G-13 or Strawberry Kush, some gas, gas.....boyyyy I needs that," laughed Rolax.

"Done, I got you, my dude. But do know that, I got to get this from my lil mans, so it's going on consignment."

"Sayless."

"Aight, my nigga keep your head up."

"Aight bruh, you do the same out there."

Kedar hung up to dial Swift's number.

"Hello?" answered Swift.

"Aye, you left home yet?"

"We backing out now, what's good?"

"You got a compressor?"

"Say nomore, I'll bring it back with me."

"'Preciate it." Kedar hung up the phone. He signed a couple more papers. Once he was done and had collected them all together, he took them over to Cara. She was attentively at work. In fact, he rarely ever saw Cara NOT working. He walked in and placed the papers on the corner of her desk. He waited until she ended her phone call. "Here you go. I looked over them, made a few adjustments, and signed them," he said.

Kedar's phone began to vibrate. He quickly checked his text; it was Rolax's info. "Oh yea....," he said as he passed Cara his phone. "Can you see to it that you set up a Jpay for me, so that I can send my partna some money?"

Cara took the phone, looked at the info, then placed his phone on the desk. "I'ma do it, but K, you can't be taking my assistant and leaving me to fend for myself. Because for things of this matter, they could tend to this, other than me cutting a conference call short, just to see what Your Royal Highness wanted."

"Humor me this shit, how is it that MY secretary has an assistant and I don't?"

"Uhhhh, because you don't do enough work to have an assistant. But..... that's a great point. I'm going to hire you a new secretary that will sit in her little cubicle, right outside of your office. So, all of these small tasks, she can tend to them."

"Why she got to have a small cubicle, what's wrong with this?" Kedar stood with his arms out.

"I have no problem with that, but if she wants to have this office here, this right HERE.....she gots to go through me. And I PROMISE you, Ima spank that ass....and WE, yes, WE....," she signaled back and forth between the two of them. "Gon have to find a new secretary."

"Why black people so violent?"

"Boy get yo' ass out of my office and let me work to pay these bills!"

"Good point," he laughed. "Just make sure that she works and looks like you."

"Oh, she gonna work, but look like me..... that's not going to happen! God outdid himself when he made me! Now, give me them damn papers, and carry your ass out to make a round or something."

"Well damn, who's the boss?" Kedar asked.

"Me! Now bye......and go make them rounds!"

"Yes ma'am!" Kedar stood to salute Cara. She burst out laughing, the two of them were extra silly at work. "Oh, where is the briefcase I had got from E?"

"It's in the corner of my closet," Cara responded.

"Thanks a lot, Cara," Kedar made his way to the closet to retrieve the case. Before doing so he walked around checking in on the employees. Swift and Stephanie were pulling up around back. He cut through the dryers to meet them. Swift was just turning off the car as Kedar walked up. Stephanie's cheeks were rosy as she got out. Kedar informed her that Cara had a job for her, finding him a secretary, as well as her own replacement.

"I'm going to need you on the lounge as soon as possible."

"Yes, sir," was her response. Stephanie took a couple of steps before she looked back and told Swift that she would talk to him later. Swift stood there blushing. He looked like a schoolboy on his first crush.

"Yo, you alright?" Kedar asked him.

"Yeah, why?"

Kedar looked at Step, then at Swift. "That's why!" He laughed.

"Nawww man, she cool peoples."

"Mmm hmm," responded Kedar.

"I'm serious. She ain't like these other chicks. You were making some good points in the office. I saw all of that and more in her."

Kedar placed his hand on Swift's shoulder. "Good choice," he stated genuinely.

"Man, bro, the thing in the trunk," Swift said, as he handed Kedar his keys. "I'm about to go check on Sam and Josh. One of them will more than likely be my replacement, but I'll get both of them up to par, so that you can decide which one you like, or neither one of them if you don't like 'em."

"I trust your process. Go ahead and get to it." Kedar gave Swift some dap. He grabbed the compressor out of the trunk and placed it in his back room along with the briefcase. As he locked the back room up, his phone began to ring. "Yeah?" he answered.

"Hey, I'm sorry we're here kind of early. I truly didn't know how far out we were, but we are in the parking lot of the restaurant."

Kedar made his way to the side. "Oh, I see you. Go ahead and get out, I'm walking towards you now." He hung up.

Kedar informed Swift that he was going on break and for him to watch over everything. He told him that if he needed anything, Cara was in her office. "I'll be back in about an hour," he said to Swift.

He caught up with the two women at the restaurant. They both looked as if they were out of place. They seemed to have dressed up just to come to Atlanta.

"What's up, K?" spoke Ms. James. "This is my friend, Dominica."

"Pleased to meet you," Dominica said.

Kedar leaned in and gave the young lady a hug. "Nice to meet you, Dominica."

"Well damn," spoke up, Ms. James. "A bitch need some love too!"

Kedar smiled, as he grabbed and embraced Ms. James, pulling her into a tight friendly hug. He lifted her from the ground.

"Boy, put me down," she joked. "You are going to mess up your suit." Kedar placed her back on the ground and she began brushing off his shirt. "See look, you got my make up all over your shirt and shit."

Kedar glanced down at his shirt. "Ain't no problem. Y'all hungry?"

"Hell yeah! A bitch is starving! On another note, I still can't believe you really going to do what he asked. I'm saying, it took him damn near two weeks to convince me to come up here, then he spoke to you, and in minutes you like okay," she said.

"That's my partna," K replied.

"I had to wait until I got paid to get the car, and let my cousin come with me."

"First she your friend. Now y'all related," Kedar stated, as he laughed and shook his head.

"Well, you know how we do, bitch give out info only on a need-to-know basis." They all laughed.

The trio walked into the restaurant. The young waitress spotted Kedar, and met him at the door.

"Would you like to dine inside, or out?"

"Inside will be just fine."

"Okay, this way to your regular table."

The women took their seats, and the young waitress handed them the menus. "Would you like your regular?" she asked Kedar.

"That would be fine," he responded.

"And would you ladies like something to drink, while you take your time to look over the menu?"

"Can I have a Grey Goose and Sprite?" Ms. James said.

"May I have a bottle of water?" stated Dominica.

"And just bring me Hennessy and coke," Kedar said.

"Will do, sir. The drinks will be here shortly."

Kedar jumped right into asking how the walk through at the prison was. Ms. James informed him that it was the same as before. "The body scanner and the x-ray machine. But they are doing it random now, for the body scanner......so they say."

"Who's at the scanner?"

"Sergeant Smith," Ms. James responded. "And she act like a real bitch too."

"Sergeant Smith......Sergeant Smith," Kedar pondered his memory. "I can't recall a Sergeant Smith."

"She was like a CO2, when you were there. She worked G Building, all the time, had the little dreads in her head. Them bitches long as hell now, though."

"Wait, who? 2 Chains?" Kedar asked.

"Yeah, her."

"Sweet! Chains made Sgt?"

"The bitch act like she want to make Warden, all the telling she doing."

"Nooo, not Chains."

"Yeah! Yesssss Chains! Can you believe that bullshit?" asked Ms. James.

"And, she detailed on your bags," Dominica added.

"You work there too?" Kedar asked.

"Well, I just got my uniform. I'm just trying to get me a couple of dollars, so I can finish paying for school. I'm trying to get into the counseling department, so I can become a P.O."

"I feel you on that," Kedar said to her. "Well how much y'all tryna get paid on these trips?"

The two women looked at each other. "Well Rolax said he was going to fuck with us, but it depends on what you give him." Kedar leaned back in his chair, listening attentively. "But we wanted $1,000 to do it," blurted out James. "We know y'all be making a killing in prison, so a band shouldn't be too much to ask for."

Kedar looked both women over. "I want y'all to understand something," he began to speak. The two women perked up in their seats. "Y'all came to me, I didn't come to y'all with this. So, with that being said, you will get your money, and I'll even put some more with it. But if you get caught, and trust, I'm going to put 110% into this so that you don't.......but if you do, you don't tell on me, and you don't tell on my partna. The money you about to receive, isn't truly for doing the job, it's really for you to keep your mouth shut. And take your hit, if you got to, because I'm gonna let you know now, I don't know nothing about no murder."

"I was way in California," Ms. James finished the statement.

"I see my nigga taught you a lot," Kedar laughed.

"Kedar, I know my business," she stated.

"Now Dominica, do you understand is the question?" he asked.

"Understand what? I don't know nothing about no damn murder."

They all laughed. "Alright then, now we in business. How does this sound? Seeing that y'all with the move, I'm going to give you both five bands a piece. Half now and the other half at the end of the month. Y'all will both drop my mans a package once a week, so that's four packs a piece for five grand. Plus, whatever money he was going to give you."

"You playing, right?" joked Dominica. She noticed he didn't smile. "Let me get this straight, you going to give me five g's to drop once a week for a month. Plus, whatever Rolax was gonna give me, is all mine? And I owe neither one of y'all nothing?"

"That's right," Kedar responded.

"So, you don't want my driver license or nothing. Nobody will be following us around?"

"If we had to go through all that, my partner wouldn't have sent you. But, to answer your question," he reached into his pocket and started peeling off green backs. "$2,500 for you and $2,500 for you." He then pulled out his phone to call Cara. She answered on the first ring.

"How can I help you, sir?"

"Look, I got some friends here from out of town. I need you to schedule two appointments at the nail and hair spot you go to. Plus, check with your folks at Lenox Mall and see if they can get my folks two or three 'fits with some new shoes. Put it on the business account, for a meeting."

"Will do, sir. I will put the reservations under your name. When is this anyway?"

"Can you get them in within the next 2 hours?"

"Anything else, sir?"

"Yes, could you please order yourself some roses, and candy? Make it from me, for being a dedicated worker."

"Roses and candy!? I'm more of a diamond tennis bracelet and earrings, kind of worker."

"Girl, get off my line."

"I will but, I'm definitely going to compliment my hard work efforts. Oh, so that you know, your new secretary will be here tomorrow. She may be a candy and flowers type, but me, I'm getting my pension, bye bye."

Kedar wrote down the address to the nail and hair spot on a napkin. "Okay, once y'all leave there, your room will be ready. Then you can hit Lenox Mall. As a matter of fact, I got some tickets to see the new Queens of Comedy. Y'all can go check it out. I'm going to be too busy handling this business." The women were speechless.

The waitress came back with his food and their drinks. "Can you be a sweetheart, and have the cook put my food in a container to go? And look, place their bill on my tab." He reached into his pocket and came back out with a 50-dollar bill. "Have my plate delivered over to the shop." The young lady took the tip and thanked him before taking the orders of the two women.

Kedar had work to do. He took a trip to Starship to see what he could use. He spotted the 2-liter dummy safe bottles. On sight and on feel it looked exactly like a two-liter drink, but the top portion comes off, leaving the entire middle of the bottle. So, he grabbed eight of them. Four Dr Peppers and four Mountain Dews. Then he set his eyes on the lunchables. They had a hidden tab that you lift up. It kept the top part of the Lunchable intact (crackers cheese, candy bar), but underneath it was hollow. The container looked like a miniature bowl, once the top was removed, and just as easy as you take it off, you could put it back on. Kedar knew for sure, that this would work so he grabbed about ten of them. He noticed a 20-ounce stainless steel coffee cup. He grabbed it and looked it over. This one was new to him. He began to look for the opening and couldn't find one. Then the young man that worked there, walked over.

"Let me help you with that."

"How does it work?" Kedar asked.

The young man signaled for him to follow. "Look, I don't suppose to show this to customers." He reached behind the counter and poured coffee into the cup. He twisted the lid on, and took a sip.

"Oh, you got jokes?" laughed Kedar

"Hey man, whatever to help my day go by."

Then it hit K, "How much for the cup?"

"Huh? They sell them at Walmart, for like five bucks."

"Well look, I'll give you 20 for that one, and ring up this stuff for me too."

"Hell, do you want some sugar and creamer too?" The cashier blurted out as he started to scan items.

"Naww the cup will be just fine." Kedar figured he could reshape the cup that sat in the stainless steel, so that the cup would be at least 2 inches deep, then that would make for the remainder of the cup to be hollowed out. A person could even walk around sipping on the little 2 inches of coffee. In fact, the steam would definitely rise. And besides, who places their coffee cup on an x-ray machine? Plus, it's stainless steel, you won't be able to see through it.

There were a million thoughts running through Kedar's head. He shot over to Walmart and grabbed a whole set of the mugs, some crazy glue, and a case of chicken ramen noodles. He made one last stop at a smoke shop. He grabbed five pounds of Bugler, some cigarillos, and a case of rolling papers. He now had everything he needed to make this move happen. He placed everything in the back room, and was waiting for business to close, so that he could hit the lab. He took his time packaging the product. He double vacuum sealed all of the bags. Kedar made sure to always switch gloves in the process so he wouldn't get any residue on the outside of the containers. It was well into 2 a.m. by the time he finished up. He went back in the office to tighten up some paperwork.

When Kedar made it home, it was about 4 a.m. He was tired as hell. He made a mental note to cuss Rolax out about this last-minute shit. Kedar fumbled with his keys before entering his home. As the door swung open, he heard a loud bark.

"Ruff!" Kedar damn near jumped out of his skin. "What the fuck?!"

he yelled.

At that moment, the lights came on.

"Ginger, what you barking at now?" A sleepy-eyed Angel came out of the back. "Oooouuuuu, you in trouble," she said.

"Huh? For what?" Kedar asked.

"Boy, you better look at the clock or one of them expensive ass watches you be wearing."

"Girl, please. Where J at?"

"In the room. You want me to get you a blanket for you and Ginger, on the couch?"

Kedar looked at Angel and rolled his eyes upwards as he walked in the room. "Whatever," he said.

As he entered the room, J was laying with her back to the door, curled up. Kedar quietly stepped out of his shoes and then his clothes. He eased the cover back. He was trying hard not to wake Jay up. All of a sudden, she turned over and sat up with a look of rage covering her face.

"Where the fuck you been, K?" was all she asked, as she crossed her arms angrily.

"For real J? Baby, I'm tired."

"Oh yeah? Your ass definitely tired, now walk your tired ass on the other side of the bed!"

Kedar got out of the bed and walked around to the other side. "Yes love? I'm here."

"Drop them drawers," J spat.

"Excuse Me?"

"Nigga you heard me. Drop 'em so I can smell yo dick! Or do you want to leave me to draw my own assumptions?"

Kedar began to smile, but he knew that J was serious. So, he pulled his briefs off and stepped out of them. He got closer to her, then dropped his penis into her waiting hand. J grabbed a hold of his penis and examined it. She lifted up his balls and all, then took a long smell of his penis. She dropped it out of her hand. "Where the fuck you been, K?" she screamed as she rolled over.

"Honestly, I've been at the shop putting something together, and before you get your panties in a bunch, here is my phone. You can go into it, and check the surveillance for today or tonight. By the way, the access code is your name and birthday. J turned back over and held her hand out.

"Come on with it," she said.

Kedar walked back around the bed to retrieve his phone. He went to the cameras and showed J how to fast forward, and rewind. "The cameras got a 72-hour lapse before they get stored into the cloud. So, you can go to any day and see it."

As J watched the cameras on the phone, Kedar asked, "Where have you been? Popping up, and showing up unannounced all over the place, I'm guessing."

"Well hell, I didn't think that I had to announce myself to come home," J responded without taking her eyes from the phone's screen. She watches the screen closely, as he entered the back room. After fast forwarding two hours, he was still in there, alone. Kedar planted two kisses on her stomach.

"You find what you was looking for yet? Now, how I see it, you need to drop your drawers and let me check where you been," he stated. J dropped the phone on her chest.

"I don't even have any on," she said as she licked her lips and spread her legs. Kedar instantly climbed in between them, and parted her lips, exposing her already swollen clitoris. He kissed her gently.

"You been wanting me?" he whispered as he placed another kiss on her.

"Yessss," J moaned.

K slipped a finger into her. It was extra tight but super wet....... wetter than normal. He placed kisses on her clit repeatedly, as he guided his index finger in and out of her. He began to suck on her clitoris furiously.

"Yes," she moaned, and arched her back upwards. "Right there, Bae." She held his head in place, rocking back and forth on his finger. She did not allow her stimulated clit to move away from his warm tongue. There was overdue and built-up tension inside of her. She screamed, as she came all over Kedar's face. J dropped her hands down and gripped the sheets, as he continued to please her.

"I'm sorry baby," she whispered.

Kedar slid a second finger inside of her, and started to massage her clit with his thumb. "Right there, baby," J moaned. Kedar was rock hard, looking at the pleasure his woman was feeling. One of her breasts slipped out of the blue Teddy that she had on, exposing her pretty nipple. He quickly cuffed it, and began sucking. "Baby, you know that spot is sensitive," J moaned. He just looked into her eyes and nodded his head. She grabbed a hold of his wrist and began to show him the rhythm that she wanted. As soon as she removed her hand, she came again. Her body wouldn't stop shaking. "Baby I want some dick," she boldly stated.

On cue, Kedar stood up, and kissed her passionately, as she pushed her tongue in his mouth. He grabbed his shaft and began to rub the head of his hard penis on her swollen clitoris. J placed her finger inside of her warm opening. She pulled juices from herself and massaged them onto Kedar's penis. The bed was now soaked. "Get it from the back, Daddy," she whispered. Kedar placed a pillow underneath her. Her ass was even bigger than before. He guided his tongue right into her wetness. He curled his tongue around so that it flicked on her clit. "Ahhhhh.... yessss.... babyyyy," she screamed.

K stood behind her, he was very gentle as he eased the head in. He could feel her insides giving way to his width. Her muscles began to cling to him like a rubber glove. When he was half way in, he could feel her pulling him deeper. Kedar started to feel her muscles flexing and throbbing on the tip of his penis and he wasn't even moving. J looked back and bit her lips, "You like my new Kegel exercise?" Kedar smiled from ear-to-ear. It felt like a mouth was inside of her. He began to slowly stroke, as she began to moan.

After a few minutes, she was throwing it back. All you heard was the slapping of their skin, as her juices filled his midsection. He was literally balls deep in her. His nuts were popping her clit every time she went back. The feeling drove her insane. She began to go faster and faster. With K stroking, and the Kegel exercises, it felt like she had his dick in a headlock. Kedar wanted desperately to relieve himself. J looked back at him, and saw the pleasure in his face. "Wait baby, not yet," she purred. "Uhhhh....," she moaned, as she sped up.

K grabbed ahold of her small waist, and began pounding her hard and fast. "Right there, bae," she moaned loudly. J stretched out her arms, grabbing on the sheets. "Yes, yes, yes, fuck me, Daddy! Fuck me!" In one motion, she came hard. At that moment, her muscles released K from their grasp. He came instantly. They came together in a euphoric bliss.

"Ahhhhh....," was all that could escape Kedar's lips. He gripped her hips tightly, allowing all of him to fill her up, then he collapsed onto her back. J looked back, and kissed him.

"Damn, you trying to have twins," she joked.

"I love you, J."

"I love you more, baby."

CHAPTER 19

The morning swung around and Kedar could smell breakfast going. He still felt Jay curled up under him. He placed a kiss on her forehead before getting out of bed. He jumped into a pair of pajamas and left the room. Angel was in the kitchen, doing her thing, and singing along with a song that played on her phone. Kedar spoke before getting himself a glass of orange juice.

"Y'all sleep too late in here," she stated.

Kedar looked over at the clock. It was just about 11 o'clock. "What you cooking?" he asked, glancing around to look at the stove.

"Boy get your ass out the kitchen," Angel yelled.

Kedar looked around. "Last time I checked, this was my kitchen."

Angel put her hands on her hips. "And the last time I checked, your pots and pans had barely been used."

"You got me on that one." He walked out and grabbed the remote to flip on the news. He watched the weather report, while Ginger sat at his feet. A few minutes later, he heard the toilet flush. Jay came up behind him, and kissed his cheek.

"Good morning, Love."

"Good morning, Bae." She strolled into the dining room and had a seat. "Girl, what you in here putting together this morning?"

144

"Something quick and simple. I got some turkey bacon and turkey sausage, cheese, grits, and toast. It's some Blueberry muffins in the bowl. She quickly fixed J a plate and placed it in front of her. Angel then made Kedar a plate and finally one for herself. As they ate, Angel got up to give Kedar his phone off of the counter. Kedar had thought that it was her phone she was jamming to all along.

Angel said, "Your phone had been ringing all morning and since you didn't answer it, I brought it out so as to not to wake y'all."

Kedar's phone began to ring at that very moment. He slid his phone over to J. With food in his mouth, he said, "Bae get that for me."

J noticed that the number didn't have a name. "Hello?"

A female on the other end asked, "May I speak to Kedar?"

"Oh, yes you may," J responded then placed the phone on speaker. "Telephone, sir." Kedar wiped his mouth.

"Yo?"

"Hey Kedar, I'm still at the hotel. I'm about to check out."

J quickly threw one of the muffins at his head. Kedar dodged, barely missing it. Ginger didn't though, she caught it in midair.

"I hate you," J yelled out.

"Woman if you don't calm the fuck down!"

"Did I call at a bad time?" The woman on the phone questioned.

"Naww, you good. I was just eating breakfast," Kedar responded.

J sat across the table with her arms crossed waiting for this conversation to proceed. Angel had just dropped her fork.

"Well first off, thank you for the tickets. Me and my cousin had a ball, and whoever hooked us up with these clothes and shit, tell them I said, we appreciate it. Rolax has been calling all morning, wanting to know if you finished up last night."

"You are very welcome, Tamara James. But go ahead and hit bro on 3-way right quick."

"Alright, let me try to catch him before count." Ms. James clicked over to dial the number.

Angel picked her fork back up and began to eat. J looked over at Kedar. She felt horrible. Tamara's sister, Shanice, had been the one to stick by her side when she had first found out that she was pregnant. Shit, it was Shanice that had given her a pregnancy test from her purse. They had all come from the same hood. She knew she had to apologize to Kedar for her behavior. "I don't know if it's the baby, or what, but my mood swings have been fucked up."

"Umm hmm," responded K.

"I'm sorry baby," she said as she batted her eyes.

"Woman you crazy."

"Nigga, I'm pregnant! I got good sense, anyway I love you."

Kedar just shook his head. "I love you more baby."

"I love you too baby," called back Rolax over the phone.

"Nigga, shut the fuck up," Kedar joked. "What up nigga?"

"Shiiiit, not you coz your ass just getting up. What happened to, the early bird catches the worm?"

"The Bird been flying all night, handling that little nothin' on nothin' for you. By the way nigga, I got your little black ass the new iPhone 5G."

"Muhfucka, stop playing!"

"Yea nigga, you owe me."

"My brother from another mother, I knew you would come through."

"Naww seriously, you owe me. That fuckin' phone was like $1,200. I want that back," Kedar firmly stated.

"Don't get yo panties in a bunch, bruh. I got you. So, what's all on the menu?"

"I got the whole entree, with the drinks."

"Bullshit."

"Since when have you known me to play?" Kedar asked. "How long you got this phone?"

"Shit all day, now!"

"Cool, I'm going to text a picture to you, but look to keep everything clear, how much you giving these folks?"

"If you say it's the whole shebang then I'm going to bless them. She told me how you looked out for them. And let me guess, I got to pay you that back too?"

"It didn't cross my mind but since you implying...... yes, you do."

"You did say the whole shebang, right? I got 9 times too?"

"Yep," K responded.

"Then cool how many trips we got them?"

"A 30-day trip."

"Shiiiit...what you promised them? The world?" Rolax joked. "Fuck it, I'll match you, 'cause I know you looked out. She just ain't said shit, yet."

"Boy, how you figure that?" James questioned.

"That's my brother, I know him."

"Well since you want to know, he promised us five g's."

"That ain't bad."

"A piece," Tamara informed Rolax.

"A piece?! Fuck it, five a piece. Half now and half later."

"That's the same shit he said."

"I told you, I know my brother."

Kedar interrupted them, "Now that's out the way, let me finish my breakfast. James pull up on me at my shop and everything will be ready for you."

"Aight, I'll see you there, K," responded Ms. James.

"Love bro," Rolax said.

"Love!" Kedar hung up the phone.

"You know I'm going with you to the shop today?" said Jay, without lifting her head from her plate.

Angel cut her eyes towards Kedar, "Five grand? Wow," she motioned with her lips.

After breakfast, they got into Kedar's BMW to go over to the shop. J sat uncomfortably in her seat.

"What's wrong?" Kedar asked her.

"Your damn baby won't stop moving! That's the main reason I came with you, hoping our baby missed its father. If that's the case then this little person would calm down."

Kedar reached over to rub her belly. "Stop troubling mommy," he said to her swollen midsection. Almost instantly, the baby calmed down a notch. However, he could still see the baby moving around in J's stomach.

A little while later, they arrived at the shop. It was busy, as usual, music blaring through the air, and people everywhere. Everyone was getting ready because the Super Bowl was being hosted in Atlanta this year. People wanted to look their best, once they stepped out, and K's Detailing was the spot that made it happen. The baby jumped vigorously with the music as J strolled through the office.

"Good morning, sir," greeted a young woman, who came from behind the desk, right in front of Kedar's office. She arose quickly and closed the distance between them. "Good morning, ma'am," she directed towards J.

J just waved her hand, trying desperately to get inside of K's office, with Angel in tow. K looked at the familiar face, he snapped as he tried to bring the name off of the tip of his tongue. "Kayla," he said.

"So, you do remember?"

"I never forget a name or face. What you got for me?"

"Well," she began to walk behind him, as they all entered into his office. She scrolled through her iPad, "I've cleared and rescheduled all of your appointments to start next week. However, the important ones can be rescheduled for this week, if need be. All of your calls are now rerouted to my desk." Kayla tapped the earpiece in her ear.

"Brunch is now pre-order every day until you require a change. Uh-hhh, let's see, Swift's replacements are in training and will return before 2:30 today. I have several messages that I can transfer to you at will."

She handed him his own iPad. "You only have a couple from a fella by the name of Rolax, and the wine brewer people would like a video conference with you. But that is on standby, whenever you're ready, sir."

J took a seat onto the couch and kicked her shoes off. She stretched out, to get a little more comfortable.

"Would you like for me to call a foot massager for you ma'am?" Kayla asked.

"Please do. I like her already," stated J.

"Anything else sir?"

"No, that will be all for now," Kedar said.

Kayla tapped the button on her headset, to dial the number for J's massage. "Well, I'm right outside sir, just buzz when you need me. Good day ladies," she said to J and Angel, as she exited.

Cara came in before Kayla could close the door. "Hey J.....and company," she said with a wide smile. "So, K how do you like your new secretary?"

"She's on point and to the tee," Kedar stated, matter of factly.

"Well, I'm glad you approve." Cara looked over at J, "Ohhhh my goodness, girl, you, okay?" she asked J, as she noticed the look of discomfort on J's face.

"His damn baby is kicking my ass! It's been jumping around so much and I don't know what to do. I swear I wish that men could just experience this shit for at least one day..... one," J cried out.

Cara began to sing an old hymn, "His Eye Is On The Sparrow" as she slowly walked toward J. Cara's voice was like music for the soul, in that moment, everyone present, hung onto her words. Kedar was unaware that she even had a voice like that. It was a mixture of love, soul, and gospel. Cara continued to sing calmly as she approached J on the couch. The baby went from bouncing to calm, the closer Cara got. Cara sat next to J and kept singing as she rubbed J's belly in a slow, circular motion. Her words and voice spoke volumes to the unborn child, who had now calmed down completely. As she closed the song out, the baby seemed to be resting peacefully inside of its mother's womb. J looked at Cara, Angel, then at Kedar.

"I'm keeping her!" The three women burst into laughter. "How did you do that?" questioned J.

"It's an old hymn that my grandmother used to sing to me. What's your plan for today Ms Jayell?" Cara asked as she looked at J.

"Hell, I'm going wherever you go just to make sure this baby stays subdued," joked J.

"Well great! Kedar needs to finally do some work today," Cara said jokingly. "I have a plan. Let's go get mani's and pedi's. I, for one, am definitely in need of some pampering and I can guarantee that you ladies can relate."

"Yes," J and Angel said in unison.

"Do you know what you having yet, J?" Cara asked.

"No, not yet," J responded.

"Good! We can plan up a gender reveal party, while we're at it! You guys couldn't have come at a better time," Cara said, as she quickly helped J get her shoes back on. She threw deuces in the air, as she, J, and Angel walked out, to have a girl's day.

Kedar received a call from Ms. James, stating that she and Dominica were parked outside. He quickly grabbed the care package from his back room, placed the articles into a plastic bag, and headed out front to meet the women. Tamara, and Dominica sat in the car, looking at all of the men that surrounded the place. There were young and old men. Grown and sexy men. Plain men and men with extra swag. The women snickered with one another as they pointed back and forth at different men. A dark-skinned brother was walking by and spotted Ms. James' curly hair that hung to her shoulders. Her yellow skin radiated, as the sun danced off of it. He stepped up to her window.

"How you ladies doing?" he said, as he licked his big pink lips.

Tamara never dropped her eyes from the way his tongue rolled over his lips. "We doing fine," she managed to say.

"That, you are," he replied as he looked each woman over. He stuck his hand into the window, "I'm Smooth. Pleased to meet you."

"I'm Tamara and this is my cousin Dominica."

"Beautiful names for two beautiful women. Where y'all from?" he questioned.

"Here and there," replied Tamara.

"Well step out of the car so I can get a full look at you," he said with a twinkle in his dark brown eyes.

Tamara straightened up her skirt before stepping out. Dominica came around from the passenger side. The women were dolled up from head to toe. Tamara wore a skirt that hung mid-thigh, making her legs appear longer than her 5'6" frame. She had hips that looked as if they were made for hula hooping. Her shirt was short, exposing her flat stomach, but had her B-cups sitting up nicely. The vanilla scent that she wore was very tantalizing and she stood with the pose that would make the 'Next Top Model' fill with envy. Smooth started to rub his hands together, admiring the sight.

Dominica walked around the car, wearing a catsuit that cover all of her 5'2", 145-pound frame. She was built with curves in all the right places, the dark-skinned woman had ass, hips, tight, and titts. The suit was zipped up to her mid chest, giving off an abundance of cleavage. She wore a gold heart chain that sat perfectly in the middle of her big breasts. She smelled just like she looked, like chocolate.

Smooth signaled for his friends to come over and check out the eye candies. The guys piled up, surrounding the ladies. Dominica began to feel uncomfortable, a big fella eyed her up and down, as Smooth took the conversation back over. "Your accent gives y'all away. Where y'all from?" Smooth asked for the second time.

"Huh? What you talkin 'bout?" Tamara inquired.

The men begin to laugh. "You sound like you're from the country," Smooth stated. For some odd reason, if someone from the city felt that you were from a country area, they thought you to be slow as hell or something. What they failed to realize is, Atlanta is below the Mason-Dixon line, and that they were still in a Confederate State. They, themselves were country as hell. Two-thirds of Atlanta is populated with immigrants from somewhere else, anyway. Smooth grabbed Tamara by the arm so tight that she was forming a red spot on her skin. "Come on now, wit' yo' country ass. A nigga trying to show you what the city like."

Tamara tried to snatch away. "Let my arm go, muthafucka!"

The heavyset dude that stood close to Dominica began to grab on his crotch while eyeing over her frame. He got bold and reached out to grab her ass. He discovered that it was soft as hell. "You ain't going to be tough like your girl, are you?"

Dominica slapped the man's hand away. "Don't fuckin' touch me," she yelled.

"Feisty, I like!"

Kedar spotted the group that surrounded the women. Swift saw the look on his partna's face, which spelled trouble. He quickly made it to his side. Kedar handed him the bag, instructed him to stay put, and hold on to the bag. Swift signaled for a couple of the workers to come over along with a couple of his partners, who were at the shop getting their whips detailed. Meanwhile, Smooth released Tamara's arm.

"Come on baby, y'all can't show us some of that southern hospitality?"

Suddenly, a voice came from the back of the crowd. "I think the women want to be left alone!"

Smooth looked around the crowd and asked who had said it.

"I did!" The crowd began to open up and Kedar came through like Moses through the parted Red Sea.

Now Smooth was about three inches or so taller than K and he quickly sized him up. He felt like he could take him. "You might need to mind your own business partna," he shouted, as he quickly closed the space in between him and Kedar. The man had a nice frame, with tattoos going across his body. He let it show on that sunny day, in Georgia. He had on a pair of short khakis and a wife beater. He locked eyes and stood toe to toe with Kedar.

Kedar matched the raging fire in his eyes and warned Smooth, "You and your folks might want to go ahead and leave." Kedar spoke through clenched teeth. Smooth looked around at his crew, and began to laugh in Kedar's face. He then drew the 40-caliber pistol that he had on his waist and shoved the barrel into Kedar's chest. "If we don't leave, then what?!"

Time felt like it had frozen. Kedar's eyes never left Smooth's. It grew so silent, that you could hear a rat piss on cotton.

CLICK......... CLACK......

"Or you and all these bitch ass niggas won't make it to see the sun fall." Murda was standing with a Draco pressed firmly against Smooth's temple.

"Who the fuck......?!" spat Smooth, as he turned to face his assailant.

Murda now pressed the barrel in his eye. "Murda fucking 2 G's bitch! Pete Gang or don't bang! Whoop!"

Throughout the crowd, all you heard in unison was a response of 'Whoop.'

Click.....Click.....Click

Smooth looked around and noticed that he was standing in the middle of ant pile of Blood Gang members. He and his team were completely surrounded and outnumbered. Smooth slowly lowered the weapon, then secured it back on his waist.

"You good, K?"

"I'm good," Kedar responded, never letting his eyes leave Smooth's.

Smooth backed away and signaled to his crew. "Let's ride! I'll see you around Murda."

Murda smiled, "Trust me, you don't want to."

Smooth hopped into his SUV with a Jag following behind him, and exited from the parking lot. Murda lowered the weapon and introduced himself to Kedar. He explained to him that his 'Big Homie,' Rolax had told him to keep an eye, and a close watch on him.

"Hey, if you ever need us, we always close by."

Kedar gave the short man dap and appreciation.

Murda rounded up his crew. "Let Big Homie know that I got some BL for him, make sure he bust at me."

"Aight," Kedar replied. Indicating that he fully understood him. BL was the abbreviation for baby love, which meant money.

Kedar turned and faced Tamara and Dominica. "Y'all good?" he asked with sincerity on his face. The women were a little shaken up, realizing how things could go from 0 to 100 real quick.

Tamara spoke up with a concerned look on her face, "Was he talking about Rolax, Rolax?"

"Ummmm....yea," Kedar said, looking her directly in her eyes, while shaking his head. He then thought about prison and how half of them used to size inmates, thinking that they were soft. They did this, abusing their position or title at work. If they only knew. Then again you would think that it would be common sense. It was at that moment that K realized, common sense wasn't that common.

Swift stepped up to his side. He had a 9mm on his hip, as he passed Kedar the bag. Kedar looked at the pistol on Swift's waist, as he took the bag from Swift's hands. Swift saw it in his eyes and read Kedar's mind. He called for one of his friends to come over then he discreetly handed the gun back to him. The young man asked Swift if he was good, then with a single nod of his head, Swift's soldier dashed back into the crowd. Things went back to normal.

"Y'all good?" Swift asked the women. They responded that they were. Swift then patted K on the shoulder. "I'm about to get back to work."

Kedar walked the women back over to their car and handed them the bag. Dominica looked in the bag, "What is this, snacks for the road?"

Kedar laughed. "Nawww lil lady, everything is packaged up. But make sure you either order a pizza or subs when y'all taking in the sodas." The bag contained four sodas, four coffee cups, eight Lunchables, and one case of soups, holding 24 soups.

Tamara reached in and grabbed one of the stainless-steel coffee mugs. Kedar showed her how to pop the top and add coffee to the container. The women were amazed. He looked at them both, "I don't need to explain how vital this is, do I?"

The women quickly reflected back over the events that had just taken place. Tamara spoke up, "Man.....I don't know nothing about no murder."

Dominica finished her statement, "I was way in fuckin' California!" Everyone laughed and gave each other a hug.

"Before you go," called back K. "Do you still have that card?"

Tamara flipped open her wallet and saw the card. "Yeah, why?"

"Do 2 Chainz still have that Cherokee truck? The silver one?"

"Yes, she still got it."

"Well look, write on the back of that card, 'who got keys to the Jeep,' and then place it on her windshield before you go to work."

Tamara scribbled the quote on the card. "Will do, sir." With that, she started up her car.

A couple blocks away, Tamara decided to get some gas. Before hitting the interstate, she pulled into a Texaco. She looked over at Dominica, "Do you want something out of here?"

"Just grab me a apple juice and some gum," she replied.

Tamara opened her door and looked left. She spotted Smooth and his crew, in the parking lot of a barbershop, kicking it like nothing ever happened. Tamara's stomach began to turn. She disliked the man to her core.

Skkkrrrrt... skkkrrrrt...the sound of tires screeching filled the air. Three Caravans pulled up and shots started to ring out instantly. Dominica ducked down inside of the car as Tamara took cover on the other side of her car. The women watched in horror, as bullets flew from the three vans into Smooth and his crew. After the bullets stopped, Tamara saw a man hop out of one of the vans. He went and stood on top of Smooth's SUV, sending bullets through the windshield. Once he was satisfied with his work, he jumped down and walked over to where Smooth was laying. He fired off the remainder of his clip into the man's body. Smooth's body twisted and jerked as the bullets hit his lifeless body. Afterwards, the gunman casually placed the gun on top of his shoulder and strolled off. Tamara jumped into the car, and hit the gas, heading towards the highway.

The women drove silently along the interstate. When they had gotten a little way down the road, Tamara finally spoke. "That shit served his ass right!"

Dominica looked over at her, "Girl you do know who that was right?"

Tamara thought about the scene and even though she couldn't see the gunman, she remembered that Draco. She also remembered that strut. It had been the same walk that Murda had when he left the parking lot of K's shop. "Who was it!? Because I damn sho don't know nothing about no fuckin' murder!"

CHAPTER 20

The next day, Tamara placed the card on 2 Chainz's windshield, as Dominica was getting out of the car with her subs. Dominica's stomach was doing flips, as she moved to the trunk of the car. Tamara was heading back to her, when Tony called her name.

"Ms. James!" he yelled.

Tamara stopped in her tracks. "Wassup Lt.?" Today was Tamara's off day but Dominica was scheduled to work.

Tony ran and caught up to her, "I need you today."

"Huh?" Tamara asked with a look of confusion on her face.

"Good morning, Dominica," he called out as they approached Tamara's car together.

"Good morning, Lieutenant," Dominica replied.

Tony stopped at the back of the car with them. "Look," he said. "I know you need the extra time. They called me in to be the O.I.C. (Officer in Charge) today, and I'm short a body. I need you today. You know I wouldn't ask, if I didn't need you."

Tamara shook her head as she tried to come up with an excuse. I don't have no lunch. my mom........."

Tony cut her off, "Dominica got food right there." He reached to grab the bag. "Shiiiiit, sodas, Lunchables...... hell. And plus isn't that your uniform right there?"

Tamara could have kicked herself in the ass for having been in such a rush to leave, that she had changed in the car before going to Atlanta.

"Listen," he said. "Grab your uniform and let's go. I promise you I'll have your car up and running by next week."

The officers for the next shift had begun to line up outside the main door. Tony gazed at the line that was heading inside to clear security. "Don't worry about that. Come on. Let's go. I have to prep for briefing."

Tony walked swiftly around the line with Tamara and Dominica in tow. He walked them through the metal detector as it went off. He threw his hand up to stop Smith, who was heading over. He then waved Tamara and Dominica through. To their surprise, the detector didn't go off for either of them. They both let out a slow, quiet sigh of relief. Tony informed Smith that he was the O.I.C. for the day, and that he was running late. He allowed Tamara to go and change into her uniform, while he and Dominica headed into briefing.

45 minutes later, Tamara and Dominica were both headed to G building, to relieve the officers. The women entered the booth, and began to clean it down from top to bottom. They wiped everything down like they would normally do. After getting themselves comfortable, they began to chat. Beads of sweat were still forming around Dominica's brows. At work Dominica was normally quiet, always held her composure, and never spoke to anyone on the job except for Tamara. She picked up on the panic in her own voice, as she spoke to Tamara.

"Tamara, girl that's all the stuff for the month, brought in at once! What the fuck?!"

Tamara pulled her chair closer to Dominica. "Man, that is Rolax problem. We getting paid to bring it, and the way I see it is, since it's all here we can go ahead and get the remainder of our money."

Dominica looked up at her, "You think he's going to have it today?"

"I really don't know, but if we push the issue, I'm sure they'll get it to us. As long as I get it this week, I'm good," Tamara replied.

Dominica's nerves had gotten the best of her. She tapped a napkin on her eyebrow to remove some of the perspiration. "How the fuck are we going to get this big ass bag to him?"

"Now that part, I still haven't figured out yet."

BOOM BOOM BOOM

Both women jumped, when someone hit the window of the booth. It was Rolax, standing there with his rag, wiping his face. Someone had come in his cell, to tell him that they had some 'real police bitches working today.' The inmate had informed him that Ms. James and Ms. Thomas were working their building.

"Shit! I thought they don't work till tomorrow or something," Rolax said.

The man replied, "Yeah, but you know this training time for the cadets, and they understaffed."

"Man damn, why they always sticking us with some bullshit?"

The inmate looked at Rolax, "Them hoes cute and all, but they need some dick. I can tell because they always come to this bitch high strung and shit. Them hoes been cleaning the booth since they came in, like the officers from last night got a disease or something."

"All I know is, we gonna have a long ass day with them bitches working," Rolax stated.

From the outside, looking in, you would think that Ms. James was a real ass. She had chumped Rolax off plenty of times, and she had written him up more times than he could remember. What no one knew was that he had told her to. They did that, just to keep down the prying eyes, and listening ears.

Tamara and Dominica sat there, staring at Rolax. Neither of them seeming to know what to do. Immediately Tamara placed her hand on her chest, and started to laugh. She was hoping that Rolax would follow suit and laugh too. He did. She grabbed one of the Dr. Pepper cans, and began waving it at Rolax. "Jackson, you play too damn much," she shouted.

Only Rolax could hear her, because the booth held in all sounds, unless you were standing directly in front of it. Nevertheless, Tamara would rather be safe than sorry. "My bad, Ms. lady. We didn't get our callouts, and I was checking on them," Rolax stated matter of factly.

Tamara had moved them to the corner of the desk. She told Rolax that she was about to separate them, and to come back in about ten minutes, so that he could pass them out. He nodded his head, and walked away. Tamara handed the callouts to Dominica and instructed her to start separating them.

"Tamara, what the hell are you up to?" Dominica inquired.

"What else? I'm trying to get this shit from around me, and see if we can get our money sooner than later."

About ten minutes later, Rolax returned half prepared for inspection, which was coming up. Tamara slid the callouts into the drawer, and looked Rolax directly in his eyes. "I got all of them," she stated.

Rolax looked at her confused, "Ok?"

He reached for the callouts; Tamara pulled the drawer back.

"Damn lady! You almost cut my fuckin' finger off," he yelled.

Tamara once again looked at him with a stern and serious look. Through clenched teeth she repeated herself, "I got all of them."

Rolax stood there, still looking at his hand, finally looked up at Tamara. "Huh?" Suddenly, it hit him. He stared at her intensely, "Wait, you got all of them, all of them?"

"Yes," she nodded. It was hard for Rolax to contain the smile that he had on his face.

"So, are they passing out monthly call outs now?" he asked.

Tamara nodded, "But we need daily pay."

Rolax grabbed the callouts, and begins to go door-to-door passing them out. Tamara came across the intercom, "Standby for first block inspection."

Flame came from his cell, wiping his face, "Man fuck! How in the fuck we end up with these bomb hoes?"

Freaky D elbowed him in the side, "They look good as fuck!"

"Yeah, but don't let the smooth taste fool you. Them bitches will book your ass faster than a rabbit fucks."

Freaky D responded, "Fuck that. Them hoes gon' have to eat it up, or write it up today."

Flame walked back into his room. "Well see you, coz them hoes definitely gon' take your ass down through there."

Rolax turned around just as Freaky D was prepping to get in that deer stand on the women. He tapped Freaky D on the shoulder. "Not today homie," he said to him.

Freaky looked at Rolax wit' a crazed looked, "Nigga please!"

Rolax told him again, "Not today! Niggas got shit to lose, and you want to play with yo lil dick to get the folks down here. Thing about it is, you know them hoes will book something. Not to-fuckin'-day."

Freaky D took a step back, "Man this my dick, and I do what I want with it! Let me do my time and you do yours!"

Rolax looked at him, and simply nodded his head in agreeance. He could clearly see now, how niggas ended up fucked up, thinking with their dicks. Any other day, Rolax would have taken Freaky D to the closet and beat him half to death, but not today. "Alright Homie," Rolax said, then turned and walked away.

Freaky D had gotten all primed up and ready to do his thing. He had the door cracked and all. He had a perfect angle of the women. He thought to himself, "It's going down today."

TAP TAP

There was a knock at the door.

"Man.....what the fuck?!" he said. He knew that whoever it was, was sure to have saw the rag on the door, indicating that he was busy. He noticed that the women were now looking his way. "Fuck! A nigga always fucking up my groove! What?!" he yelled out. There was no response, only another tap at the door. Freaky D adjusted his clothes and walked to the door with an attitude. He swung his door open, with aggression. "What the fuck you want?!"

There were about ten Bloods standing at the door. Flame was leading the way. Freaky questioned Flame, "What the fuck is this Flame?" He saw that four of the men were clutching. Freaky D knew Flame from their hometown, Sandersville, Ga. At this current moment, Flame wasn't the person that he thought he had known. Flame looked around at his 'Blood Brothers,' "Y'all hold up."

The men all looked like some angry pit bulls, that were off the leash, and ready to attack. Flame knew that if Freaky D so much as breathed the wrong way, the men would instantly tear into him, with no remorse.

"Freaky D...... I don't know what you said to Rolax, but home team, you got to pack your shit! The only reason I'm here is to stop these niggas from killing you. Man, where was your head? You disrespected the biggest Blood on the compound," Flame informed Freaky D.

"Man, it was not like that. Where Rolax at, let me holla at him right quick," Freaky D responded.

"Nigga, talk to me, I'll speak for him," one of the feisty ones that was clutching spoke out.

Freaky was no fighter, but he would. However, he for damn sure was no fool. "Naw, you got it." he called back. "Flame, can I pack my own shit?"

"That's why I'm here. Nobody is going to fuck with you as long as you start putting it together."

Ten minutes later, while they were running block, the Cert team was there to take Freaky D to the hole for refusing housing. Flame carried his stuff for him. Tamara stood on the walk, signing the inmates out for session. The Lieutenant came down, and informed her that he appreciated the lookout. He also asked her to sign the DR for 'Refusal of Housing' that had been issued to Freaky D.

"They putting him on the door?" he asked.

"Naw, actually he volunteered to go. He said he didn't want to be in here," Tamara responded.

"But ain't that Flame 2G's carrying his stuff?" Lt asked.

"Yea, but I think they from the same spot, because we had to wait while he went back to get him food from his own cell."

"Aight," responded Lt. "Oh, Johnson called and said that he was running late, but he'll be here by 12, so what do you want to do?"

"I'm good. I'll stay," Tamara responded.

Tony put a smile on his face. "Thanks," he said then turned and walked away.

Tamara continued to sign people out. Rolax was the last one, so Tamara walked him all the way to the gate. She took this opportunity because she had to lock the gate once the last man went through.

"You got all that shit, for real?" he asked while walking in front of her.

"I got the whole month with me. When do we get our money?" Tamara didn't waste any time asking.

"Give me 48hrs and I got y'all in full. That's my word, on Blood."

"I believe you," she said. "But you can't open this shit up until tonight, not while we are on shift."

"All right, no problem," Rolax said.

Tamara was satisfied with his response, but then something crossed her mind. "But how you gonna get it from me?" she questioned.

Rolax thought for a minute, "Have you taken out the trash yet?"

"No," Tamara replied.

"Well, wait until I come back then call me to the booth for the trash. Go ahead and put it all in there."

"Won't that look suspicious?"

"The way you been working me this morning, they'll think I'm trying to work my way out of a DR. Oh, and you still gonna give me one for failure to follow, don't forget to write the wrong GDC number."

In Rolax's mind the plan worked to perfection. He emptied the trash and placed the bag into his net bag with his clothes. He had just gotten the bag of clothes from laundry. He casually strolled right back into the dorm. Several minutes later someone called out, "12 on the floor, shower side! Coming at 206!"

160

That indicated that there were officers coming, and they were headed for cell 206.

It wasn't ten minutes later, Rolax was on the floor raising all kinds of hell about the DR that Ms. Thomas had just served him. He went back into his room and told everyone to 'stay the fuck from around him,' just before he slammed his door. Rolax pulled everything out of the bag, and eyed the contents in awe. He opened the soda bottle first, and his eyes lit up seeing the exotic weed double bundled up. "Ohhh damn!" was all that he could say.

He knew from there, what was in the other bottles. He examined the coffee cups next. He flipped one marked 'Double R' over and over, trying to get inside of it. When he finally got it opened, a brand-new iPhone popped out. "Yes! My boy done put me in the game." At that moment, he quickly dialed K's number to let him know that he had received the goods.

"Hello," Kedar answered.

"What up my dude?" Rolax said smiling.

"Boy! What up?! How you get your phone early? I thought it wasn't due until tomorrow," Kedar questioned.

"Man look, bruh, I got the whole thing. Everything that you sent. I got it all today."

Kedar looked at his watch, "Boy it ain't even 10 o'clock yet?"

"I know right, but I'm going to put it up and hit you 'bout 8 tonight. They want the money in 48 hours."

Kedar laughed. "Well nigga, you need to get on yo' shit. You really got the whole month drop in a day?" he questioned to be sure.

"Hell yea and nigga I ain't seen this much shit even when you was here," Rolax joked. "Bad as I want to bust this gas open, I got to relax until they leave. It ain't been no gas, gas in a while."

Kedar leaned back in his seat, "Well look, handle your business. And I did think about yo' soft ass. It should be two soups in there marked 'Double R.' They contain 'per se' in them. So, you need to secure the rest of that shit before you open up the 'per se'. It has seven of gas, 1/2 can, a lighter, and five wraps in one of them bags."

Rolax dug through the bag. "My nigga," he smiled. "Got it. What you want me to do with these bottles and coffee cups? I can wag with the Lunchables tho."

Kedar thought for a minute. "Has the trash gone out, yet?" he asked.

"I just took it out," responded Rolax.

"Well before they call session, take that shit out, and put all the cups and bottles in the trash outside. Bro, make sure you put it on the trash cart so niggas don't stumble up on it."

"Already," responded Rolex. "How much I owe you bro?"

"We'll sort that out later. Handle yo' business."

Kedar was relieved that the situation worked out. It took balls of steel to walk that much shit through. Rolax was sitting on about four pounds of gas, two pounds of meth, and ten cans of Bugler. If that ain't Chain Gang rich I don't know what is, Kedar thought. Kedar remembered his conversation with Angel, so he dialed Divine's number. He knew that at the facility that Divine was in, they seldom, or if at all, put their phones up. Divine answered on the first ring.

"Peace God."

"Peace, peace," quoted Kedar. "I need your help."

"No pressure, I'm there for you."

"That nigga Rico still in your dorm?"

"Yep."

"Well look, do you feel like making sure he gets something? But you got to act like it came from you."

"Aight."

"You still got that cheap-ass flip?"

"My shit ain't cheap, but yea I got it."

"Aight look, when it comes to you, I'm going to give you a set price, but make sure you fuck with my partna Mustang, down in the K Building. Make sure that Rico gets half, tho'."

Divine heard someone calling his name, looking for a haircut. "Whatever you need, I'ma do it for you, my brother. I gotta go tho', they calling my name now."

"Thanks, my man."

"No problem."

About four months had gone by and everything was on the up-and-up. Rolax had added several more officers to his team, Lt. and Chain were now on board. Rolax was eating, hand-over-fist. He now had the entire compound on smash. The first 'Jump Off' made him blow up, overnight. His sister had been dropping off money weekly. Kedar had long ago stopped counting. The same was to be said about the other institution, as well. Divine ran a nice, quiet, tight shift. Angel had a glow of happiness on her. Apparently, Rico was breaking bread tremendously, although he still hadn't told her how he had come up. Kedar had introduced Divine to Cara, they hit it off instantly. She wrote him frequently, and they stayed on the phone. She didn't need or want anything from him, and he felt the same, but that didn't stop him from sending flowers to her from time to time.

All of Kedar's businesses had taken flight. Erica, Stephanie, and Swift had the lounge doing numbers. Plus, the alcohol vendor with Cara was finalized. Kedar began to distance himself from the illegal shit. He introduced Big Joey to Escobar but he made sure that he explained to Escobar the rates. Escobar, in return, made sure that Kedar got all of the overhead. Escobar started hitting Big Joey with more and more. All was good.

J was at her gender reveal party, hosted by Cara. Cara had to have spent an arm and a leg because she had a whole floor at the Belmont Hotel. She had done this, so that after the party, everyone had a spot to lay and chill. A couple of J's closest friends were there and some of Cara's friends were there as well.

Kedar was at his lounge kicking back. He sat with Swift, enjoying a bottle. They were celebrating a new accomplishment. They stood and shared drinks, as Swift asked, "Have y'all come up with any names yet?"

Kedar sipped the wine, "She came up with a few. I did too, but honestly my guy, all I really want is to have a healthy child, with ten fingers and ten toes."

"I heard that," said Swift, as they tipped glasses. Swift leaned in towards Kedar, "Let me tell you something."

"What up?" Kedar asked.

"Man, I appreciate you."

Kedar reached over to touch his forehead. "You alright?" Kedar questioned Swift.

"Bruh, stop playing!" Swift replied, as he moved his hand. "I'm serious man, I had one foot in the ground, before you showed me love. Now look at me." Swift opened his jacket, and did a full spin. "I couldn't have made it or done it without you man. I'm forever indebted."

Kedar gave off his signature Colgate smile, "You want to show me your appreciation? Then simply keep your head screwed on right and stand like a man." He leaned in and embraced his new business partner and new friend. "I see you and Stephanie hitting it off."

Swift couldn't help but smile, "Bro, she really makes my day, and night. Real shit! She easy to get along with. I recently found out that she don't have no problem with voicing how she feels. She really is the true definition of a real woman and she's so gentle." Swift began to smile.

"Looks like that ass in love to me," joked Kedar.

"What can I say?" Swift said matter of factly.

Blues was packed. You pretty much had to have a reservation now to get in. Erica did her best to promote this one and she was successful. Stephanie offered a discount to the ladies that she knew frequented the lounge, and she made sure that while they were there, they were good. All types of upscale men filled the lounge, looking to get even the simplest conversation from the caliber of women there. You would be surprised at how many men wanted a woman with brains backing him. Several of the women that Stephanie had gone to school with were now dating celebrities, or someone with power. It was all thanks to the lounge.

Smooth R&B played through the speakers, Kedar turned and saw a 'Welcome Home' banner hanging over in the VIP section.

"What's that?" he tilted his cup in the directions of the VIP section.

Swift looked over, "Ohhhh, some dude named......." the bartender cut in.

"Telephone sir, it's Miss Stephanie. She said that neither one of you two have been answering the phone."

The men looked at each other, as Swift took the call. Kedar told the bartender to send two bottles, compliment of the lounge, to the gentleman that came home. Swift placed one finger in his ear, "What?" he yelled, trying to hear what Stephanie was saying. "When.....Where?! Aight, we on the way right now!" He hung up the phone, and turned to Kedar, with a look of panic on his face.

"What's wrong?" Kedar asked.

"Man, J going into labor, they headed towards Grady now!"

"Oh shit!" Kedar started patting his pockets for his keys.

Swift pulled out his keys, "My car parked in front, by the door."

Kedar switched keys with him, "I'm going to go ahead and go, you stay and wrap everything up. Meet me at the hospital later."

Kedar bee-lined out of the club on his way to the aid of his woman and unborn child. Little did he know, in the corner of the club some eyes were locked in on him.

A young fella tapped his homeboy's shoulder, "Is that who I think it is?"

"Who?" His partna asked.

Just then the waitress strolled up with two bottles of Don P. The men looked at each other, then at the waitress. "Who paying for that?" one of the men asked.

The waitress smiled, "Compliments from the owner, sir. He said to tell you congratulations on coming home."

One man took a bottle from the bucket of ice. "Where is he? So, we can at least share a cup with him."

The young lady looked around and spotted Kedar heading out. "There's Mr. Kedar right there heading out of the door."

A look of vengeance spread across the man's face. Kedar had been in the presence of death, and he didn't even know it. Dre, whom he had stuck right before he left prison, was in the same room with him, sharing the same air.

Dre sent Mario after him. Mario cut through the crowd of people, but he was too slow. He saw Kedar as he sped off in a black Jag.

"Fuck!!!!!" he screamed.

Mario made it back to Dre and told him that the mission was a no go. Dre slapped Mario across the table then straightened himself out before speaking.

"I want that nigga dead!!!!" he barked.

Swift came into the VIP section with three large security guards, and asked the men if everything was ok.

Dre started to fix Mario's clothes, replied, "We good. My partna here missed the man that purchased these bottles, and I really wanted to show him my appreciation."

"Aight, cool," Swift responded. "Well, my mans had an emergency that he was obligated to tend to. If it weren't for that, I'm more than sure that he would've shared a drink with you fellas. So just enjoy the rest of your night and anything that you fellas want or need, is on the house tonight."

Dre stood facing Swift and shook his hand. "I'm Andre," he said.

"And I'm Swift, the manager." For some strange reason, the man's handshake wasn't matching his eyes. Swift wrote it off as paranoia, or even that the men had drank too much alcohol. "You fellas enjoy the rest of your night," he said before he walked away.

Kedar made it with time to spare. J was on the table, legs wide. He got down by her side and placed his forehead against hers. "I love you," he said.

J looked at him with sweat pouring off of her head, "I hate you," she screamed as another contraction hit her.

CHAPTER 21

Four hours later, a 4lbs 6oz bundle of joy was born. They named her Serenity. She was a preemie and could fit in the palm of Kedar's hand. She looked so fragile and right then, at that exact moment, his whole life changed as he looked at his daughter. She had her mother's eyes but all other features belonged to him. Serenity had to stay in the hospital for the next month. It stung Kedar to his heart to see his daughter with the tubes running into her nose and seeing her in an incubator. She looked so helpless. He made a promise to always protect her from this cruel world. Serenity had pretty much gotten her weight up and was feeding on her own. She had also been able to keep her body temperature normal outside of the incubator, within the first two weeks, but for precaution and observation, they kept her for two additional weeks. The day to take her home had finally arrived.

Swift had arrived to congratulate Kedar, as well as to see his new niece. He did the favor of pulling K's truck around to the entrance, so that Kedar could help J and the baby downstairs. He admires his niece and then tells J, "I'm glad that she took your looks and not her father's, wit' his ugly ass," he joked. Swift then informed them that he would trail them home. Kedar and Swift embraced before they started up the vehicles to leave the hospital.

J rode in the backseat with Serenity. Kedar frequently looked in his rearview mirror at the two women, who now had become his living existence. After Serenity had dozed off, J leaned up and kissed Kedar on the cheek.

Kedar smiled, "What was that for?" he asked.

J cut her eyes back at their daughter, "I love you."

"Hmmmp, now you love me? You told me you hated me in the hospital," he joked.

"Well at that moment, I did hate yo' ass but now I love you," J smiled and said as she placed more kisses on K's neck while he drove.

"All right now, that's how you got the first one."

J looked back at Serenity, "Babygirl, how you feel about a brother?" she whispered to her daughter.

Kedar smiled ear to ear, hearing J ask that question to their sleeping daughter. Moments later they were getting off of 85 North. They pulled into the gated community not long afterwards.

"We got to talk about our living arrangements, right?" J questioned from the back.

"Overstood." Kedar responded. K turned the corner and parked across the bottom of their stairs that led up to his apartment. He jetted upstairs to unlock the door while J brought Serenity up into the house. K went back outside to grab the remainder of J's bags. As he opened the passenger door, he saw some men in the reflection of the window. They hopped out of a Ram 1500. Kedar figured they had just moved in recently.

BOOM!!!!!!!

The first bullet barely missed Kedar's head and shattered his window.

BOOM BOOM Tat Tat Tat!!!!!!!!!!!!!

K quickly hit the ground as the bullets rattled off of his truck. The men were now walking down on K but Swift intervened. Swift had pulled his Jag between the men and Kedar. He hopped out and used his car for cover as he checked on K. "You hit?" he asked frantically.

"Naww," K responded as he patted himself, checking just to be sure. He could hear J crying at the door, screaming his name. "Get in the house," he yelled back. Bullets were flying in the direction of the stairs. Swift pulled out a .40 caliber from under his shirt. "Fuck this." He got close up on his car, and started sending bullets across its hood.

BOOM BOOM BOOM!!!!!!!!!!!!!!!

The bullets slowed down hitting the car and truck. That gave Swift time to peek over, and now take aim. A bullet skipped across his hood, and a fragment hit his right cheek. "Motherfucker!" he yelled.

BOOM BOOM BOOM!!!!!!!!!!!!!

Swift sent bullets flying towards his attacker, striking the intruder through a parked car's window. His friend let off some cover shots coming Swift's way. Swift quickly ducked but not before busting a couple more times. "Fuck!! I'm out," he said looking at Kedar.

A few seconds later, they heard a sound neither one of them had ever been happier hearing. Literally. For the first time in their lives, Kedar and Swift were glad to hear police sirens. An officer called over the intercom for the intruder to place his weapon down. They had not expected the response to the request be a series of bullets coming their way.

Kedar quickly dashed for the stairs to go and check on his girls. The firepower was too much for the officers, so the men got away. Gwinnett County had never been on the losing side. They didn't even care about all of the bullets that were in lodged into the vehicles. They took Swift downtown, but Kedar went and got him shortly after. It saved Swift in a way, that his gun was actually legal. Although, they did still charge him with destruction of private property. Kedar was boiling over. He could barely hold the steering wheel as he drove. Someone had committed the ultimate sin. They had crossed a line of no return. He pondered his mind as they rode, trying to figure out who and why. Kedar had J and the baby to go and stay at Cara's for a while. Cara lived in Buckhead. In her development you needed a code and a card to even enter the building. Security was all over the property and in the building on every level. Matter of fact, Cara's suite was actually on the same floor as one of the Senators.

Swift looked over at Kedar. He could see the fire in his eyes.

"Fuuuuck!!!!!" Kedar screamed, as he hit the steering wheel. A nigga gon' die bruh!"

Swift had gotten a look at one of the assailants. He was more than sure that he had seen the man before. Out of nowhere it hit him, like a blindsided tackle. Swift snapped his finger, "Bruh, do you know a nigga name Andre or Mario?"

Kedar checked his mental database, "I can't say I do." He was trying to place the names. "Why do you ask?"

"Remember when J was having Serenity, the cat name Mario was trying to catch up to you at the club, he missed you though. When he returned, the dude Andre slapped the fuck out of him."

"You talking about at Blues?"

"Yeah, bro. Remember the nigga you sent the bottle to? The welcome home party?"

Kedar damn near swerved, quickly reaching to grab his phone. He dialed Divine's number.

"Peace God," Divine answered.

"Yo D, did that nigga Dre jump?"

"Hold on, let me check right quick." A few moments later he returned to the phone, "Say God, big facts, he did, a little less than 45 days ago. Why, what's good bro?"

"That bitch ass nigga just shot at me and to top it off I was just coming home with Serenity and J!" Kedar bit down on his lip so hard, it began to bleed. "Get what info you can get on him, for me. I'm paying top dollar for any, and I do mean any, information on that bitch ass nigga!"

There was a pause on the phone. "God, your money is no good this way, but I'm going to get all of the information you need," Divine replied. He didn't want to lead on to the fact that he had just heard the same info about an hour ago. News spread quicker in prison than it does on the street. He hadn't wanted to entertain the ones that were talking, because he figured it was some bullshit. However, receiving this call, he knew Dre was going to wish he had died by the time this storm settled. About family, this was a category six hurricane coming straight at Dre, and whoever else was in the way.

Dre had done his homework on Kedar. He knew where he lived. He knew about the detail shop, the restaurant, and he even knew about the club. He made sure his crew posted up at every one of them. Dre was originally born and bred out of Atlanta. This was his playground and stomping ground. He was amazed though, by how many people knew K, but that didn't stop shit. The man tried to take his life. The whole time Dre sat in ICU, he was praying for God to spare his life. He died twice on that table. Just when all hope was gone, he prayed to the devil since God hadn't seemed to have heard him. "Satan spare my life so that I can do your will," he had stated out loud. After that, he awoke stable with a new and even darker side to himself fully present.

Dre had tortured at least ten people to extract all of the information he had on Kedar, that wasn't even including his secretary. During one of her lunch-breaks, he jumped out on the young lady. He had taken her to one of his duck offs on the westside. While there, he slapped Kayla around like a rag doll. She broke, and gave him all of the information he needed. Afterwards, he raped her. He figured, "Hell, ain't no sense in letting no good pussy go to waste."

When Dre was done having his way with the young woman, he had let his friends have what was left. Finally, after all of the sexual assault on the young woman was done, he had gone into the room and placed two bullets in her skull himself. Dre then threw the woman off in the alley like throwing away trash. So, he was overly anxious, when he had gotten the call that Mario had spotted him leaving Grady.

As he ducked off to watch all movement, he had spotted the C.O. that was working the day Kedar had stuck him. He gazed over all of her curves that came with the baby fat. Her ass had really spread. He couldn't help but think of how he was going to enjoy fuckin' Kedar's bitch in his face, right before he killed both of them. Dre would have just settled for killing Kedar, but now fucking J after all the times she had refused him, would serve as a two for one. Swift came in dumping shots like O-dog. Dre was coming around back, until goddamn Gwinnett's Finest came. At that point Dre had to let off the shots so that Mario and the crew could get away. Ever since then, this nigga been hard to find, like a rice grain in snow.

Dre sat in the spot, explaining to his crew that he would not tolerate another fuck up of that magnitude. He walked around the room, looking at the pack of wolves that he had recruited. Dre scowled at Mario, "That shot you took to the leg, served yo' ass right nigga! Matter of fact if you weren't my first cousin, I would have shot yo' ass first before I shot at the police.... just because you fucked up!"

"My bad cuz," whispered Mario.

"Fuck yo bad!" spat Dre.

"I told that nigga, Dre...." said Squirrel, a young shooter from Pittsburg.

Dre crossed the room and was on top of Squirrel like a lion on a gazelle. "And you still didn't stop him?!" he spat with rage in his eyes. Dre grabbed Squirrel's gun off of his waist and shoved it into his mouth, knocking out one of his teeth.

Dre growled through clinched teeth, "If you allow him to fuck up again, he won't be the only one dead!" Squirrel threw his hands up in surrender. Dre continued, "Now if any one of you niggas make the same mistake, it will be fatal!" He looked around into the eyes of all the wolves in the room. To drive his point home, he squeezed the trigger.

BOOM!!!!!!!!!

The shot pushed Squirrel's brains out through the back of his head, plastering fragments all over the wall.

Dre threw the bloody murder weapon over into Mario's lap. "Now clean up your fuck up," he said to Mario. "Next time, I will be sending flowers to my aunt for your fuckin' funeral. Now let's ride."

The men all got up. Dre had grown tired of looking for Kedar. It was time he made Kedar come to him. Dre and his crew pulled into Blues' parking lot. He had everyone spread out, cars covered every angle of the club. Dre rolled into the club with four of his guys and grabbed a VIP booth. The waitress came over to take their order of what they would be having for the night. Immediately, one of the men were rude and blew weed smoke into the young waitress's face, "We'll have a sip of you."

The group of men burst into laughter. Dre brought order back to the group, "Naw shawty, seriously, just bring us a bottle of Moe."

The woman grabbed the money and quickly sped off. She walked back to the bar and rang up the order. Stephanie was walking by. The waitress stopped her and pleaded to her, "Please don't fire me. If I take a drug test and it comes back positive, please, please don't fire me."

"Why not? You know we have a no drug policy here," Stephanie re-iterated.

The young waitress went on to explain how the guys in the VIP section constantly kept blowing smoke in her face. Stephanie looked over and saw how distraught all the men were acting. She decided to go over to the table. "How are you gentlemen doing tonight?" Stephanie asked.

Dre looked at the luscious, slim woman. He began to grab onto his crotch. "And who you might be, shawty?"

"I'm one of the managers here."

Dre looked over at the waitress by the bar. She looked worried. "Well, great," he replied. "I'm glad you're here. I have a complaint about our waitress."

Stephanie switched her stance then crossed her arms, "Is that right?"

"In fact, it is, see....my mans here was being a gentleman to the lil bitch and she copped an attitude," Dre retorted.

Stephanie's face screwed up because he referred to the waitress as a 'bitch'. Not only had this young lady been here since they opened Blues but she was considered one of, if not, their top waitress. Stephanie looked down at Dre, "Understood, but I'm going to need for you to put the marijuana out, while you're in here."

Dre eyed the woma' then took a long pull from the blunt, and put it out. "No problem, ma'am."

"Thank you," she replied. "And I'll be sure to change your waitress."

Dre reached up, and grabbed Stephanie by the wrist. "How about you be our waitress?"

Stephanie snatched away, "Don't touch me!"

Dre blew smoke into her face then popped her on the ass. "Go be a good hostess and fetch our drinks."

Stephanie stormed off in utter disgust of the disrespect that the men showed. She went straight to her office. Her hand was shaking as she dialed Swift's number.

Kedar got up out of bed. He looked over at J and Serenity, as they lay sleeping in Cara's master bedroom. He kissed his daughter and then kissed J on the forehead. He went out of the room in his pajamas, to the fully stocked bar that Cara had. K poured himself a glass then threw it back. Afterwards, he just took the whole bottle to the chair and began drinking from it. He placed the big 50 caliber handgun in his lap and continued to drink. His mind was going at a rate of a million thoughts per second, as he continued to drink, holding the bottle in his left, as he fingered the trigger of the gun with his right hand.

Cara got up and walked out of her guest room to get her a bottle of water. She was startled by Kedar, sitting in the dark. She almost choked on her water, "Fuck!!!!.....Kedar why in the fuck you sitting in the dark?" She made her way from the kitchen to over where K was sitting. He continued to drink without saying a word. Cara looked at him with the gun in his lap.

Kedar finally looked up at her. "Thank you, Cara, for everything you have done for me."

Cara looked down into Kedar's eyes and realized there was another side to him, something dark, but yet she could still see the gentle side of him. Right now, she knew that was the one she was looking to appeal to. "You're welcome, but I need to be thanking you. You helped me find myself, K. I was lost before you. However, with your company, it helped me find a part of myself that was lost. So therefore, I owe you. You helped me bring a dream of mine to reality. I am forever indebted to you for that. Don't get me wrong......" she continued. ".......I can't imagine what you're going through, but some things are better left alone."

Cara was starting to see K's eyes return to normal as she spoke. It was as if he was trying to find the silver lining of his situation in Cara's words.

Suddenly, his eyes began to grow dark again, as he spoke. "Cara, he took shots at me," he spat as he beat his chest with his fist. "Not only that......," he rose up from where he was seated and began to pace the floor. ".........that nigga took a shot at J!" Kedar's volume kicked up a notch, right then, he transformed. His eyes were completely black. There was a rage present that wouldn't allow him to return to normal. "That bitch ass nigga took a shot at my daughter!!!!!!" K barked.

As Cara looked up at Kedar, she actually saw him now, as he stood. He seemed to have grown two feet. It was then that she knew there was no coming back. K was now in savage mode and he was all in on killing this Dre character. Cara tried one last effort to persuade him, "But Kedar, you got to think about J. What type of predicament you will leave her in.....and then think about your daughter. That sweet innocent baby."

"I AM!!!!!!!! Them being innocent is why this bitch gotta die NOW!!!!" he barked back.

As long as she had known him, he had never raised his voice at her. It cut her deep. She loved K from her soul, more like a big brother or a father now, a real protector for her. Kedar had filled the shoes of all the men that had left her. Cara spoke, barely above a whisper this time, "I'm scared to lose you," she said as tears began to trickle down her face. In between sobs, she pleaded, "Don't be selfish! I don't deserve to lose you. J doesn't deserve to lose you, and mostly Serenity doesn't deserve to lose you. I know what it's like growing up without a father!"

Kedar slowly placed the bottle down and pulled Cara into his arms. "Shhhhh......ain't nothing going to happen to me." He now had an up close and personal view of some of the things that drove Cara, as well as her way of thinking, and her actions. At that moment, his phone began to vibrate on the table. Kedar spotted Swift's name on the screen. He wiped the tears away from Cara's face before answering the phone. "Hello?"

"Yah yah yah," was all that Kedar heard. Swift was screaming into the receiver.

"Calm down bro, breathe. You gotta calm down, and talk slow."

Swift had to get himself together, as he leveled his breathing. "The nuts on this nigga is ridiculous! He is at Blues now, and to top it all off, the bitch is being disrespectful! Homes grabbed my girl ass or some shit like that. She called me panicking. On my life, that muhfucka is dying tonight!"

"Aight," replied Kedar. "Where are you?"

"I'm in the parking lot of Cara's building with the crew!"

Kedar took a step back, "Call security at the club. Make sure they bolt the place down. I'm on my way downstairs now!" He hung up the phone. Kedar beelined to the closet in the living room to grab his gear.

CHAPTER 22

     J had been standing in the hallway the whole time. She came up be-
hind Cara and grabbed her hand. By the time Kedar looked up, he was staring in
both of the women's pleading eyes. J looked deep into K's eyes. She had seen
that look before. It was the same look he had, the day that he had stabbed Dre
up. She had a full understanding that there was no turning him back now. She
walked over and hugged him. J swung Cara around to the other side, to hug him
as well. The women embraced him firmly. Kedar leaned down, and kissed Cara's
forehead then kissed J passionately on the lips. "I love y'all," he said quietly.

     Several of K's men were already there, keeping a close eye on Dre.
The club was closing, and some people had already made their way out of the
lounge. Dre sat with a disappointed look on his face, "Bitch ass nigga, I'm going
to get his ass tho'," he thought to himself, as he signaled for his team to pack it
up. Dre saw the young lady that was his waitress earlier by the bar. He walked up
on her, "Thank you for your services." Then he balled up a $20 bill and hit her in
the back of the head with it. "Broke bitch!"

     The teary-eyed waitress turned around, "Why do you disrespect wom-
en in that manner?" She struggled getting her words out, then tried pleading to
him. "Don't you have a sister, aunt, or even a mother for that fact?"

     Dre looked back at the woman and began to laugh in her face. "First of all, bitch, I don't have no sister, but I do have a mama with her broke, crack rock smoking ass! So, I guess I'm right in viewing you bitches the way I do!" He laughed.

The poor woman couldn't do anything but drop her head. A security guard walked up and placed his hand on her shoulder. "I think it's time for you to go," he stated to Dre.

The young woman was glad that someone had come to her aid. She grabbed her purse and belongings.

Dre looked up at the 6'6" bouncer and laughed. The man stood his ground on informing Dre that it was about time that he and his crew left, also signaling towards the door.

Dre pulled out a spliff and fired it up. He had brandished the firearm on his waistline, in the process of getting his lighter from his pocket. As he took a long toke from the spliff, he eyed the bouncer intensely. He blew the smoke in the bouncer's face, "Unless you bulletproof, if you ever see me talking to a bitch, leave your cape at home....fuck nigga! Even then, I got some shit that hit worse than Kryptonite for yo' ass!" Dre had rounded up his entire crew. They were about ten cars deep waiting on him to come out.

Dre's Range Rover was the third car in the ten-car Caravan. Once he stepped out of the club, he took another pull of the spliff, before passing it. "We got to go get something to eat, man I'm hungrier than a motherfucker!" He took in a deep breath, acknowledging his hunger pains, before one of his guys opened the passenger door for him. Dre was making himself comfortable........

PEWWW...PEWWW

The man that had just closed his door, dropped dead. The men that were not in vehicles, drew their weapons, and spinned them around, aiming frantically. They were looking to see which direction the bullets had just come from. At the entrance of the club, Dre noticed the waitress hadn't left, and that she was standing behind the big-ass bodyguard. A sinister smile came across the bodyguard's face. Dre rolled down his window, and just as it was cracking, the bodyguard called out to him. "I hope you're wearing your vest," as he continued to smile.

Dre drew his weapon and immediately sent bullets flying his way. He wasn't quick enough, the bodyguard had already closed the doors and locked it down. Dre screamed over to his driver, "Get us out of here!" As the words left his mouth, a bullet went flying through the driver's chest and exited out of his back. Panic began to set in on Dre but survival mode overrode it. Big Joey gave the man to his right, a high-five for the shot he had just made from the rooftop, with the AR-15.

Big Joey had gotten the call from the pen, from Divine. He immediately loaded up a team to go aid and assist the man who helped him become a dominant power in PA. Cars turned the corner from the north and south. With shooters on the roof, Dre was boxed in. Dre quickly formed his unit around him. The men were in the shape of a diamond, facing north and south. Once the cars stopped, the real shooting began. Kedar came from the north with the team, and Swift came from the south. Kedar had made a statement to his men that Dre was his. Swift wasn't hearing that, since the man had placed his repulsive hands on his woman. Swift moved like a swift fox, dropping two of the stragglers that were not in the ranking. He was on a rampage like a madman, but his own team was constantly dropping.

Dre smiled to himself; he knew that the man wasn't ready for this type of brawl. Dre was ex-army, and he trained his raw shooters in that manner. A few bullets went whizzing by his head, dropping the man to Dre's left. "Fuck!" Dre thought to himself, then quickly called out to his men to unload everything they had in the direction of the snipers.

TATTAT TAT TAT TAT TAT...........

The men annihilated the corner of the building, knocking chunks out of the concrete. Big Joey and his shooter took cover. Big Joey spoke out to his partner, "God damn, they packing!"

His partner agrees, then reminded him, "Yeah they are, but they got to reload shortly."

As if on cue, two of Dre's men went to their knees to reload their weapons. The snipers perched the gun back on the ledge. "Gotcha!" Dre snickered, as he sent bullets flying their way.

BOOM BOOM!!!!!!!!!!!!!!!!!!!!

The first shot hit the man in the shoulder, sending him back to the ground.

"Fuck, Fuck, Fuck!" Big Joey screamed. The man was bleeding badly. Big Joey quickly put pressure on the wound. "I got you," he said as he started to help his injured colleague out of the game.

Dre had one of the vehicles swing around and provide a little defense from the south. Swift's men were now dropping like flies. Swift was too far ahead of his group to back up. Dre spotted him open and alone. He sent a bullet flying through Swift's leg.

"Ahhhhhh," Swift screamed out in pain, as he hit the concrete. He scrambled around to find some cover. "Shit," he moaned through clenched teeth. Swift ripped his shirt and tied a piece above the leg wound. He now sat with his back against the car. He checked his magazine in the firearm. Bullets were hammering the car, he peeked around and quickly jumped back as bullets came his way. "Fuck," he thought.

Kedar could see his man was pinned down, with the group advancing on him. He decided to split his team in half and push forward towards Dre. Dre took notice of the move and broke off one third of his rank and pushed forward with the rest. Kedar and the small group were like sitting ducks, isolated. Dre became more aggressive in his advance. He had quickly knocked off the entire second-rank that Kedar had split. Now his target, and main focus was on Kedar, being that he had spotted him in the other group.

Kedar saw nothing but images of his daughters, J, and Cara flash in front of his mental. He knew that he could not leave them alone in this world. Kedar began to take all of his shots with precision, one shot, one kill. He was dropping Dre's advancements slowly but surely. However, the number was overwhelming.

TAT TAT TAT TAT TAT!!!!!

An array of bullets began to ring out. "What the fuck?!" Dre thought as he quickly turned to see bodies dropping behind him. The security guards had come out of the club with street sweepers, killing all of the men that had Swift cornered. Now they were knocking off his entire flock. There was no cover for him. Bullets began to whistle overhead. Big Joey had gotten his comrade to safety, picked up the AR-15 again, and began firing. Kedar saw the turn of events, so he came from behind cover, and advanced.

When K knew that he had full advantage, he shouted towards Dre, "Put the gun down nigga, nobody else got to die!"

One of Dre's men looked at him. "Boss, we can live to fig......"

Dre cut him off by sending a bullet through his eye. "Fucking coward," he said as he spit on the man's corpse. He noticed that his clip had run dry. He looked to another one of his men, "Give me a clip, and cover me."

Dre made a dash for a nearby alley. As quickly as he ran off, the man that had been standing next to him was gunned down. Dre fired shots over his shoulder as he bolted for the dark alleyway. Kedar took another precision shot, and hit Dre in the leg. Dre fell to the ground. His body going to one side, and his gun flying to the other.

Kedar walked across the bodies that lay sprawled out on the ground, from the chaos. Along the way, he shot a man who was wounded, but still drawing his gun for dear life. He checked his clip as he approached the alley. Dre looked like a deer in headlights. He tried to hurry and grab his gun. Kedar sent out a shot that struck him in the hand, just as he grabbed the gun.

Dre's hand felt like lightning had just struck it, sending pain through his entire body. He rolled around on the ground in agony. It took all that he had for him to sit upright. He locked eyes with Kedar, "Fuck you bitch ass nigga!" Dre spat.

"Naw, fuck you!" Kedar sent three shots into his chest. Swift came to Kedar's side with the help of one of their men. Kedar looked over at him, "You good?" he asked Swift.

Swift shook it off, "It's just a flesh wound."

Kedar leaned over to give his friend a hug. "I'm glad you made it through, bro'. Now, let's get you somewhere to get that shit looked at." Before Swift could turn, he saw Dre raise up with his gun in his hand.

BOOM!!!! BOOM!!! BOOM!!!

Swift pushed Kedar to the side, and sent two bullets into Dre's neck. As Dre lay still, Swift wobbled over and gave his face the rest of the clip. The police sirens began to ring loudly. It sounded as if they were right above them.

It had been a little less than a year ago when Kedar was in prison at Autry State. He had found himself right back behind the wall. Kedar had ended up with a two-year revocation of his probation for being in the presence of a firearm. He had stated that he was only trying to assist an injured person Although, there were no witnesses to state that he partook in any of the action, bullets were everywhere. The judge figured that he had to have been there. The judge wasn't stupid and he wasn't going to just let him walk either. J had quit her job so that she could bring Serenity to see her father. Cara was on the other side of the couple, visiting Divine, they all knew that one day, they would all be in the free world together.

Cara had exercised some of her connects to help Swift out. As the manager, and part owner of the club, he was held partially responsible for the events that occurred. Swift had stated to the courts that he was a victim. He took his case to trial and was facing party to a crime of murder. With the display of Cara's attorney friend, he ended up with a ten do five for a part to a crime of aggravated assault, a lesser offense. Stephanie vowed to be by his side, and she was making good on it. She even asked Swift to marry her. He turned her down, but came back and asked her to marry him. Swift believed that, that was the way it was supposed to be. Him asking her.

Cara had a secret. While the gang sat together during visitation, she pondered on how to break the news. She looked at Divine and Kedar before speaking, "I want y'all to know," she began. "That I'm running for governor."

Kedar's mouth dropped, "So you just jump over mayor, huh?"

"Why not?" Cara said, looking at him. "You said shoot for the stars!"

Kedar looked over at her again, "Well, hell you should've ran for president then. Trump made it."

Cara tapped at her temple for a moment, "You might be right......" The whole group burst into laughter. "........and Jay is going to be my campaign leader."

"No, the fuck I will not. I don't know the first thing about no damn politics," J replied as she bounced Serenity on her lap.

Cara looked at her. "If you with this muthafucka, it is political," she joked.

An officer came over and told them to bring it down a notch. The crew looked at each other, as Angel winked. An idea came across Kedar's mind, "Hell I might as well make the best of it while I'm here." Rolax was still in Macon State. They had sent Swift to Coastal. It came across Kedar's mind to corner the market behind the wall. He could easily recruit workers and obtain product by the truckload.

J looked at him in a daze, "What you thinking about?"

He spread that million-dollar smile across his face, "How much I love you, and my angel." He leaned over and kissed his daughter's forehead.

J cut her eyes at him, "Yea right. I'm not crazy. You got something on your mind, I know you."

Kedar's mouth dropped, "Whaaaaaaat?" he questioned with sarcasm written on his face.

MORE ADVENTURES WITH KEDAR COMING SOON....